WICHITA UNDERCOVER

WICHITA DETECTIVE
BOOK THREE

PATRICK ANDREWS

ROUGH
EDGES
PRESS

This novel is dedicated to the Wichita Eagle newspaper of the 1950s, where the author first earned money for writing

WICHITA
UNDERCOVER

"Dwayne, you couldn't find a single person in Wichita, Kansas who would be surprised by learning that you've been taking part in illegal activities."

– Steve Williams, F.B.I. Agent

CHAPTER 1

The beginning of the year 1948 A.D. arrived in Wichita, Kansas, in a blaze of celestial brilliance. At least it seemed that way to Dwayne Wheeler, a local private detective with dubious moral standards.

He had just finished the best caper of his career after teaming up with an officer from his former World War II army military police unit. He ended up with a five-thousand-dollar bonus for his participation in that complicated modus operandi of international crime. This was twice the yearly earnings of the average American. He also received a 1940 Buick Sedan to replace his beat-up 1932 Pontiac coupe.

Dwayne's mood of exhilaration about the new year increased even more within a short period of time. The reason for this additional gladness was that Kansas finally rescinded their laws prohibiting of the sale of intoxicating liquor. Additionally, this change authorized the establishment of taverns that were permitted to serve beer. Cocktails were not allowed, but people could go to package stores and purchase hard liquor to mix their own.

This momentous legalization that had originated in the smoke-filled backrooms of Kansas politics, came about for several reasons. The first and most important rationale was that after World War II, Kansans were not in the mood to endure preposterous laws and regulations forced on them by certain religious sects of society. Most people considered churchgoers as quintessential hypocrites. There was a saying in Kansas back in those days regarding a potentially impossible or improbable event; it went, "That's gonna happen when the Baptists started drinking in front of each other." The only shortcoming of this deregulation was that the taverns and liquor stores were not permitted to conduct business on Sundays.

But the other, more important reason for the rescission of the liquor laws was the amount of taxes that could be raised through the sale of alcoholic beverages. During the dry years the only commercial enterprise that profited from the marketing and distribution of liquor were the bootleggers. Now in early 1948, those gentlemen knew their lucrative merchandising operations were about to be blown away like a haystack in a tornado.

————

IN LESS THAN A MONTH AFTER THE NEW LAW went into effect, Dwayne had picked out a recently established downtown tavern as his favorite place to imbibe 3.2 beer. This tavern was called the Beachcomber. It was owned by Bret Underwood, a young Wichitan who had moved to Los Angeles to work as a bartender. His goal was to save enough money to open up a bar in California. But when he heard Kansas had gone wet, he hurried back to his hometown to go into business for himself. That was a lot less costly than establishing a bar on the west coast.

Bret designed the interior of the Beachcomber Tavern with an oceanic motif of small fake palm trees, a fishing net over the bar and a large seascape painted on the walls. He chose that ambiance because it would appeal to land-locked Kansans.

Additionally, opening at seven a.m. attracted down-town businessmen to come in for eye-openers before beginning their day's work. They brought in flasks of whiskey or brandy to pour into their servings of beer or coffee. These well-to-do tipplers had no reason to fear the authorities for bending the new ruling. Their prestigious positions in Wichita commerce afforded them protection from law enforcement.

———

FOR THE TIME BEING, IT WAS IMPERATIVE FOR Dwayne to keep the five grand from his illegal activities out of sight. After all, the money could be accurately described as "ill-gotten gains" by people with less open-minded attitudes than Dwayne's. Thus he carefully and surreptitiously used enough of the funds to move out of his cheap rooming house and find a furnished apartment. He located a suitable habitat a few blocks south of the Beachcomber Tavern on Market Street. It was a one-bedroom place with a small kitchenette, living room, and bath that suited his bachelor lifestyle.

In addition, just to be on the safe side, he kept his decrepit office in the rundown Snodgrass Building on the western edge of downtown. Numerous times in the past, he had been locked out of the place for nonpayment of rent. Maintaining this shabby headquarters would make him appear as if he were still short of money as usual.

THE NEXT THING ON THIS TO-DO LIST WAS TO make some paybacks to some people who had been kind to him and his mother after his father died. The first was Tommy Brady, a former Salvation Army member who lived on a farm near the small town of Augusta; and the second was the Kairouz family of Lebanese Christian grocers who ran a small store in north Wichita.

Dwayne's late father had been a barber at a large shop downtown. Unfortunately, the elder Wheeler met his end under the wheels of a taxi cab. He had been more than a little inebriated on a Saturday night when he stepped off a curb while attempting to cross a downtown street against a red light.

This tragedy happened in 1936, leaving sixteen-year-old Dwayne and his mother destitute and desperate. Mother and son were forced to move to a cheap downtown hotel near the warehouse district. She found employment in a nearby laundry while he dropped out of school to work odd jobs to bring money into the household. They received help from the Salvation Army in getting clothing and other material support. Liberal credit was afforded them by that kind Lebanese family.

More heartbreak struck again in 1940 when Dwayne became a full-fledged orphan. His mother died from a particularly vicious form of stomach cancer that killed her in the three months between diagnosis and death. Left completely on his own, Dwayne wanted to get away from Wichita and the misery he had endured in the city. He enlisted in the small professional U.S. Army of pre-World War II, and the young man ended up as a military policeman at Fort Benning, Georgia.

Now, driving east on U.S. Highway 54, Dwayne traveled toward the small town of Augusta. Just beyond the community, he turned north onto a dirt country road, wending his way to the entrance of a farmyard. He turned in and continued up to the house.

A knock on the door was answered by a short, tough-looking old guy whose craggy face broke into a wide grin. This was Tommy Brady, a former Salvation Army member who had inherited the bucolic property with his late wife Margie.

"Dwayne! C'mon in!"

Dwayne was led into the kitchen and invited to take a seat at the table. "How're things going, Tommy?"

"The Lord shineth his face upon me," Tommy replied.

When Tommy met Margie in San Francisco, he was a carousing boatswain in the U.S. Navy and the middleweight boxing champion of the Pacific Fleet. He saw the future love-of-his-life in a Salvation Army street band as he headed for a whorehouse on the Barbary Coast. His immediate fascination with the comely young woman led first to an acceptance of Christ as his savior, a romance, a marriage and a long career in the Salvation Army until finally retiring to the farm in Kansas.

He and Margie inherited the property from her father where they lived for a decade until Margie passed away. Tommy, left alone in the world, rented out tracts of land to farmers, giving him a comfortable living.

The old guy had some hot coffee on the stove, and he poured out a couple of cups, joining Dwayne at the table. "I seen the article in the *Eagle* about you solving the murder of that professor. You been doing a lot of good for yourself, ain't you?"

Dwayne nodded. "And you helped me out by letting me hole up here on that bookie murder caper." He took a sip of the strong brew, then reached into his jacket pocket and pulled out an envelope. "This is for you, Tommy."

Tommy was surprised. "What is this?"

"There's five one-hunnerd dollar bills in there."

"Okay," Tommy said. "D'you want me to hold 'em for you?"

"Nope. They're for you to keep and—as they say—squander or save."

Tommy leaned back in his chair. "You're giving me five hunnerd dollars? What for?"

"For all the kindness you showed my mother and me during the darkest hours of our lives."

"I can't take this, Dwayne. It's a nice gift, but I was doing my Christian duty."

Dwayne finished his coffee and stood up. "Then give it to your church. To the Salvation Army. Buy Care Packages and send 'em overseas to the poor folks in Europe." He walked to the door, pausing to wave goodbye.

Dwayne drove back to the highway, returning to Wichita. He continued through the city, turning north to continue to Fifteenth Street near Wichita High School North. He slowed down, then spotted the small store he was searching for. The sign on the front said: **KAIROUZ FOOD MARKET**.

Dwayne parked at the curb and got out of the Buick. He experienced a warm feeling as he gazed at the storefront. When Dwayne returned to Wichita after his discharge from the army, he found out the owner Eliza Kairouz and his wife Marie had lost their son who was killed in action at Omaha Beach on D-Day.

Dwayne walked into the store and looked around. A short, dark bald man appeared from the back then stopped. "Dwayne!" he yelled out. "Dwayne Wheeler!"

Dwayne grinned. "Yeah. It's me, Mister Kairouz."

Mrs. Kairouz, shorter and stouter than her husband, came out to see what the commotion was all about. When she saw Dwayne she hurried to him and gave him a hug. "What a nice surprise. We read about you in the paper. All the time, we read about you in the paper!"

"I've meant to come see you," Dwayne said. "But I don't get up to this part of town very often. I heard about Charlie. I'm so sorry."

"Life and death always go together," Mr. Kairouz said. "It is like when your mama die. And like when our Charlie die." He shrugged. "What can we do, eh?"

"We're helpless," Dwayne agreed. "I remember how kind you were to my mother and me. You gave us credit when we needed food, and you never pressed us for the money."

Mrs. Kairouz patted his cheek. "We know you are good people and will pay."

Dwayne pulled another envelope from his jacket. "I want to give you this to show my appreciation. I have had some very good luck and want to share it with you." He gave the envelope to Mr. Kairouz and headed for the door. "I'll come back and visit when I can."

Dwayne walked to the car and had just opened the door when the couple came out. Mr. Kairouz waved the envelope. "There is five hundred dollars here, Dwayne. I think you make mistake."

Dwayne shook his head. "It's no mistake, Mister Kairouz."

They watched him drive away. "He paid us too

much," Mr. Kairouz said. "We should give him some of it back."

Mrs. Kairouz shook her head. "Dwayne is a good boy. He would feel bad if we did that."

They walked slowly back into the market, now feeling deep sorrow about Dwayne's mother and their son.

CHAPTER 2

The next morning at nine o'clock, Dwayne walked through the front door of the rundown Snodgrass Building. A climb up to the third floor on the badly worn stairs plus a few steps down a hallway brought him to his office. The door to his small headquarters bore a hand-painted plywood sign. Dwayne had taken a stencil sheet and dabbed on the letters to identify his business.

DWAYNE WHEELER
PRIVATE INVESTIGATOR
CONFIDENTIAL SERVICES

The interior of the office contained a battered second-hand desk and three chairs; one in the back for the shamus and two in front for clients. He closed the door and tossed his fedora on the hat rack in the corner. After settling behind the desk, he lit a Lucky Strike cigarette and exhaled a cloud of smoke. With those preliminaries taken care of, he dialed his answering service.

A perky female voice responded, "Reliable Answering Service, this is Millie. How may I help you?"

"This is Dwayne Wheeler, any calls?"

"One moment, please." A brief pause. "You have one call from a Mister Jessie Pickens. His number is—"

Dwayne interrupted. "I have his number. Thank you."

Jessie Pickens was the proprietor of a redneck night club called Western Danceland. It was located just outside the southern city limits of Wichita. The club was notorious for drunken brawls, loud music, stabbings and even a few shootings. The Sedgwick County Sheriff's Department's records showed that in the previous year of 1947 there had been five murders in the parking lot that resulted from confrontations among the patrons.

The latest in hillbilly music could be heard inside the large building between the fracases. These bands played on a stage behind a wire mesh screen. This protected the *artistes* when critics in the audience expressed disenchantment of their performances by hurling objects at them. Since the new liquor laws, this now included empty beer bottles.

Dwayne dialed the number and Jessie Pickens answered. "Yeah?"

"Hi, Jessie, this is Dwayne. My answering service says you want to speak to me."

"Oh, God, yeah, Dwayne! I got a real serious situation. I don't want to talk about it over the phone. How soon can you get down here?"

"I can be there in twenty or so minutes. Is this a job?"

"Dwayne, it is a *big* job!"

———

THE EMPTY PARKING LOT LOOKED STRANGE TO Dwayne as he drove across it to the Western Danceland building. He was used to seeing it at night, full of cars. He drove up to the door and stopped, noting Jessie Pickens waiting for him. The owner was frantically motioning for the shamus to hurry.

Dwayne joined him and they went inside, past the bar and into the office. The shamus was surprised to see Jessie's wife Lorene sitting at the side of the desk in a folding chair. The woman, an alcoholic, had a disturbing habit of disappearing for days at a time, then calling Jessie to pick her up in some cheap hotel or motor lodge where she'd been abandoned by the latest guy or guys screwing her. Their sixteen-year-old daughter Mary Sue was a bit more sophisticated. Her thing was to run off with big rig truck drivers from the nearby Highway 81 Truck Stop. Jessie never had to go after her; Mary Sue always caught a ride back.

"We got big troubles, Dwayne," Jessie said.

Lorene said nothing, only sobbing into her hankie.

"What's going on?" Dwayne asked.

"Mary Sue has run off with a truck driver," Jessie said. "And this time it's serious."

"I see," Dwayne remarked, thinking it was serious any time a teenage girl went on trips with strange truck drivers. "How long has she been gone this time?"

"I figger ten or so days," Jessie replied. "Or two weeks maybe. Could be a little shorter'n a month."

Lorene spoke up in a loud voice. "She's with Darrell Bodine, Dwayne. One of the other drivers stopped by here and told us that Darrell has locked her up and is pimping her."

"How d'you know she's locked up?"

"Hell's bells, Dwayne!" Jessie exclaimed. "How else is

he gonna hold her a pris'ner 'cept to keep her in his truck?"

Dwayne was thoughtful for a moment. "Mmm, if she can't get out of the cab, that means this guy Bodine has removed the inside door handles. And he's probably pulled out the lock knobs, too."

"Well," Jessie said, "he's sure as hell done something or other to keep her penned up like 'at."

"Now looky here," Dwayne said, "I don't want to make you two mad, but are you sure she's not doing this on purpose? Maybe to please this Bodine guy or just to make some money."

"Johnny stopped his rig near Darrell's a week ago outside of Enid, Oklahoma," Jessie said. "He said he heard some commotion in the cab and it was Mary Sue crying and begging to be let loose."

"Who's Johnny?" Dwayne asked.

"Johnny Devans," Jessie replied. "He's a decent guy. Married with kids. Lives in Hutchinson. Anyhow, he said Darrell was hitting her. Then later, Darrell was going around bringing other truckers and letting them get into the sleeper with her."

Lorene was now weeping openly. "You got to get her away and bring her home to us, Dwayne!"

"Now just how'm I supposed to figure out where they are?"

Jessie answered, "The best chance you got is U.S. 81 between Oklahoma City and the junction of U.S. 6." He reached in a desk drawer and pulled out a roadmap, handing it to the shamus.

Dwayne took the map and studied it. "Damn, Jessie, that's from Oklahoma clear up through Kansas and into Nebraska." He checked the distance scale in the legend.

"That's almost four hunnerd miles! I could be out there two or three weeks. Maybe even a full month or more."

"Dwayne!" Lorene cried. "We'll pay whatever you want! Name your price! You got to rescue our little girl from white slavery."

"You better call the cops," Dwayne advised them.

Jessie shook his head. "We don't want publicity about this. It'd bring shame and disgrace to our Mary Sue. That's why we want you to take care of it."

Dwayne knew the real reason behind their worry. If the Sedgwick County Family Services found out the full and true story of Mary Sue's activities, both Jessie and Lorene would be in deep trouble. He was thoughtful for a moment. "I charge twenty-five dollars a day and expenses. That means you pay for my meals, my lodging, gasoline, and ever'thing."

"That's fine," Jessie said.

"Who does this Darrell Bodine work for?"

"He's an independent," Jessie explained. "He's got 'Darrell Bodine-Owner and Operator' painted on the door of his rig."

"What kind of truck does he have?"

"It's a '41 Dodge Semi," Jessie replied. "Johnny described it to us. It's dark blue. The lettering on the door is yeller."

"Okay. What does Darrell Bodine look like?"

"Short and husky with black hair," Jessie replied. "His face is pock-marked pretty bad from pimples when he was a kid."

"Please help us, Dwayne!" Lorene pleaded. "If you get her back we'll give you free beer anytime you come in here."

Jessie interrupted. "Well, maybe not permanent. For a little while anyway."

"I told you what I charge," Dwayne said. "And I'll need a hunnerd dollar advance."

"That's no problem," Jessie assured him.

"And I'll need a picture of Mary Sue. I've never seen her."

Lorene reached into her purse and pulled out a studio portrait of Jessie, her, and the girl. "Here. This was took about six months back."

Dwayne studied the color photograph. Mary Sue was not a particularly pretty girl. She had red hair—like her father Jessie—and was plump with a wide face, heavily covered with freckles. But Dwayne figured any horny trucker on the road would find her desirable.

"Okay," he said. "Here's how I'm gonna do this. I'll drive down to Oklahoma City and check out all the truck stops on the way back here to Wichita. I'll take some time to update you two, do laundry, check for phone calls, and take a one or two day break. Then I'll drive up to U.S. 6 in Nebraska. And if I can't find her up there, I'll turn around and drive back to Wichita and check in to see if she's back with you."

"That's a grand plan, Dwayne," Jessie said. "You take all the time you need."

"I'll start first thing in the morning."

He left the building and could hear Lorene's wailing though the window as he got into the Buick.

———

DWAYNE WENT TO HIS APARTMENT TO PACK FOR the trip, turning to his special stock of handy items. These were kept in an old valise that held such things as false moustaches, eyeglasses of various sorts, and other items for disguise. The shamus decided he would take along a moustache and heavy framed spectacles in case he needed to vary his appearance.

His various styles of special clothing were hung in the closet with his everyday wear. These were items he'd picked up as purchases in second hand stores. They consisted of garments and headgear he had bought to assume different roles in his capers. Dwayne decided that, instead of his usual suit and fedora, he would wear an old ball cap, khaki work shirt, and blue jeans so that he might walk among parked vehicles at a truck stop without attracting too much attention. He also included oil-stained overalls so he could be taken for a mechanic as well. Besides clothing, he would take his Army Colt .45 semi-automatic pistol in a shoulder holster. He also included brass knuckles and a leather sap filled with small ball bearings. These were tools of his trade to be used in case Bodine refused to give up his young girlfriend without a struggle.

While packing, Dwayne turned his thoughts to the operational procedures to employ. It was simple; he would pull into a truck stop and check out the parking lot, the restaurant and the area around the fuel pumps and garage where repairs are made. If he didn't find Mary Sue within six weeks, he would consider the caper a failure. There was always the chance that Darrell Bodine might get a new trucking contract that would alter his route.

After finishing the preparations, Dwayne walked up Market Street to the Dockum Drug Store to eat at the lunch counter. He wanted to order his favorite mid-day meal of a grilled cheese sandwich and French-fries, but Dockum only served potato chips. And they didn't have the Orange Crush he preferred either, so he had to settle for the sandwich, chips, and a fountain coke.

With his appetite appeased, he crossed the street to the

Beachcomber Tavern and went in for a few beers before returning to his apartment. The lights were dim in the interior and he noted a new barmaid on duty. He slid onto a stool. "How about a Schlitz?" he asked, laying a quarter on the bar.

"You got it," the barmaid answered. She appeared to be in her early thirties with a plumpish figure that was well-proportioned. Not a beauty, but sexy with a nice rack. Her hair was blonde and cut short as was in the latest style. The shoulder length tresses that the movie actress Veronica Lake had made so popular were now *passé*.

When he was served, Dwayne held out his hand. "Dwayne Wheeler."

The woman shook with him. "Nancy." She started to walk away, then stopped and came back. "Did you say Dwayne Wheeler?"

"Yep."

"You're that detective, ain't you? Bret told me about you being a reg'lar customer."

"I hope nothing he said was bad."

"Not a bit! He really bragged you up."

There was only one other person at the bar at that time of day, so Dwayne and Nancy were able to chat as he consumed the brew. He learned her last name was Turner, she was divorced, had a ten-year-old daughter by the name of Holly, and she lived with her mother in a rented duplex just north of downtown.

"Are you the same as a policeman?" Nancy asked, handing him his second bottle.

"No, I'm a private eye. A shamus. I do special investigations for folks that hire me."

"Oh!" she said excited. "Like in the movies and the radio, huh?"

"Yeah. I'm just like Sam Spade."

"I've heard that program on the radio a few times," Nancy remarked brightly. "On Sunday nights, right?"

"Right."

They continued a quiet conversation, and Dwayne paced his drinking to keep from getting drunk. "What time do you get off?"

"Five o'clock. Bret says I'm gonna be working the day shift for awhile."

"Would you like to go out for a bite to eat? The Continental Grill on East Douglas is a great place to chow down."

"I have to get home. I ride the bus and it takes a while."

"I can give you a ride."

"I don't like to stay out too late. It makes my mom worry."

"That's okay," Dwayne said. "I'll take you home right after we eat."

She didn't hesitate. "I'll have to call my mom to tell her I'll be a little bit late."

"No problem," Dwayne said, sensing he would get to know her a lot better. But it would require a bit of finesse on his part. "We could even get some burgers and fries to take out for your mother and...what's your daughter's name?"

"Holly."

"And she's a ten-year-old, right?"

"Gosh," Nancy said. "You don't forget nothing, do you? I guess that's how detectives are."

"Yep."

Dwayne sipped his beer slowly and deliberately, then at a quarter to five he finished the last one. "I'll go down the street and get my car. Then we can head for the Continental."

––––––––

IT WAS A LITTLE AFTER SIX P.M. WHEN DWAYNE pulled the Buick up in front of the duplex where Nancy lived with her mother and daughter. The smell of hamburgers and fries in a paper sack filled the interior of the automobile.

The couple went up to the door and Nancy led the way into the interior. Dwayne followed her, and saw the grandmother and daughter on the sofa listening to the radio.

"Hi," Dwayne greeted, well aware of the close scrutiny he was being given.

"Mom," Nancy said. "This is Dwayne Wheeler. Dwayne, this is my mother Maggie and my little girl Holly."

Holly spoke up sharply. "I am *not* a little girl!"

"I'll say not," Dwayne said. "You're a young lady. That's what you are."

The girl smiled and Dwayne knew he'd just made a friend.

"You're not married, are you?" he asked her.

Holly burst out laughing. "No!"

"Do you have a fiancé?"

"What's that?" she asked.

"When a boy asks you to marry him, he's your fiancé."

"Ugh! I hate boys! They're loud and dumb!"

Dwayne grinned. "I think you're right about that."

"Hello, Mister Wheeler," Maggie Turner said. "It's nice to meet you."

Holly suddenly jumped up. "I smell hamburgers and French fries!"

Dwayne held out the sack. "We have a couple of milkshakes, too."

Nancy took the take-out food into the kitchenette and got some plates. Mrs. Turner and Holly followed, sitting down at the table. The little girl wasted no time in grabbing some fries and treating herself to a big helping.

Nancy put on a pot of coffee as Dwayne joined Holly and Mrs. Turner. The girl handed him one of her fries and he gave her a wink as he accepted it. She winked back. "You're handsome!"

"Am I?" Dwayne remarked. "Well, you're a sweetie for saying that."

Nancy, spooning coffee into the brewing basket, said, "Dwayne is a detective, mother. My boss Bret Underwood told me he's solved a lot of cases in Wichita."

Mrs. Turner, who didn't fully grasp the meaning of what Nancy said, nodded with a smile. "That's nice."

As soon as the coffee had perked, Nancy poured cups for her and Dwayne. He sipped the brew, enjoying himself in the company of the three females. Nancy was the talkative one while Mrs. Turner and Holly munched on their burgers and fries between swallows of strawberry milkshakes.

Fifteen minutes passed and the food was consumed. Holly sucked on the straw of her milkshake until it gurgled empty. Mrs. Turner gathered up the sacks, paper cups and wrappers, taking it all to the kitchen wastebasket.

Dwayne checked his watch. He wanted to get a good night's sleep since he was planning on leaving at five o'clock the next morning. And it was always wise not to remain too long when meeting a new woman friend's family. "I have to start a job early tomorrow, so I'd better go home and get ready. I'm going out of town."

"Are you after a crook, Dwayne?" Nancy asked.

"It's involves a missing girl," he replied, standing up.

"Really?" Nancy exclaimed. "Is she kidnapped?"

"That's what I have to find out," Dwayne said. "I can't really talk about my capers. I have to keep my clients' names a secret."

"I'll walk you to the door."

"Me, too!" Holly said, taking Dwayne's hand.

He made his final goodbyes, then left the duplex for the Buick, already deciding he wanted to get to know Nancy better and much more intimately.

Chapter 3

By two o'clock the next afternoon Dwayne arrived at the first truck stop on his tour. It was a large installation located on the south side of Oklahoma City. From there he would travel northward to Wichita, checking out similar facilities along U.S. Highway 81 before taking his first break in the caper.

After a couple of hours, he reached a truck stop on the south side of Kingfisher, Oklahoma and parked on the far edge of the site. The trucks with their diesel engines running were in the large lot at the front of the restaurant. Once these motors reached operating temperatures, they were not turned off except for lengthy halts. It took time to get them restarted; especially in cold weather.

Professional truck drivers are orderly when they park in the crowded area of a truck stop. They shared a tendency to stay in column formations to avoid hemming anybody in. On-time deliveries were religion with them, consequently they made sure nearby vehicles had an unobstructed way back to the highway.

Dwayne's pistol was in a shoulder holster under his

shirt while the sap and brass knuckles were in his front trouser pockets. He strolled casually between the trucks as he sought a blue tractor with the words **DARRELL BODINE: OWNER AND OPERATOR** painted in yellow on the doors. Unfortunately, that particular vehicle was not among the others.

Dwayne's stomach was rumbling and he decided to eat at the restaurant before resuming his quest. He went inside, sitting off to one side of the long counter, keeping his ears open for any discussion among the truckers regarding some guy pimping a young girl.

A waitress walked up showing a wide smile. "What's your pleasure, hon?"

"A grilled cheese sandwich, fries, and an Orange Crush," Dwayne responded.

After being served, he chewed the food slowly between sips of the pop. Twenty-five minutes later the shamus left a twenty-five cent tip, then went back outside. He weaved his way through the trucks once more until reaching his car. He lit a cigarette and sat on the fender to see if Bodine might show up. A waste of time. He flipped the butt away, and got in the Buick to continue north.

———

DWAYNE SPENT A TOTAL OF THREE DAYS thoroughly checking truck stops as he worked his way up to Wichita. The shamus visited the towns of Enid, Oklahoma, and Wellington, Kansas. After that, he investigated truck stops in the Wichita area before ending that stage of the hunt.

The next phase of the caper would be the longest and most time-consuming. This involved traveling from Wichita up to the junction of U.S. Highways 81 and 6 in

Nebraska. It meant driving a bit over 500 miles while visiting numerous locations.

Dwayne decided to see Jessie and Lorene Pickens before going back to his apartment. There was always the chance that Mary Sue might have returned home. It was late afternoon when he pulled into the parking lot, and he noted a Sedgwick County Sheriff's patrol car parked in front of the Western Danceland building. He went inside and saw Jessie talking to Deputy Sheriff Dave Mason.

Dave nodded to Dwayne, taking note of how he was dressed. "Hi, Dwayne. Have you been moonlighting at an honest job?"

Dwayne grinned. "No. This is my casual look. How d'you like it?"

"Classy," Dave said. He turned back to Jessie. "Okay. Now who knifed who last night? We've got both perpetrators locked up, each claiming the other started the fight."

Jessie shrugged. "It looked to me like they done it to each other at the exact same time."

Dave scowled. "Don't give me that shit, Jessie! Who knifed who *first*?"

"Oh!" Jessie said. "You mean *first*!" He was thoughtful for a moment. "I don't remember."

"Listen up, Jessie. You're skating on thin ice right now. There's been too much trouble out here as it is. And there's never any reliable witnesses. How'd you like to be shut down for about three months?"

"Uh...I don't think I'd like that, Dave."

The deputy knew he would get nowhere with the owner. "Okay. I'm turning in a report based on what *you* said. We'll see what the sheriff is gonna do about it." He closed up his notebook, looking at Dwayne. "Nice seeing you again."

"Same here."

The deputy went back to his car, and Jessie gave Dwayne an imploring look. "I guess you didn't find Mary Sue, huh?"

Dwayne shook his head. "I've got to take a couple of days off to tend to other business. I'll tell you when I start the north run to Nebraska. Okay?"

"Okay," Jessie said. "Do your best, Dwayne. Please! And don't turn any information over to the law."

"I don't have to reveal the clients on my capers," he assured Jessie, thinking to himself, *the miserable bastard is more worried about getting arrested for contributing to the delinquency of a minor than getting Mary Sue back.* He spoke aloud, saying, "I'll see you in a bit."

———

THE FIRST THING DWAYNE DID AFTER returning to his apartment was to check the hiding place of his cash. He had removed the inside jamb of his closet door and hollowed out a rectangular hole for the money. He counted $3,840 dollars—the correct amount—then returned it and pushed the jamb back into place.

Next he turned to taking a bath. After a good soaking and scrubbing, he patted himself dry, then got into a clean shirt, underwear and socks before pulling a suit from a cleaner's garment bag. He hurriedly donned the clothing, then left his apartment. Destination: The Beachcomber Tavern. It was three-forty-five, meaning Nancy would be there for the next hour and fifteen minutes.

Four businessmen were sitting at the bar when Dwayne walked in. Bret Underwood was talking to two of them while Nancy stood by the cash register, ready to serve refills. She smiled and waved when she saw Dwayne, obviously pleased by his appearance.

"A bottle of Schlitz, if you please, madam," he requested, taking a stool.

"Right away, sir," Nancy replied. She served him, then leaned on the bar. "So how's your caper?"

"In progress," he replied in sotto voce.

Nancy lowered her own voice. "I remember you said you like to keep stuff like that under your hat."

"Yeah," he whispered. "I can tell you about it when we're alone." He took a swallow of beer, then spoke normally. "How's about another supper at the Continental Grill? What if we go to a movie afterward?"

"That would make me too late," she said.

"Well, then, we could go up to my place for a couple of drinks after we eat. Then I'll take you home." He braced himself in case she was going to be offended by a suggestion to go to his apartment.

"Okay! I can tell mom we went to a movie even though there won't be enough time to really do it."

"Good idea," Dwayne said. "I never would have thought of that."

As soon as they left the Continental Grill and drove over to his apartment, Dwayne mixed a couple of scotch and sodas. His favorite drink was Jack Daniels neat but he figured a cocktail would be more to a woman's taste. They sat together on the sofa, slowly imbibing the libations as they listened to a country-western disk jockey on the radio.

Dwayne didn't want to waste any of the short hour they would spend together, and after a few moments he shifted closer to her. To his delight, she also moved toward him. He sat his drink down and put his free hand under her chin, lifting her face up. He kissed her lightly, then more passionately as she responded with the same sense of haste.

After a moment, she pulled back slowly. "Have you got a rubber? The last thing I want is to end up pregnant. That's how I got Holly."

"I have some. Yeah."

The couple made love that evening like all people did when it was the first time. They weren't quite sure what pleased the other partner, so they proceeded slowly through the lovemaking as relaxed and friendly as possible.

———

WHEN HE TOOK HER BACK TO THE DUPLEX AT eight o'clock, Maggie Turner and Holly were waiting up for them. Nancy had made sure to freshen her makeup and run a brush through her hair before leaving the apartment. She wanted it to appear as if they had really done nothing more than see a movie. Dwayne stayed only long enough to respond to Holly's request for a hug, then he headed back to his digs to prepare for the trip north.

CHAPTER 4

Dwayne, clad in his outfit for the Mary Sue Caper, drove twenty-five miles north of Wichita to Newton where U.S. 81 veered to the northwest. He found his first truck stop on the south side of the small town of Moundridge.

Dwayne drove onto the site, following his usual practice of parking his Buick in an inconspicuous spot. The shamus gave the semi-trucks a quick glance before beginning a walk-through of the vehicles. After a twenty-minute stroll, he found no semi tractor that matched the description of Darrell Bodine's rig. He had known the caper was going to be difficult, but he was frustrated nevertheless.

Dwayne went back to his car, deciding to have some coffee from his thermos. After a sip, he lit up a Lucky Strike and settled back in the car seat. His mind turned to thoughts of his new paramour Nancy Turner. She would be his first steady sexual partner since the breakup with his former girlfriend Donna Sue Connors. He and Donna Sue had been soul mates during the time she worked as a waitress at the Jayhawker Restaurant across Douglas Avenue from the OK Barbershop. This tonsorial establishment had been a second headquarters for him during times he was locked out of his office when behind in the rent. The owner Ernie Bascombe let him use the phone since Dwayne's father had worked as a barber in that same place before being run over and killed.

Dwayne and Donna Sue had a lot in common until she decided to move up in the world to be a secretary. After getting a high school equivalency diploma, she attended a secretarial school and upon graduation was hired by Brian Murchison of Murchison Enterprises, a Wichita petroleum company. This took Donna Sue completely out of the environment she had shared with Dwayne, and the couple drifted apart. Dwayne was sure that she and Murchison were now an item.

After the breakup, he began going to Jessie Pickens' Western Danceland and sought sex with drunken female rednecks between dances. He would take the women out to his car in the parking lot. These encounters offered relief from horniness, but the ritual of meeting the women, dancing with them while getting them drunk became tedious.

All that was over with since he was now linked up with Nancy. His apartment served as the perfect love nest where they could enjoy unhurried and comfortable sex while Nancy's mother and daughter thought they were at the movies.

Now, finished with both the coffee and cigarette, Dwayne turned his mind back to the job at hand. He drove from the parking lot to the highway, going through the town of McPherson where U.S. 81 turned due north again.

———

DWAYNE FOUND HIS NEXT STOP A COUPLE OF miles past the small city of Salina. It was late afternoon and past the lunch hour, so there weren't many trucks parked at the place. A few were gassing up as the shamus stepped from his Buick to take a closer look. A couple of truckers were conversing at the front of the parked vehicles not far from the restaurant. Dwayne took a roundabout route and approached them, giving the impression he was coming from his own rig.

"How's it going, boys?" he asked, strolling up.

They were a friendly duo, and one answered, "Same ol' shit, buddy."

The second guy nodded a hello. "How's it going with you?"

Dwayne chuckled. "I'm anxious to get home. I've been gone about three weeks and got another two to go. I got some dirty laundry and a stiff dick for the old lady to take care of."

"Well," the first said with a wink, "if you cain't wait, there's a guy up past the Nebraska line that's got a chubby little redhead that'll take care of that stiff dick."

Dwayne showed no outward reaction to the news. "No shit? I'm headed that way."

"The guy's at the Sunrise Truck Center between the weigh station and the town of Hebron."

"I might just check that out," Dwayne said. He chuckled again. "At least after I get me something to eat."

He gave the two a wave, then walked toward the restaurant. When he was out of their sight, he turned and headed back to his car. A check of the roadmap showed he had about a hundred and sixteen miles to go before he would reach Darrell Bodine's truck. Although there was no speed limit on open highways in Kansas, he would be forced to slow down and creep through a half dozen hamlets before he reached the Nebraska state line.

It was just as well. Bodine would wait for dark to put Mary Sue to work.

———

IT WAS LATE DUSK WHEN DWAYNE TURNED OFF U.S. 81 and drove into the Sunrise Truck Center to park his Buick. He stopped in the shadows outside the illumination of the stadium lights that lit up the site.

When he got out of the car, he noted a tan-colored '41 Chevrolet panel truck among the other vehicles. It seemed familiar, then he recalled that he had seen it previously in Oklahoma during his first trip. If it was the same one, then it probably belonged to a traveling salesman who preferred to eat at truck stops. He loosened the pistol in the shoulder holster and reached in his pocket to make sure the brass knuckles and sap were easily accessible.

Dwayne went down to the last trucks in the rows of similar vehicles, and made his way between them, looking in both directions for the blue truck. As he turned from one row to enter another, a man stepped into view. "Hey, buddy, are you looking for a good time?"

Dwayne, thinking he was about to be invited to participate in a homosexual act, gave the guy a quick glance then stopped. He knew it was Darrell Bodine from the description given him by Jessie Pickens. "Sure. I ain't seen my old lady for three weeks."

"Well, I got a young chubby gal that likes to fuck," Bodine said. "Two bucks gets you a go at her. You got a rubber?"

"No."

"I'll sell you one for fifty cents. I don't want the gal to get knocked up or catch anything."

"Okay. But I want to see her first."

"O'course, buddy. And I guarantee you'll get some good loving from her. C'mon."

Dwayne was surprised when Bodine led him out of the rows of trucks back to where the cars were parked. And when he was taken to the tan panel truck, he realized that the pimp wasn't using his big rig to haul Mary Sue around. This vehicle made his pimping easier and safer.

When they reached the vehicle, Bodine pulled some keys out of his pocket and unlocked the back doors. Dwayne peered in and saw Mary Sue seated on a mattress. He recognized her from the family portrait. She quickly got to her knees and pulled open the worn, oversized corduroy robe she was wearing, revealing her nudity.

"C'mon," she said in a dull monotone. "I got what you want."

Dwayne paid the two and a half dollars and got in. Bodine slammed the door shut and could be heard walking away, his footsteps crunching on the gravel. Mary Sue lay down and spread her legs to receive him, but Dwayne reached out and pulled her up to a sitting position.

"Mary Sue, I'm here to take you back to your parents. They hired me to find you."

"What?"

"You heard me," Dwayne said impatiently. "Get dressed as quick as you can."

"My clothes are locked up in the cab. This robe is all I have back here. I ain't even got any shoes."

"Okay. That guy is Darrell Bodine, ain't he?"

"Uh huh."

"Well, when he gets back here and opens the door, I'll

make my move. After I take care of him, I'll carry you back to my car."

"Darrell's tough. And he's mean, too."

"Yeah. I got a look at him," Dwayne said, pulling the pistol from its holster. Next he got the brass knuckles out of his pocket and slipped them on his right hand.

The two sat quietly, not speaking any more. Ten minutes later the sound of footsteps could be heard. The left door was opened and Bodine announced, "Time's up."

"It sure is," Dwayne said, stepping out. He slammed the knucks as hard as he could into the husky trucker's face.

Bodine staggered back but managed to stay on his feet. His eyes were watering from the attack, but not enough to keep him from seeing that his assailant was pointing a pistol at him. Mary Sue, bare-footed, gingerly stepped down on the gravel.

Dwayne motioned with his pistol, saying, "Get in the back or I'll blow your goddamn head off."

"You son of a bitch!" Bodine cursed in a hoarse voice.

"If I kill you, the law won't do nothing to me," Dwayne said. "I'm a private detective hired by her folks to bring her home. And you're a white slaver."

Bodine knew the game was up. He climbed into the back of the panel truck. Dwayne slammed the door shut. "If you as much as stick your head out of there, I'll put a slug in it."

He holstered the weapon, then picked the girl up and hurried over to his Buick.

CHAPTER 5

Mary Sue sat silently on the passenger side of the sedan. Her feet were drawn up to keep them warm under the corduroy robe. Dwayne glanced over at her now and then as he drove south toward Wichita. The girl gazed out the window at the dark countryside, sniffing a bit.

Dwayne asked, "Are you getting a cold?"

"I'm getting over one."

"I guess you ain't been wearing a lot of clothes, huh?"

"Just this goddamn robe," the sixteen-year-old replied matter-of-factly. "Are you gonna want to fuck?"

"Jesus Christ! Didn't you hear me say I'm taking you back to your folks."

"Yeah."

"Well, I sure as hell ain't gonna have sex with you then turn you over to your mom and dad."

Mary Sue shrugged. "Suit yourself."

"Let me tell you something, Missy. You're lucky you ain't been hurt. Or even murdered. I guess you won't be running off with truck drivers no more, huh?"

"Hell yes I will! It's the only fun I have."

"For God's sake, Mary Sue! Look how you ended up this time."

"Aw! It wasn't so bad."

It hadn't taken Dwayne long to figure out the girl's family life was miserable. Her dad obviously didn't love her while an alcoholic mother, who at least showed some affection for her, had a habit of running off with men for short periods of time.

———

DWAYNE PULLED INTO THE WESTERN Danceland parking lot at 2 a.m. Mary Sue had been dozing, and woke up when he came to a stop at the back of the night club. It was closing time and he waited until the crowd walked or staggered out to their cars. After fifteen minutes, he nudged Mary Sue. "Let's go."

The girl got out of the car and walked around to the front door without waiting for him. Dwayne had to hurry to catch up with her. A drunken redneck gave the girl a leer as they passed him. The bouncer Benny Gordon was about to go back inside when he noticed them.

"You found her, huh?" Benny remarked.

"I found her, yeah."

Dwayne put his hand on the girl's back and steered her toward the office door. When they entered, Jessie and Lorene Pickens were counting the cash from the bar register.

Lorene let out a happy squeal and rushed to her daughter, giving the girl a frantic hug. "You're back, darling! You're back!" When she noted the robe and the fact Mary Sue was barefooted, she glared at Dwayne. "What did you do to her?"

"I found her and brought her back," he snapped. "That's what I did to her."

Mary Sue yawned. "Can I have a beer?"

"Sure," Jessie answered. "Go on out to the cooler and grab one." As soon as she left, he turned to Dwayne. "The girl seems all right."

"None the worse for wear," Dwayne replied. "I found her at a truck stop in Nebraska. Bodine wasn't keeping her in his rig. He had a panel truck with a mattress in the back."

"Okay," Jessie said, not really interested in all the details. "How much of my advance am I getting back?"

"*Getting back!* You owe me, bud! I put six days into this caper."

Mary Sue returned to the office drinking a bottle of Pabst beer.

Jessie brooded for a moment. "Okay. I owe you fifty bucks."

"More'n that. My meals and gas come to ten dollars for gas and six for meals and incidentals. That comes to a hunnerd and sixty-six dollars."

Jessie frowned. "You said twenty-five bucks a day."

"Plus gas, meals, and expenses," Dwayne reminded him.

Mary Sue yelled, "Don't you cheat my daddy!"

"Right," Jessie said. "I'm only giving you fifty bucks."

"Okay," Dwayne said. "Suit yourself." Then he fell back into a lie he always told clients who were trying to stiff him. "I'm required by law to write up my capers and turn 'em into the Kansas Bureau of Investigation. I was gonna give you a pass on that little procedure, but now I'll give the K.B.I. a full account of how your teenage daughter always runs off with truck drivers and this time was made to prostitute herself. What we have here is endangerment of a minor and all that shit."

Lorene yelled at her husband, "Pay him the hunnerd and sixty-six dollars, Jessie!"

"Okay, Lorene." He frowned at the shamus. "That ain't a bit fair, Dwayne."

Dwayne's voice was strained. "I ought to beat the living shit out you, Jessie. You rotten son of a bitch! You try to rob me, then insult me by acting like I cheated you."

Dwayne stepped toward the club owner, but the guy quickly reached over to the cash box on the desk and pulled out some bills. He nervously counted out a hundred and sixty-six dollars. Dwayne took the money and headed for the door.

Jessie suddenly yelled out, "You can forget that free beer we promised you!"

———

THE NEXT DAY DWAYNE WENT TO HIS OFFICE, settled down behind his desk, and began the day by phoning his answering service. Millie, his assigned contact at the Reliable Answering Service, informed him there were no messages. The shamus was relieved by the negative report. The tediousness of the caper to bring Mary Sue back had left him more than just a little agitated. He didn't feel like taking on any work that day.

He put his feet up on his desk, lit a cigarette and began languidly smoking. Once more his thoughts drifted to Nancy Turner. She had turned out to be a delightful sexual playmate. Dwayne had learned a hard lesson in the past where women were concerned. They enjoyed sex and freely put out to guys they liked. However, there was a limit to this acquiescence. The ladies required solicitous treatment such as compliments and other things they wanted to hear. They also appreciated good times outside of the bedroom such as dancing, movies, eating out, etcetera, etcetera. There was no way a guy could get out of that if he wanted to continue with the sex.

Dwayne crushed the cigarette butt in the ashtray on his desk, deciding it was now time to take Nancy out on the town. And what better a place in Wichita than the Roadhouse Night Club. He reached for the phone to make a reservation.

———

THE MORNING PASSED AS DWAYNE DOZED IN HIS chair. He slept uneasily and woke up from time to time because of the discomfort. At noon he drove over to the Continental Grill to grab a quick lunch. The shamus enjoyed his much preferred grilled cheese sandwich with French fries. After finishing off the main course, he chose a slab of cherry pie for desert. When that was polished off, he left the restaurant to go to the Beachcomber.

Dwayne walked into the tavern in time to see Nancy set a bottle of Miller Highlife beer—advertised as the "Champaign of Beers"—in front of a customer. The guy was a large, overweight businessman, who gave her some appreciative attention. Dwayne couldn't hear what he was saying, but the expression on Nancy's face indicated she was not amused.

Dwayne spoke up. "How about some service down here?"

The sound of his voice made Nancy grin with delight and relief. She hurried away from the corpulent Casanova, stopping by the cooler to grab a bottle of Schlitz. "Here you go, hon."

"Thank you," Dwayne said.

"Well? Is your caper over with?"

"Yeah. And I was paid in cash so I thought that this Saturday night would be the perfect time for you and me to spend an evening at the Roadhouse."

Nancy's eyes opened wide. "You mean that ritzy night club?"

"That's right," Dwayne replied. "And it's just the place for a lady like you."

"Oh, Dwayne! I don't have an evening gown or nothing like that!"

"People don't dress up formal for the Roadhouse," he explained. "Put on what you'd wear for going to church or downtown on a shopping trip."

"I got a dress I think will be okay," Nancy said. "I don't want to embarrass you, Dwayne."

"With a good looking gal like you on my arm, I'd never be embarrassed."

Nancy almost laughed aloud with delight. "You say nice things, Dwayne!"

"Did I tell you that I'm good friends with Elmer Pettibone, the owner of the Roadhouse?"

Nancy was impressed. "I guess as a private detective you get around Wichita, huh?"

"I sure do. Now if we were going someplace like the Prairie Wind Golf and Tennis Club, we'd have to really dress up." He winked at her. "But I ain't a member and never will be. So I don't think we'll ever go there."

"That's okay. I'm not comfortable around snooty people."

"Let's see," Dwayne mused. "You get off work at five o'clock, right? So I'll pick you up around eight."

The fat drinker finished off his beer and stomped

angrily out of the tavern, hoping the barmaid had sensed his disdain for her.

———

DWAYNE CALLED ON NANCY AT THE DUPLEX A few minutes before eight o'clock. Her mother Maggie opened the door and gave him a wide smile of welcome. "Hi, Dwayne. C'mon in. Nancy's still dressing."

"Thanks, Maggie." He had noticed that the woman had sad eyes. It reminded him of his mother when she and he were struggling after his father's death. No doubt Mrs. Turner had endured her share of misery and sadness, too.

Dwayne went in and took a seat on the sofa beside Holly. He gave her a friendly wink. "How's things going for you?"

"Okay."

"Has anything special happened since I saw you last?"

The question launched Holly into a long spiel, giving a complete account of the previous week at school. She got an A+ in a spelling test, the teacher read a chapter of the novel *The Secret Garden* as she always did after lunch, the class began learning long division, and a boy in the back of the room threw up.

Dwayne found himself falling under Holly's charms. She was a cute little girl, thoroughly likeable and showed an obvious affection for him. The shamus knew that if he kept seeing her, the child would soon have him wrapped around her little finger.

Nancy made an appearance from the bedroom. "Hi, Dwayne. I'm ready."

Dwayne's eyes opened wide. "Wow! You really look nice, Nancy."

"Thank you. Bret let me off early so's I could go get my hair done."

"Well, they done it real good."

Nancy wore a simple beige frock that buttoned down the front. It had a yellow collar and a dark brown narrow belt with a small buckle. Dwayne was glad he had taken the Buick to the corner gas station for washing and waxing. He was also glad he was wearing a new suit he had recently purchased.

"You're gonna be the belle of the ball at the Roadhouse Night Club tonight," he said.

"I doubt that," Nancy remarked. "I bought this outfit out of a Monkey-Ward catalog." She looked at her mother and daughter, giving them a little wave. "We'll be really late, so don't wait up."

THE OWNER AND OPERATOR OF THE ROADHOUSE Night Club was Elmer Pettibone, who had been Wichita's premier bootlegger before the dry laws were dropped off the books. He was an old associate of Dwayne's, having used him to make pickups of illegal liquor down in Texas on numerous occasions. There were also a few times when Dwayne acted as a bodyguard and collected overdue debts for the man. Those jobs required no finesse. Dwayne always collected by employing convincing intimidation, punctuated with a display of his brass knuckles.

The nightclub was just beyond the northern city limits on Arkansas Avenue. Although the building was a cement block structure, it was popular with cliquey patrons of the Wichita community. The location was far enough off the road to be out of sight behind some cottonwoods and oaks.

Dwayne pulled off Arkansas Avenue and drove down to the parking lot beyond the grove of trees. All the automobiles were brand new '48 models now in production since the auto plants retooled after manufacturing military vehicles during the war. Dwayne found a place to park between two Cadillacs. After helping Nancy out of the car, he escorted her around to the entrance of the night club.

Two burly doormen by the names of Jack Wallace and Denny Tarball stood guard at the front door. They knew all the Wichitans allowed in the club by sight. If an unknown showed up, the pair issued a refusal of entry in a courteous but resolute manner. Persons who showed even the slightest irritation at not being allowed to enter the club were immediately seized and frog-marched out to their cars. Any serious struggles ended with the belligerent getting a thorough punch up before the sheriff's department was called to arrest him as a trespasser.

The two guardians gave the couple a friendly grin. "Hey, Dwayne," Jack Wallace said. "I saw your name on the reservation list for tonight. So what's up?"

"A little celebration," Dwayne replied. "This is Nancy Turner."

"Hi, Nancy," Denny Tarball greeted.

Dwayne introduced them to Nancy, remarking, "These two guys make sure the customers are the right sort."

"By the way," Jack said. "You can actually order real cocktails now instead of beer. Customers don't have to bring their own liquor and buy set-ups."

Dwayne laughed. "I see law enforcement has been greased, huh?"

"You know Elmer Pettibone," Jack said. "The guy knows his way around."

"Like any smart bootlegger or bookie," Denny added.

"By the way," Jack said. "There's a maître d' now. But the same gals are waiting tables."

"Thanks for the info," Dwayne said. He turned to Nancy. "Shall we go in?"

"I can't wait!"

Dennis opened the door for them and Dwayne let Nancy precede him into the building. After Dwayne gave up his fedora at the hatcheck counter, they continued into the club proper. Nancy had never been in a class place like the Roadhouse, and was thrilled by the glitzy interior. "This is wonderful!"

The furnishings and decor were first class in a charming out-of-date art deco fashion. A large dance floor occupied the center of the interior with a well-stocked bar off to one side. A small bandstand was adjacent to the bar. At that moment the dance orchestra with a piano, saxophone, double bass and drums was playing *In the Mood* for a crowd of appreciative dancers.

Sure enough there was a maître d'. The man's voice was courteous yet businesslike. "Good evening. Have you a reservation?"

"We sure do," Dwayne replied. "Under the name Wheeler."

The maître d' checked his list. "Ah, yes! Your name is written in red ink, Mister Wheeler. That means you are a special friend of Mister Pettibone." He turned and snapped his fingers. The gesture produced the immediate appearance of a waitress.

"Hi, Dwayne," she said cheerfully.

"Hi, Teresa. This is Nancy Turner."

"Hi, Nancy," Teresa said. She looked at Dwayne. "We haven't seen you for awhile. C'mon, I'll take you to your table." She ushered them to a ringside location midway between the band and the door. "Are you ready for a cocktail?"

"You bet!" Dwayne said enthusiastically. He looked at Nancy. "What's your pleasure, sweetie?"

Nancy was embarrassed. "I don't know. What did you fix for me at your apartment?"

Dwayne turned to Teresa. "Bring us two scotch and sodas, please."

"You got it."

Teresa went off for the drinks just as the band began playing another number. This one was *Moonlight in Vermont*.

"A slow tune!" Dwayne said. "Let's take a whirl." He took Nancy's hand and led her out to the dance floor. "I can't do that jitterbug stuff. The slow tunes are my favorites."

"Mine, too," Nancy said.

At the end of the song, they returned to their table to find their drinks and a snack bowl of mixed nuts and pretzels. Dwayne chuckled. "The eats are free. Pettibone knows it makes folks thirsty and they'll drink more."

The evening evolved into rounds of cocktails and trips to the dance floor. This was interspersed with quiet conversation as the two grew to know each other better in the bright moments of the evening.

It was around one a.m. and a song Dwayne and Nancy were dancing to ended. They walked toward their table with Dwayne's arm around her waist.

"Dwayne!"

They stopped and Dwayne caught his breath when he saw who had called out his name. It was his former girlfriend Donna Sue Connors. She was with her boss Brian Murchison the CEO of Murchison Enterprises. He was a man Dwayne resented somewhat unfairly. Murchison hadn't taken Donna Sue away from him since they had already split up when he came on the scene.

Murchison showed a genuinely friendly smile. "Congratulations, Dwayne! That was great work you did on solving the murder of that professor. I read about it in both the *Eagle* and the *Beacon*."

"Thanks, Brian," Dwayne mumbled. "Uh...this is Nancy Turner."

Nancy sensed the tension and did not fail to notice that Donna Sue wore what was obviously a very expensive dress even if it wasn't an evening gown. Murchison invited the couple to join them at their table, but Dwayne turned him down, saying they were getting ready to leave.

Nancy was glad Dwayne wanted to go. Her feminine instincts screamed at her that Dwayne and Donna Sue had once been lovers. Her self-esteem had taken a nose dive by the fact she was not as pretty as Donna Sue and her simple frock was dismal in comparison with what the other woman wore.

The evening was over.

CHAPTER 6

When Dwayne walked into his office on Monday morning, he carried a Styrofoam cup of coffee he had purchased at Dockum's Drugstore across from the police station. The caffeine-laden brew required a cigarette as an accompaniment. After the first sip, he lit up the requisite Lucky Strike and leaned back in his chair.

Nancy had been quiet after they left the Roadhouse the night before. Dwayne knew that Murchison and Donna Sue had overwhelmed her with their beauty and attire. He wasn't sure of Nancy's background, but it was obvious she had humble beginnings. No doubt she thought most people looked down on her. He knew that awful feeling from his own early life.

Now, after taking a final swig of coffee, he dialed his answering service. The operator Millie was on duty as usual. "You have one call, Mister Wheeler. It's from a woman by the name of Rachel. She said you have her number."

"I do. Thanks."

He hung up and gave the matter some consideration.

This was an unusual summons. Rachel Brooks worked for Venus Services. This was a swanky call girl service run by a Mrs. Davies who was the *grande dame* of local prostitution. Dwayne had worked for the lady on several occasions, including running off a would-be blackmailer. He quickly looked up the number in his notebook and dialed.

"Venus Services," came the answer in a sultry voice.

"Hi, Rachel," Dwayne said. "I hear you want to talk to me."

"Oh, hi, Dwayne! I sure do. Mrs. Davies wants to see you. She says she'll send Karl to pick you up over here."

"I'm on my way, doll!"

———

THE CALL GIRL COMMUNICATIONS CENTER WAS nestled in a far corner of the Harry Street Medical Arts Center east of Hillside. Dwayne pulled into the complex, making sure he didn't park directly in front of the unmarked Venus Services office. Mrs. Davies wanted the place to maintain an empty appearance. This clandestine enterprise operated twenty-four hours every day of the week. Rachel was there most of the time, but three more women also handled the telephone chores.

Dwayne walked down to the office and pressed the doorbell in a signal pattern that identified him as an insider. The summons was quickly answered by Rachel who opened the door automatically with an electronic button on her desk.

"Hi, Dwayne," Rachel Brooks greeted. She was a small, slim brunette in her mid-thirties. She had been a call girl for several years, popular with the clients because of her striking good looks. But a serious car crash had left her legs badly scarred. She walked with a noticeable limp and always wore slacks. "Karl is on his way."

The man Karl was Mrs. Davies' chauffeur who drove the lady's pristine 1934 Duisenberg limousine. Mrs. Davies always sent the chauffeur to pick up her invited guests. The lady did not want cars driving down the long, curving driveway to her house.

A quarter of an hour passed before the coded doorbell signal sounded. Rachel buzzed it open. "Hello, Karl."

"How do you do, Miss Brooks," the chauffeur replied. He was a gaunt elderly man wearing an old-fashioned chauffeur's outfit complete with billed cap but without the leather gaiters. He turned to Dwayne. "Mrs. Davies is in a hurry to see you, sir."

They stepped out the door and walked down to the limo. Dwayne slipped into the back seat as the chauffeur fired up the big car's twelve-cylinder engine.

Mrs. Belle Davies lived on a secluded country estate just past Thirty-Seventh Street in north Wichita. Her large two-story house was almost invisible from the road because of a high wall and tall trees. The entrance to the property was a heavy iron gate with an armed guard in attendance.

Karl drove to the gate and waited for it to be opened. Then he headed directly to the house where a butler waited at the steps of the small concrete porch. The man opened the passenger door for Dwayne to exit the vehicle. The greeter was heavy set and most dignified. He had an expression on his round face as if he smelled something unpleasant. "This way, Mr. Wheeler. I am Dawkins."

"Yeah. I remember you from other visits, Dawkins."

They entered the house, crossed a foyer and went down to a waiting room. The butler said, "Make yourself comfortable, Mr. Wheeler. I shall collect you presently."

The room was a well-furnished parlor with a deep carpet. A large portrait of a young woman dressed as a flapper of a bygone era hung on one wall. Dwayne knew the image was Mrs. Davies as a young woman. He admired the lady's beauty as he sat down on the sofa and waited to be ushered into her presence.

Belle Davies' clientele consisted of Wichita's wealthiest businessmen as well as special customers who visited the city from time to time. Since Wichita was the only metropolitan center in that part of the state, it was the hub of commerce in that very lucrative region. No customer—local or out-of-towner—ever had any contact with the *grande dame* or got a glimpse of Rachel. All their requests for services were done over the phone.

No one was sure of Mrs. Davies' age, but it was a known fact that she had been in silent movies. This meant she was most likely in her fifties. Her arrival in Wichita was a mystery, but some insisted that she had been paid off to get out of Hollywood because of intimate knowledge regarding a famous personage's death.

The butler appeared in the door. "Mrs. Davies will see you now, sir."

Dwayne followed him out into the hall, and farther into the interior of the house. Dawkins stopped and indicated a room that Dwayne was expected to enter. When he walked in, he saw the lady sitting at her desk. As always he was impressed how her beauty had matured in a most flattering way. Her secretary Kathryn Carruthers stood next to her.

Mrs. Davies offered a slight smile. "I believe you know Miss Carruthers."

"I sure do," Dwayne replied. "How are you, Miss?"

"I am fine, thank you. It is so good to see you again."

"Please sit down, Mister Wheeler," Mrs. Davies

invited. Her voice was gracious and feminine but exhibited a commanding tone.

Dwayne seated himself in a plush easy chair. "What can I do for you, Missus Davies?"

"There is a situation that has been revealed to me," the lady began. "A cruel criminal organization is controlling many unfortunate young women." She paused as if pained to continue. "They are forced to act as prostitutes at truck stops."

Dwayne's eyes opened wide. "I know about that...in a way, that is...I recently brought the daughter of a client back to her family. She was being prostituted at truck stops like you said."

"Was she addicted to heroin?"

"Not that I could tell," Dwayne replied. "She seemed all right except for being worn out."

"Perhaps yours is a different situation," Mrs. Davies informed him. "The young women I am talking about are addicted to the drug. In order to feed their habits, they must work for the criminals who inject them after each period of work."

"I'm not real familiar with heroin."

"It is a horrible narcotic that ensnares its victims in the strongest of addictions."

Dwayne shrugged. "Can't they just run away and stop taking the stuff?"

"The withdrawal from the drug is one of extreme agony. The addict will do anything for another dose to take away the torment."

"Jesus!"

"I would like you to investigate this horrible state of affairs," Mrs. Davies said. "I need you to gather enough evidence to have those vicious pimps put in jail."

"Where'd you get this information, Missus Davies?"

"I can understand your professional curiosity, Mister Wheeler," she stated. "However, I cannot elaborate except to say I was informed of the situation by friends and associates who must not be revealed. We all share concern about young women who are not particularly attractive that work in the basest stratum of prostitution. Those are the ones who are under the power of pimps and other whoremasters. It is a situation that is outright slavery."

"I understand."

"I realize I cannot provide you with adequate information of the who, what and where of this outrage. No doubt the job will be most difficult and time consuming. I am certain you have the skill to conduct the investigation and gather evidence to bring those malfeasants to justice. You always served my interests in a very professional way; that is to say 'successfully.' Are you able to accept this employment?"

"Yes, ma'am."

"In that case I shall advance you five hundred dollars, Mister Wheeler."

"I don't need near that much right now, Missus Davies."

"I *shall* advance you five hundred dollars," she repeated in a firm imposing tone.

"Yes, ma'am. Thank you."

"How soon can you start?"

"Immediately if not sooner," Dwayne replied, grinning. "That's a saying they have in the army."

"How interesting," she replied wryly.

Mrs. Davies got up, turning to her secretary. "Please give the money to Mister Wheeler." With that final statement, she left the room.

Miss Carruthers handed Dwayne an envelope. "By the way, how is Donna Sue?"

"We've broken up."

"Oh! I'm sorry to hear that."

A year or so back Dwayne had requested Mrs. Davies to allow Donna Sue to take refuge in her house when she was threatened by the Kansas City mob. It was a caper that had begun with a bookie's murder. Donna Sue and Miss Carruthers had become friends during that time.

Dwayne stuck the money into his inside jacket pocket. "Well, I'm on my way."

"I shall summon Karl to drive you back to your car."

AFTER KARL DROPPED HIM OFF, DWAYNE immediately drove downtown to call on one of his best contacts. This was Lieutenant Ben Forester who headed up the Wichita Police Department's homicide bureau. Although this newest caper did not concern murder—at least it didn't seem to—Forester, as a ranking officer, was privy to much of the criminal activity that went on in Wichita and the state of Kansas.

Dwayne nodded to the desk sergeant as he entered the building, then went up the stairs to the second floor where homicide was located. When he walked through the door he encountered an old nemesis. This was Detective Sergeant Al Gallagher. He and Dwayne shared a mutual hatred of each other. Gallagher was at his desk hunting-and-pecking on a typewriter while filling out a case report.

Dwayne stopped and looked at him. "Unsolved is spelled U-N-S-O-L-V-E-D, Gallagher. But you've probably written that down so often you got it memorized."

"I got two words for you, shamus," the sergeant growled. "And they ain't 'happy birthday'."

Dwayne snorted, "Putting two words together is the biggest sentence you can form, ain't it?" With that said, he continued through the desks to an office at the end of the large room. He could see Lieutenant Ben Forester through the glass window. He rapped on the door and stepped inside. "How's it going, Ben?"

Forester looked up. "Hey, Dwayne. What's up?"

"I need some information. D'you know anything about prostitution at truck stops?"

"I know it goes on," the lieutenant replied. "But no details. Why?"

"I got a client that's concerned about it," Dwayne said. "And there's heroin involved."

Forester was thoughtful for a moment. "That sounds like an interstate crime to me. Have you thought of contacting the Feds?"

Dwayne shook his head. "No. I just got the caper. I was hoping maybe you knew something."

"There hasn't been any mention in the latest bulletins. You remember F.B.I. Agent Steve Williams, don't you?"

"Sure do."

"If I were you, I'd go see him," Forester suggested. "I'm not aware of anything going on in Wichita or Sedgwick County involving truck stop whores."

"I'll check him out. Thanks. See you later."

"Right," Forester said. "By the way, you didn't speak to Gallagher when you walked in, did you?"

"Yeah."

"Damn! That means he's gonna be in a bad mood for the rest of the day."

———

THE F.B.I.'S WICHITA OFFICE WAS LOCATED ON the third floor of the Wheeler Kelly Hagny Building on South Market Street. Dwayne had worked with Agent Steve Williams there on a couple of capers. One involved the attempted takeover of Wichita by the Kansas City mob and the other concerned a war criminal.

A secretary was at her desk in the outer office when Dwayne walked in. "Hi. I'd like to see Steve, please."

The woman gave him a cold look. "What does this concern, sir?"

Dwayne showed the P.I. badge he had purchased in a pawn shop a few years before. It wasn't official or legal, but gave a better impression than a small license that didn't even have his picture on it. "It involves an interstate matter. I've worked with Steve before. My name is Dwayne Wheeler."

"Have a seat, sir," she said. The woman got up and knocked on the door leading to an inner office. She went in and quickly returned with Williams at her side.

"C'mon in, Dwayne," the man said. "Long time. No see. As our oriental brothers say."

They entered his office and both sat down. Dwayne wasted no time. "I've got a client who has hired me to look into prostitution at truck stops. "What I need—"

"Prostitution at truck stops?" Williams interrupted.

"Well, yeah," Dwayne said. "I checked with Lieutenant Forester at the Wichita Police Department and he said I should talk to you about it. It's prob'ly interstate. And heroin is involved. So I—"

Williams interrupted him again. "Well! Let's discuss this, shall we, Dwayne?" He leaned forward. "Who is this client of yours?"

"I can't tell you that, Steve."

"Okay, I understand. Just give me the gist of the matter."

"It's like I said," Dwayne replied a bit irritably. "There's whores working at truck stops. In Kansas. The women are addicted to heroin. I been hired to check things out. To get some evidence."

"Y'know, Dwayne," Williams said. "That's very, very interesting. Can you come back here tomorrow afternoon?"

"Yeah," Dwayne asked, puzzled. "Why?"

"Just come back and we can delve into this matter a bit deeper."

Dwayne stood up. "Sure. No problem."

He walked out of the inner office and was surprised to see that the agent was right behind him. Williams escorted him to the outer door. "Okay, Dwayne. Don't forget. Tomorrow afternoon. Let's say about two o'clock. Okay?"

"Okay."

CHAPTER 7

When Dwayne arrived at the Beachcomber Tavern, the only people in the place were Nancy and her boss Bret Underwood. He was down at the end of the bar doing a crossword puzzle.

The shamus slid onto a barstool just as Nancy sat a bottle of Schlitz beer in front of him. "What's new?"

"A caper I can't talk about."

Nancy giggled. "Are you gonna solve it by sitting on that stool?"

He grinned back. "I wish I could." He took a couple of quick swallows from the bottle. "How's it going?"

"Okay," she replied. After a moment of silence, she asked, "Was that lady Donna Sue an old flame of yours?"

"Yeah."

"She seems nice."

"Donna Sue used to be a waitress at the Jayhawker Restaurant on West Douglas," he stated. "Actually it was a diner. She worked at Boeing Aircraft during the war. When it ended, she lost her job and went back to being a waitress."

Nancy was surprised. "She sure don't look like the type to sling hash."

"Well, that's what she did. But Donna Sue wanted to step up in life so she got a high school equivalent certificate and took a course on how to be a secretary and got a job. She works for Murchison now."

"How's come you two broke up?" she asked, then her face reddened. "I'm sorry. I know it's none of my business."

"That's all right," Dwayne assured her. "A lot changed between us when she quit being a waitress. Things wasn't the same at all. Sometimes that happens." He chuckled. "It happens *a lot* to me."

"Well, I ain't gonna be stepping up in the world," Nancy declared. "That's for sure."

"I don't know much about you."

"I was born in Oklahoma," Nancy said. "My daddy was a roughneck in the oil fields. He was mean and drunk half the time. He made pretty good money but spent it all on liquor and women. I had to leave school in the eighth grade and get a job as a cleaning girl in a motor lodge outside of Muskogee."

"I bet that didn't pay much, huh?"

"It sure didn't," she said. "I had to keep at it though. It was the best I could do and there was four other kids too young to work."

"We got a lot in common," Dwayne told her. "My dad was run over and killed by a taxi when he was drunk. My mom and me had a hard time. She died when I was twenty and I joined the army. And here I am. That's all I got to say about it."

"And that's all I got to say about me," Nancy said. "I guess it was easy for you to figure I wasn't married when I got pregnant. I kept Holly instead of giving her away for adoption. My daddy got killed in a work accident down in east Texas and mama got an insurance settlement. Me and mama and Holly came to Wichita about a year ago. We're living on the insurance and what I earn here. We're doing all right now."

He shoved the empty beer bottle forward. "Can I have another?"

She grinned. "I don't know. You got a quarter?"

"Yes, ma'am."

"Then you get one more Schlitz." She walked over the cooler and retrieved the beer. After prying off the cap she brought it back.

Dwayne took a drink. "You want to come over to my place this evening?"

"I do," she replied. "Take me home and I can tell mama we're going to the movies like we always do."

"She must think we're real movie fans, huh?"

"Mama knows what we're doing," Nancy explained with a giggle. "The movie lie is for Holly."

A couple of customers walked in and settled down in a booth. Nancy walked around the bar and stopped beside him for a moment before going to the newcomers. "We have to talk tonight."

Oh, shit! Dwayne thought.

———

DWAYNE EJACULATED AND FINISHED HUMPING.

Nancy, who had put her arms around his shoulders during coitus, opened them up to allow him to roll off her. As usual, he got a pack of Lucky Strikes off the nightstand, took one, and lit it. She squirmed her way to a sitting position and reached down to pull the sheet up over her.

He glanced at her. "How come you always cover up when we finish?"

"I guess I'm modest."

He looked at the clock. "It's only nine o'clock. Since it's early—"

She interrupted. "This is the last time I'm doing this."

"Doing what?"

"Getting into bed and letting you fuck me."

Uh oh! his mind said to him. He cleared his throat. "What brought this on?"

"I ain't going through another one of these so-called romances," Nancy pronounced, close to tears. "If you really want me, you'll get serious about us."

"I *am* serious about us," Dwayne insisted.

"Goddamn it!" she yelled. "I don't want no more boyfriends! I want a man who'll be *my* man! I want a man who'll marry me and settle down with me!" She began sobbing. "How much...more do...I gotta go through...this bullshit?"

"Well," Dwayne said hesitantly, "it's not that simple."

She wiped at her tears. "What are you talking about?"

"Well...you got a kid and your mother, too."

Nancy turned and faced him. "That's low, Dwayne! That's so goddamn low it's mean!" She got out of bed and went across the room to the chair where her clothes were draped. "Take me home!"

Dwayne snuffed out the cigarette, then got up to get his own clothing.

———

DWAYNE WHEELER SHOWED UP AT THE F.B.I. office at a quarter to two for his appointment with Agent Steve Williams. When he stepped into the outer office from the hallway, the receptionist greeted him. "You're expected, Mister Wheeler. Go right in."

Dwayne entered the inner office to see F.B.I. agent Steve William obviously waiting for him. "Take a load off, Dwayne." He waited until the visitor had taken a chair. "You told me you're working on a case regarding prostitution at truck stops. How much information do you have to go on?"

"Not a goddamn bit."

"Okay. The F.B.I. is involved in a situation similar to what you described. And it's in Kansas."

"Hey!" Dwayne exclaimed. "Maybe it's the same one."

"It most likely is," Williams agreed. "Now I'm gonna ask you one more time. D'you mind identifying your client?"

"Yeah. I mind."

"Fair enough. D'you consider this person reliable?"

"My client is in a position to have accurate, up-to-date info on this situation," Dwayne said. "And the client mentioned heroin being used to control the whores."

"And what exactly does this client want you to do for him?"

"To get enough evidence to close the operation down," Dwayne answered.

"Are you willing to quit working for your client?"

Dwayne frowned. "Why the hell would I do that?"

"Because after a telephone conference I learned the F.B.I. wants you to go undercover on this truck stop and heroin case. Anyhow, there's not a doubt in my mind that your client is talking about the same group of pimps."

"I believe you're right," Dwayne said. "And it's the interstate side of the caper that's making it a Federal job, right?"

"Right," Williams said. "But there's more to it than

that. The group running the racket is an Irish gang from Boston called the Derbies. We have an agent that's been infiltrated into their midst for the past couple of years. They've transferred him and a few others to this part of the country." Williams paused and gave Dwayne a meaningful look. "We want you to join him."

Dwayne was impressed. "Will I get a cover name and all that?"

"You won't need one," Williams said. "In fact, you can be your real self. We'll set up a cover story for you. We'll issue a press release stating that your P.I. license has been suspended for several serious violations."

"Are you sure people will believe that?"

"Dwayne," Williams replied, "you couldn't find a single person in Wichita, Kansas, who would be surprised by learning that you've been taking part in illegal activities."

Dwayne made no comment.

"The cover story is that you and our guy served together in the Army. You were both military policemen who became mixed up in the black market. Which is exactly what *you* did."

"Oh," Dwayne said. "You know about that, huh?"

"Yeah."

I bet you don't know my commanding officer was in it with me, Dwayne thought.

"So we can say you two kept in touch after the war and he's called you now and then since he was in Kansas," Williams informed him. "When you lost your license you wanted to know if he could find work for you. So he invited you to come up and he'd introduce you to the others. They'll welcome a local guy since ever'body else is Boston Irish and aren't real familiar with the area. Frankly they stand out like a Nazis at a bar mitzvah."

Dwayne thought fast. He knew he'd be put on a Federal payroll. And he also had the advance money from Mrs. Davies who wouldn't let him return as much as a dime of it to her.

"I'll do it."

CHAPTER 8

Dwayne went straight back to his apartment after the interview with Steve Williams. He had a serious situation to tend to before going undercover. This dilemma was all about Nancy Turner.

He felt terrible about what had happened the night before. It was another case of him being confronted by an emotional woman and not knowing the proper way to handle the problem. In all those past incidents he'd regretted his reactions the next day.

Dwayne liked her little daughter Holly a great deal. She was a vivacious, charming ten-year-old who had caught his fancy. He also had a genuine affection for Mrs. Turner. The widow had suffered terribly from mistreatment by a brutish husband. No doubt he slapped her around and made her life miserable.

After serious contemplation Dwayne had an idea how to set things right. And the undercover caper couldn't have come at a better time. He planned to mollify Nancy before leaving on the assignment. This would give her plenty of time to think about their relationship.

He went to the closet where his money was stashed in the door jamb, and retrieved the envelope with the five hundred dollars that Mrs. Davies had advanced him. He pulled a hundred out and put the remainder back into the hiding place.

With that done, he left for the Beachcomber.

———

DWAYNE TIMED HIS ARRIVAL AT THE TAVERN exactly right. It was fifteen minutes before the end of Nancy's shift. He walked in and caught her eye as he settled himself at the bar. Nancy brought him a Schlitz as usual. But instead of exchanging any remarks, she took the quarter he'd laid down on the bar and started to walk away.

"Nancy, I got to talk to you."

She stopped and turned, giving him a suspicious look. "What about?"

"I'm sorry about last night," he said. "I wasn't very nice and I feel bad about it."

The stern expression on her face relaxed slightly, and she stated, "You were terrible to me."

"I know."

She glared at him, waiting to see what else he had to say.

"How about if we go to the Continental Grill after you get off? It's kind of like our special place. Y'know what I mean? And I'll take you home right after we eat."

She hesitated, then nodded an affirmative answer.

Ten minutes later the couple walked out to Dwayne's car. He held the door open for her, then walked around and got in. He showed a grin. "Continental Grill, here we come!"

Nancy remained stoic.

Dwayne drove up to East Douglas and turned toward the restaurant. He wanted desperately to lighten the mood. "Oh, boy! I'm hungry. How about you?"

She made no answer.

After he found a parking place, they went inside and he saw an empty booth in the back where they could converse without being overheard. They sat down across from each other rather than side-by-side. This was instigated by Nancy who did not slide over for him. He accepted the snub with a smile, turning his attention to the juke box.

"Whatcha wanta hear?" he asked cheerfully.

"Nothing."

"Me either," Dwayne replied. "Same old songs as always, huh?"

A waitress appeared. "Hi, folks. What can I get you?" She noticed Nancy's rancor and the woman's feminine instincts kicked in. Here was a couple in crisis. That meant getting their order ASAP. People aren't quite as talkative or aggressive when eating.

Dwayne asked for his usual Orange Crush, grilled cheese sandwich, and French fries. Nancy ordered a chicken salad sandwich, coleslaw, and ice tea. After the waitress left, she asked, "Why do you always order the same thing?"

He ignored her peevishness. "Habit, I guess."

Nancy gazed out the window at the traffic passing by. She sensed he had a reason for the dinner date, but she wasn't going to encourage him to explain himself. As far as she was concerned, he had a long way to go to make up for his bad behavior. They had no conversation while waiting for the food.

When the waitress reappeared with their orders and

set the plates in front of them, the silence continued. Eventually Dwayne took a sip of the Orange Crush, then said, "I'm gonna be out of town for awhile."

Nancy made no comment.

"I'm afraid I'm in kind of a jam," he told her, picking up a single French fry.

Nancy was suddenly curious. "What's going on?"

"A misunderstanding," Dwayne replied. "I'll be back in a month at the earliest. But it'll probably be longer'n that. I can't be sure."

"It sounds serious."

"It could be. In the meantime, I got something for you." He pulled the envelope from his jacket and laid it by her plate.

"What's this?" Nancy asked.

"A hunnerd dollars."

Her temper flared and she replied in an angry undertone. "I am *not* a whore!"

"No! No!" he whispered frantically. "I'm not asking you to come back to my apartment. This is for you and Holly and your mom. I got a big payout from my last caper. I figured you could use it. I'm taking you straight home like I said. Right after we eat. Honest."

Nancy calmed down. She could see he was sincere, and even if he wanted to have sex, he certainly wouldn't pay a hundred dollars for it. She gazed straight into his eyes. "This is becoming confusing, Dwayne."

"I know," he replied contritely. "Obviously we're not going to be able to see each other while I'm gone. I figured it would be a break for us both to do some serious thinking. This is extra money I want to share with you. I don't want nothing for it."

Nancy looked into the envelope at the five twenty-dollar bills. Her practical side kicked in as it does for all needy people when financial assistance is suddenly available. "Thank you, Dwayne."

"You're welcome."

"When we get to the house you should come in for a cup of coffee," she suggested. "Holly is always pleased when you visit. So is my mom."

"Sure! Let's get some food-to-go for 'em."

Now, with a better humor in the booth, the couple finished their meal.

———

WHEN DWAYNE AND NANCY ENTERED THE duplex, he held up a bag and sang out, "Get you hamburgers! Get your French fries! Get 'em while they're hot!"

"Yay!" Holly yelled. She ran up and hugged Dwayne around the waist. "You're the nicest man in the whole wide world!"

Maggie Turner took the sack. "I'll take care of this. Anybody for coffee?"

"You bet," Dwayne answered.

"I'll help you, Mama," Nancy offered.

Dwayne, taking Holly's hand, knew Nancy would show her mother the hundred dollars. He and Holly sat down on the sofa, and she snuggled against him. He smiled at her. "I kept a secret when I brought that bag in."

"Really? What's your secret?"

He hesitated. "Well...there's milkshakes in there, too."

Holly cheered again, then quickly changed the subject. "You want to hear what I did? I got a hundred on my spelling test today."

"That's great, sweetie. You're a real smart girl."

"I was the only one. Another girl named Janet was next with ninety-five. I don't like her. She thinks she's better than anybody else. She always gets new dresses and shoes and shows them off. Mama buys our clothes at the Salvation Army store."

"Hey!" Dwayne exclaimed. "That's where my mama bought ours, too."

"Really and truly?"

"Sure. That's nothing to be ashamed of. In fact, it's pretty smart. There's good bargains at the Salvation Army."

"What are bargains?"

"That's when you get more for what you pay."

Nancy called out, "Ever'thing's ready."

Dwayne took Holly's hand again, and they headed for the kitchen. Everyone sat down and Maggie and Holly turned their attention to the hamburgers, fries and milk-shakes. Dwayne and Nancy sipped cups of fresh-brewed coffee.

Maggie gave him a fond look. "Thank you, Dwayne. Thank you for ever'thing."

"Dwayne is going on a trip," Nancy announced. "He'll be gone for awhile."

This worried Holly. "You won't be away for a long time, will you?"

"Aw, no," Dwayne answered. "I'll be back just as soon as I can."

Nancy smiled at her daughter. "I know something you don't know!"

"What?" the girl asked.

"Your grandma and me have decided to get a telephone!"

"Wow!" Holly happily squealed. "We never had one before!"

Dwayne winked at her. "Who're you gonna call first?"

"You!" the girl exclaimed. "Just as soon as you get back!"

The group settled in for a pleasant evening as Dwayne basked in the glow of affectionate glances from Nancy. And Holly. And Maggie.

CHAPTER 9

A few days later, a news article appeared in the morning edition of the *Wichita Eagle* followed by another similar one in the evening *Wichita Beacon*. The subject matter of the articles was also broadcast on all the local radio news programs.

Local Private Detective Loses License After Charges of Misconduct by K.B.I.

Agent Harry Philbin of the Kansas Bureau of Investigation announced that Dwayne Wheeler, a private investigator in Wichita, has had his license revoked. Investigations revealed fraud and extortion committed by Wheeler in a criminal case yet to be disclosed.

The private investigator, who has solved several well-known murder cases in the city, has been under surveillance by both the K.B.I. and the F.B.I. for several months. If found guilty, the private eye could face a long prison sentence.

The accused could not be contacted for a statement regarding this incident.

Dwayne had gone through a final briefing with Steve Williams. He learned the criminal organization he would infiltrate was a Boston outfit called the Derbies. The boss was Johnny Cullen, a man in his sixties, who had been wily enough to escape more than a dozen attempts on his life since the days of national prohibition. Cullen was a clever survivor, always cool when the organization faced the greatest danger from other gangs. However, despite the leader's cunning, the Derbies had never been able to establish a strong presence in their hometown. Thus it appeared that Cullen had decided to move to another part of the country to establish a prostitution racket at truck stops.

The F.B.I. surmised that after giving the matter some deep thought, the gang boss decided Kansas was the best place for his plan. The state was in the middle of the country and two main highways U.S. 40 and U.S. 81 crossed each other in that area. Cullen sent a team of his best men to Kansas but he and his second-in-command stayed in the Boston neighborhood where the Derbies had been for decades.

The F.B.I. informant who infiltrated the gang had a difficult assignment since Cullen played his cards close to his chest. The only information the agent had gleaned was the hooker racket at truck stops. However, the F.B.I. was sure that was just a cover for more complicated criminal activities that might possibly be sponsored by an eastern Mafia crime family. The Feds needed to confirm or dismiss that rumor to the extent they were willing to take their time before making arrests.

Now Dwayne was back on U.S. 81. His destination was a truck stop with a telephone exchange east of Salina, Kansas on U.S. 40. This was where the gang in Kansas made phone calls to Boss Cullen back east. As luck would have it, the guy charged with those communications was no less a personage than the F.B.I. infiltrator himself. As far as Dwayne was concerned, that showed the agent had been able to penetrate deep into the Derbies' organization. He had to be a cool and courageous operative if he'd been in the assignment for almost two years and not yet been compromised.

Dwayne reached Salina and turned east on U.S. 40, continuing to his destination. He spotted it after fifteen minutes and pulled into the parking lot in front of the telephone exchange. It was close to the ten a.m. appointment for him to meet the mysterious undercover guy.

The shamus walked in and looked around, noting the place was empty except for a woman at a counter in the back. He rightly assumed this was where customers arranged for calls to be made. Two banks of five telephone booths each were aligned along both sides of the room. A row of folding chairs was at the front of the building, and Dwayne walked over to them and sat down.

The lady on duty noticed him. "Can I help you?"

"No thanks. I'm waiting for a friend."

He checked his watch just as the door opened. A man walked in, going up to the counter. He was a short tough-looking guy with ruddy features and sandy hair. Dwayne watched as he made arrangements for a call with the woman. When that was done, the guy walked back to the chairs to wait for his requested connection to be made.

He looked at Dwayne. "Hiya. Are you making a call?"

"I'm thinking about it," Dwayne replied. "But I can't remember the number."

That was the challenge and password arranged for their meeting. The stranger nodded to him. "You must be Dwayne Wheeler."

"Yeah. They never gave me your name."

"Terry McCarthy. I just put in a call back east. As soon as I'm finished, we can go over to the restaurant and talk."

The woman called out, "Sir, your collect call to Boston is connected. Go to booth three please."

"All right. Thank you."

McCarthy went to the booth and pulled out a pencil and notebook before sitting down. Dwayne watched as he took the handset off the cradle and spoke into the mouth-piece. He did very little talking, only speaking a few words occasionally as he took notes. After fifteen minutes he hung up and left the booth.

"Let's go next door for some coffee," McCarthy said. "I guess they told you there's a good chance the Big Boss is gonna call me back to Boston."

This startled Dwayne. "No. Williams never told me about that."

"I guess this is gonna make it more difficult for you."

"It sure as hell is."

When the two walked into the restaurant it was busy with truck drivers, and they went down to the far end of the counter. A bleached blonde waitress took their orders for coffee and donuts. As they waited, McCarthy commented, "So you were involved in the black market in Germany after the war. How'd you get away with only a discharge for the convenience of the government?"

"They wanted to get rid of me as fast as possible,"

Dwayne replied. "When I got back to Wichita I couldn't get on the police department without an honorable discharge. That's why I ended up with a license as a private investigator."

The waitress reappeared with their order. "Anything else, guys?"

"That'll do it," McCarthy said. He turned back to Dwayne as the woman went to wait on other customers. "That discharge was okay for a P.I. license, huh?"

Dwayne shook his head. "I put down I had an honorable discharge. It was all done by mail between Wichita and Topeka."

McCarthy grinned. "You're a resourceful fellah, Wheeler. But don't think I look down on you. You've pulled off some damn fine detective work according to what the Bureau told me."

Dwayne was getting impatient. "I'd like to hear about the set-up I'm about to step into."

"Okay. We're running a prostitution ring at this truck stop. We're an Irish gang called the Derbies."

"That's an odd name," Dwayne opined. "Is there some meaning behind it?"

"Yeah. It seems that a long time back they all wore derby hats with green bands around the crowns."

Dwayne chuckled. "Saint Patrick's Day ever'day, huh?"

"It seems that way. Anyhow, the Derbies are actually working for a Mafia family located in New York City. I'm not sure at this point, but I think this prostitution thing is going to become part of a coast-to-coast smuggling operation."

That aroused Dwayne's curiosity. "What kind of smuggling?"

"Narcotics," McCarthy answered. "As a matter of fact,

we have four whores and all are addicted to heroin and that's how we control 'em."

"Is that all you've got? Just four?"

"As far as I know," McCarthy replied. "If there's other teams out there, I'm not aware of 'em. Our group is working out of a former religious retreat north of U.S. 40."

"A *religious* retreat?"

"Yeah. It was owned by a fundamentalist Christian group. They called it the Christ the King Retreat. We just call it the Retreat."

"That doesn't seem like the best choice for a hideout." Dwayne stated.

"It's pretty well hidden. To get there you have to turn north off the highway and go a ways down a dirt country road. Then you follow a narrow track that goes through a bunch of trees and crosses a creek. There's a main house with a parlor, kitchen and a couple of offices on the bottom floor. All the bedrooms are on the second floor."

"What about the bathrooms?"

"Modern but only the two upstairs are for most of us," McCarthy replied. "One is for us and the other for the whores. The chief has his own along with a bedroom downstairs."

"Where does the water come from?"

"There's a large well with a gasoline motor pump. The sewage system is a cesspool. We don't have any garages, but we park under a line of carports. And we have propane gas for cooking and heating. A truck from a nearby town fills the tank once a month."

"Isn't that risky?"

"No. We have a gatehouse at the entrance to the property. Some of our guys are there twenty-four hours a day. They escort the gas man to and from the tank."

"Nice set up," Dwayne commented. "Did the gang buy it?"

"Yeah. And we got a good deal on it, too. Nobody had use for property in a hard-to-reach place."

"It all sounds like a hell of an expense," Dwayne said.

"We're making a hell of a lot of money," McCarthy said. "So we're not short on funds. So what you and I have to do, is figure out what the big picture is in this operation."

"I notice you saw 'we' a lot," Dwayne remarked. "You must really consider yourself a member of the Derby Gang."

"Yeah," McCarthy said. "And you will, too, after awhile." He dunked his donut. "By the way, Dwayne, we better use our first names. We're supposed to be old army buddies, remember?"

"Okay, Terry."

They finished their coffee and went out to the parking lot. Dwayne was surprised to see that McCarthy was driving a brand new 1948 Nash "woody" station wagon. He let out a low whistle. "Wow! You guys are making good money all right."

"Yep," McCarthy replied. "We drove it all the way out here from Boston. Note the Massachusetts license plates."

"Oh, yeah."

"Follow me," McCarthy said, "and I'll take you to your new home."

They drove out of the truck stop with Dwayne following. When they reached the junction where U.S. Highways 40 and 81 crisscrossed, the pair continued west on 40. They went thirty miles then slowed and turned north on a country road.

After being allowed to pass the gatehouse by an obviously armed guard, it was only a short distance to a roomy-looking wooden building. They continued around to the back and parked. Dwayne got out of the Buick holding a copy of the *Wichita Eagle*. He handed the newspaper to McCarthy. "I'm disappointed they didn't put my picture with the write-up."

McCarthy checked out the article about Dwayne's misconduct. "It was a good idea to bring this with you. It backs up our cover story. C'mon. I'll take you in and introduce you to the chief."

They entered the large building, stepping into a combination kitchen and dining room. A large dining table was situated in the center of the area. Ten chairs were arranged around it and there was a counter with shelves mounted to the wall. A stove and sink were off to the side.

One man was seated at the table, and he looked at Dwayne with obvious curiosity. The guy had a bottle of Irish whiskey in front of him.

"Jimmy," McCarthy said. "This is the guy I told you about." He handed the newspaper to him. "Take a look at what they're saying about him in Wichita."

The man, Jimmy Sheehan, read the article. He finished with a chuckle. "So you're on the lam, huh, Wheeler?"

"Well," Dwayne replied, "let's put it this way. A few members of law enforcement would like to have a long talk with me."

"I know the feeling," Sheehan said. "Terry tells me him and you was in the army together. Military police, right?"

Dwayne gave an affirmative nod. "We both got busted over black market dealings in Germany after the shooting stopped."

"You must be Irish, Wheeler," Sheehan surmised. "I know a coupla families in South Boston by that name."

Dwayne shrugged. "I don't know what kind of name I got."

"Well, let's get down to the nitty-gritty. Terry said you're looking for work."

"Yeah. But it's got to give me some cover, y'know what I mean?"

"I know exactly what you mean. And working with us is gonna fill the bill for you."

McCarthy spoke up with a necessary lie. "He don't know what we do, Jimmy. I never told him."

Sheehan gave him a serious look. "That was real wise of you, Terry." He turned his attention back to Dwayne. "We're pimps. That's the bottom line. But it's a big business."

Dwayne played a role of puzzlement. "Is this a whorehouse? It don't look like one to me."

"The gals sleep in rooms upstairs. Fact is, there's four of 'em snoozing up there right now."

McCarthy interjected, "We work a certain truck stop, Dwayne. And here in Kansas there's one hell of a lot of trucks that come and go in all directions. Them guys get horny when they're away from home. So we provide a service for 'em."

"It sounds like a real money-maker all right," Dwayne said, showing some enthusiasm.

"We're part of a big team," Sheehan said. "A decision has to be made about you. But that's only routine. By the way, if you get the itch, you can always go to one of the girls' rooms for a bit of fun. They ain't good looking and it's a real let down if you got a pretty wife or girlfriend back home."

"Or both," McCarthy said with a laugh.

"How much do they charge?"

Sheehan chuckled. "We get all the cash they earn. The

rule is that we get free pussy. We make up for it by providing something else they crave. If you join us, you'll get the full picture."

"C'mon, Dwayne," McCarthy said. "Let's get your luggage. There's an extra bed in my room."

They went out to the Buick and Dwayne got a pair of suitcases from the trunk. McCarthy led the way to his room. It had two beds with a wardrobe in the middle. Dwayne put his luggage on the bed without covers. "I guess I'm home, huh?"

"Yeah," McCarthy said. "I got some bedding for you. It's in the wardrobe. I'll put it on my expense account."

"Thanks," Dwayne responded. "When do you think you'll be going back east?"

"I don't know for sure," McCarthy said. "I wasn't given a particular date. When I heard about you, I figured Williams had better move fast to get you up here."

"By the way," Dwayne said, "how much do the girls charge for their customers at the truck stops?"

"Five bucks."

"That seems kind of pricey for quick couplings in the cabs of trucks."

McCarty laughed. "You can bet those guys charge the dough to their operating expenses in one way or another. The girls generally do oral sex and masturbation since most of the truckers are married. Those guys don't want to take any venereal disease home from intercourse."

"That makes good sense," Dwayne commented. "How much can one girl make in an evening?"

"Between fifty to seventy dollars is about average. And you have to remember those trucks roll seven days a week."

McCarthy sat down on the other bed, speaking in a low voice. "You heard Jimmy say we're part of a team.

That means this is gonna turn into a real complicated assignment."

"Are you telling me this could take a long time?"

"Hell, I've been inserted in here for eighteen months. So empty your suitcases and put your clothes in the wardrobe, ol' buddy. You're gonna be here for awhile." He winked. "I'll send you a postcard from Boston."

CHAPTER 10

When Dwayne and McCarthy went to the kitchen that evening, there were three men sitting with Jimmy Sheehan at the table which was now set for eating. An older man was at the stove, tending to cooking chores.

Sheehan noticed Dwayne looking at him. "That's Charlie O'Donnell. He's the oldest member of our organization. He used to run the numbers racket for us back in Boston. At one time he had about twenty civilians working for him."

"Civilians?" Dwayne queried.

"That's what we call outsiders," McCarthy explained.

Charlie turned and looked at Dwayne. "You're the new guy, huh? How's it going so far?"

"Okay."

Sheehan continued, "Charlie was brought into the Kansas operation so the rest of the gang wouldn't attract too much attention by eating out or shopping. He goes into Salina once a week to purchase the groceries he needs." He pointed to the others at the table. "Them guys are Frank Quinn, Tim Fagin, and Duke Glencannon."

"Howdy," Dwayne said. He noticed that Glencannon was a particularly tough-looking individual with heavy shoulders and a broken nose.

The man gave Dwayne a friendly grin. "Jimmy showed us your news clipping." He snorted a laugh. "You're gonna fit right in here."

"He sure as hell is," Frank Quinn agreed.

"Yeah!" Tim Fagin echoed.

The supper Charlie prepared that night was surprisingly good. It was one of his versions of Irish stew that was delicious and filling. He was also adept at baking bread.

Charlie walked over and set the pot on the table along with a platter that held the supper rolls, then went back to the stove and filled up four bowls with the stew. He sat them on a large tray.

Sheehan explained, "Charlie takes that up to the girls in their rooms. Them broads don't eat much since the dope cuts down their appetites."

"That's right," Glencannon said. "But if one gets too skinny, we got ways of putting more weight on her."

Tim Fagin chortled. "If they lose their appetites their tits shrink. That means they aren't so appealing to the truckers."

"Not to worry though," Glencannon said. "A couple of sessions of force-feeding solves that problem."

Dwayne knew the procedure involved forcing a tube down the throat into the stomach. A funnel was at the other end in which a pitcher of soup could be poured.

Sheehan tore a roll in half and dunked it in the stew. He took a bite and looked at Dwayne. "I'm gonna send you out with the guys this evening. They're gonna take the girls to the truck stop. That way you can see how we operate."

"Good," Dwayne said. "I'm looking forward to it."

"We'll meet you behind the house at the car ports," Glencannon said. "At seven o'clock."

———

IT WAS A QUARTER TO SEVEN WHEN DWAYNE left the room he shared with McCarthy, to go out to the back of the lodge house. Frank Quinn and Tim Fagin with the four women were waiting for him. Jimmy Sheehan was there, too.

When Dwayne walked up, Sheehan noticed he was wearing an old ball cap, a khaki work shirt and blue jeans. The others were clad in sport jackets and trousers.

"You're kinda informal, ain't you, Dwayne?"

"This way I'll be able to walk around a truck stop without attracting too much attention."

Sheehan grinned. "By God! You are indeed a clever guy. I think ever'body that takes the girls out should dress up that way."

"I can take 'em to a second hand store to buy some work duds if you want."

"Okay!" Sheehan replied enthusiastically. Then he cautioned him. "But you still gotta stay away from the truck stop restaurant. If you go in there too often, the people who work there will recognize you eventually. Anyhow, I'll see you guys in the morning." He walked back toward the house.

Dwayne took note of the females. They fit the image of unattractive women being in the lower caste of prostitution as described by Mrs. Davies. Each was clad in a blouse unbuttoned to the waist. None wore brassieres. Their skirts were short with wide hems to facilitate being lifted for intercourse. Dwayne was sure they weren't wearing panties.

"We'll leave as soon as Duke gets here," Tim Fagin said. "All set to go, Dwayne?"

"Yeah. I'm anxious to see exactly how you guys run this operation."

Frank Quinn said, "We'll show you the when, where and why."

"I think I know why," Dwayne remarked with a grin.

The two gang members chuckled. Quinn pointed to the girls. "Introduce yourselves to the new guy."

"I'm Fay." She was thin and drab looking, with carelessly applied make up.

The next one had the look of a tough tomboy. "My name is Tammy."

"Hello," the third, a sleepy-looking type, greeted. "I'm Carla."

"Wilma," the fourth announced. She seemed to be aggressive and combative.

"My pleasure, ladies," Dwayne said. He felt a sudden uneasiness at the sight of the prostitutes. There was a haggard, hopeless appearance shared by all of them. However, this would not be obvious in the semi-darkness of the truck stop at night.

Duke Glencannon walked up with a box of sack lunches for breaks during the night. "Okay, girls, did you remember to bring rubbers?" He had them open their purses and show him. "And don't forget to use 'em. If you get knocked up or clapped up, you're gonna find yourselves in deep shit. So turn down any customer who won't use one."

With that final announcement, Glencannon led the way over to the Nash station wagon. "Ever'body get in."

"I really like that vehicle!" Dwayne exclaimed, glad to turn away from the hapless women. "You guys travel in style!"

"You bet," Glencannon said. "We got good money backing us. You're in a first class organization, Dwayne."

"I'm in? I didn't know I had been accepted."

"I guess Jimmy didn't make that clear at supper. But you're one of the guys now." He paused. "How come you're dressed like that?"

"It's easier to move around a truck stop without getting a lot of looks," Dwayne explained again.

Tim Fagin spoke up. "Jimmy wants him to take us all to a used clothing store to buy clothes like he's wearing."

"Okay," Glencannon said. "Whatever Jimmy wants, Jimmy gets." He winked at Dwayne. "Either that or somebody gets an ass kicking."

———

IT WAS A HALF HOUR DRIVE TO THE TRUCK STOP along U.S. 40. Glencannon turned into the parking lot, skirting the semis, coming to a stop out of the glare of the stadium lights that lit the area.

Everyone got out of the car and stretched their legs. The girls pulled down their blouse fronts to show maximum cleavage. "Okay," Glencannon said. "Get to work, ladies."

The females were practiced in trolling for customers. They split up and each walked her own line of trucks. Glencannon spoke to Dwayne. "You follow Fay. Keep back out of the way so the customers can't see you. If some son of a bitch starts to rough her up, move in fast and take care of the situation. But try not to make too much of a ruckus. It'll attract undue attention."

"I gotcha," the shamus replied.

Dwayne got behind the girl and walked slowly keeping a discreet distance. She scored quickly, approaching a couple of truckers who had been returning to their vehicles after eating. Dwayne couldn't hear the conversation, but Fay got into the cab with one and was with him a bit less than five minutes. The next guy took her twice as long, then she got out and straightened her skirt to continue.

The evening's work shift was in full swing. The women came back to the station wagon for their sack lunches and a break when it was convenient. Dwayne noted they only ate half the sandwiches Charlie had made for them. But they did drink full cups of coffee from the thermos jug.

———

THE GROUP WAS BACK AT THE HOUSE AT A LITTLE past four a.m. Glencannon invited Dwayne to go with him for the last chore of the night. The two went into Sheehan's office where a small safe sat beside the desk.

"Close your eyes," Glencannon said.

Dwayne complied, knowing he wasn't supposed to watch him work the dial.

"Okay, you can open 'em now."

Dwayne saw him standing with a small leather valise. "What's that?"

"It's the girls' reward," Glencannon explained. "Smack it's called. Brown sugar and skag. But what it all means is heroin. We keep it locked away so as not to tempt any unauthorized highs. Let's take the goodies to the girls."

He led the way upstairs with Dwayne close behind. When they reached the second floor, the shamus did a very obvious double-take. All the women stood in the hallway, stripped naked.

Glencannon glanced at Dwayne. "Sometimes one of 'em will try to keep some of the money for herself." He opened the case and pulled out a rubber glove.

The females were made to squat to make sure there was nothing hidden in their anuses. Next Glencannon slipped on the glove and inserted his fingers into vaginas to inspect that part of their anatomy. All were empty.

Dwayne was sickened by the humiliation of the searches even though the procedure didn't seem to bother the women.

Glencannon announced, "Okay. It's time for your reward." He handed the valise to Tammy to pass out the paraphernalia. Then he and Dwayne went back downstairs. "By the way," Glencannon said, "we made a grand total of 210 dollars tonight."

When Dwayne got back to his room, he got out a notebook and pencil. McCarthy woke up and looked at him. "What the hell are you doing?"

"I'm figuring out something," Dwayne said beginning a multiplication problem. "We made 210 dollars tonight. If this was an average night, we're pulling in 75,650 dollars a year." He scribbled some more. "And if it's a leap year, the amount comes to 76,860 bucks."

McCarthy yawned. "And that's just here. We've got to find out how many operations this gang is running." He yawned again. "G'night, Dwayne."

"G'night, Terry."

CHAPTER 11

At noon on the same day they had returned from the truck stop, Dwayne was awakened by Terry McCarthy. The shamus opened his eyes and looked up. He yawned, stretched and asked, "What's going on?"

"Jimmy wants to see you."

Dwayne sat up and swung his legs over the side of the bed. McCarthy waited for him to get dressed, then they went downstairs to the kitchen. Jimmy Sheehan was seated at the table, pouring a shot of Irish whiskey into his coffee. "Hi there, Dwayne."

"Hi," Dwayne said. "Is that a pot of joe on the stove?"

"Sure is," Sheehan answered. "Help yourself."

Dwayne took a cup from several that hung on hooks by the cabinets. He poured himself a coffee, then joined the boss at the table. "What's up?"

"I been thinking about your idea for the guys to wear clothes like the truckers do."

"Or they can dress like mechanics. It's almost as good."

"Naw," Sheehan stated. "I think it's best if they look

like they drive the big rigs. So here's what I want you to do. Go into Salina and buy several sets of them outfits."

Dwayne had what he thought was a better idea. "I think we should go to another town. Salina is too close to our operating area, and it might make folks curious."

"Okay. Where do you want to go?"

"Hutchinson," Dwayne told him. "It's about seventy miles south of here on State Seventeen. And I want to take the other three guys with me so they can get the right fit. And we're gonna have to buy used, worn clothing in second-hand stores. Brand new work outfits would stand out as much as sports coats and slacks."

"Won't it look strange for a bunch of guys to suddenly show up in a store to buy work duds?"

"Not with the right cover story," Dwayne countered. "I can say we're on our way to Colorado to work on a—" He thought a moment, then continued. "—to work on a new mountain highway through the Rockies. And I have another idea. We ought to start using another vehicle other than that fancy Nash station wagon to go to the truck stop. It stands out like a race horse in a herd of mules."

"Our other car is a Ford coupe and it ain't big enough haul seven people," Sheehan explained. "Charlie uses it for his grocery runs."

"Well, I don't want to use my Buick," Dwayne said. "It ain't new but it's a swell looking car. Besides, the license plates can be traced to me. Anyhow, even though it's bigger'n Charlie's car, we couldn't fit ever'body in it either."

"What've you got in mind?"

"A panel truck of some kind," Dwayne explained. "I had a caper where a pimp was hauling around a whore in a truck like that. We could pick up a couple of second-hand sofas and put them in a panel truck, and ever'body would be comfortable going to and from the truck stop."

"So how much would that cost?"

"For a reliable used model, I figure a hundred and fifty to two hundred bucks."

"We can do that," Sheehan said. "And how much are we gonna spend on them old clothes?"

"Let's see. I already got my own, but we'll need six sets so the other guys won't have to wear the same ones all the time. That'll come to around ten to twenty bucks. It'd be cheaper if we didn't need hats, but drivers always got some kind of headgear."

"Okay," Sheehan agreed. "It's a done deal. I'll give you the money after you get back from the truck stop tomorrow morning."

"I'm gonna be driving the panel truck back from Hutchinson," Dwayne said. "And Glencannon will drive the Nash station wagon both ways. That's a hunnerd and thirty miles or so round trip. Him and me have got to be rested or we might fall asleep and run off the road."

"No problem. Me and McCarthy can take your places at the truck stop tonight. You two be ready to go as soon as we get back. The other guys can catch some sleep during the trip."

Duke Glencannon walked in and fetched himself a cup of coffee before sitting down. "Anything new?"

"Yeah," Sheehan answered. "You ain't going to the truck stop tonight."

"What's that all about?"

Sheehan explained the trip to Hutchinson, and Glencannon agreed it was an excellent idea. "A week or so ago I seen some truckers standing around and looking at the station wagon. It attracts attention all right."

"There's one thing I want to point out," Sheehan said.

"Even if you're in clothes that make you look like truck drivers, do not go into the restaurant. *Ever*! Your faces will start getting recognized and the waitresses will wonder why you're there so often."

Further conversation was interrupted when Fay walked in, carrying the valise. She had the look of exhaustion and illness about her as she handed the container over to Glencannon. He took it from her. "I'll get some fresh smack and be up there in a jiffy."

The woman, satisfied she and the others would get the first injections of the day left the kitchen. Dwayne watched her, remembering what Mrs. Davies had told him about heroin addicted prostitutes. And she'd been right. It really was a miserable existence with the only relief being periods of high from the narcotic.

———

THE NEXT MORNING AT SIX O'CLOCK, WITH Glencannon at the wheel, the Nash traveled down the dirt road toward U.S. 40. Dwayne was riding shotgun while Tim Fagin and Frank Quinn sat in the middle row of seats dozing. The two were tired after being awake all night at the truck stop.

Dwayne navigated, directing Glencannon eastward on U.S. 40 to Salina. From there they turned south on U.S. 81 that was also a part of Kansas 17. They stuck with the state highway when it veered off three miles south of McPherson. This would take them all the way to Hutchinson through the small towns of Inman, Buhler and Medora.

Kansas had no speed limits on the highways, but it cost them time slowing down when going through the trio of rural communities. And a couple of times farmers on tractors blocked the two-lane highway while going from one field to another in their day's work.

The Boston gangster Duke Glencannon sniggered at the area. "Who the hell would want to live way out here in the middle of nowhere? It's nothing but open country."

"Are you kidding?" Dwayne remarked. "That land you're calling open country is profitable wheat farms. All them farmers are rich."

"No shit?"

"No shit," Dwayne answered. "But the way they live don't show it. The big thrills in their life is going to church, watching movies on Saturday nights, and cheering the local high school sports teams."

"Well," Glencannon surmised, "they can bet on the games for a bit more excitement."

"They consider gambling a sin."

"I hope they at least fuck their old ladies."

"Sure," Dwayne said with a wink. "But that's only because they need kids to help with the chores."

Glencannon laughed. "C'mon! Ever'body likes sex."

"Right," Dwayne said. He looked out at the flat Kansas terrain. "Y'know, when I'm away from Wichita and out in the country where I can see from horizon to horizon, I feel like I could run for a hunnerd miles without ever getting tired."

"Yeah! Now that you mention it, I get that same feeling."

———

WHEN THEY REACHED THE OUTSKIRTS OF Hutchinson Dwayne noticed a commercial vehicle lot. It was a dealership with farm equipment and trucks for sale.

"I bet we can find a panel truck in there. We'll take care of that little matter on the way back."

In a few moments they were rolling slowly along Main Street until Dwayne sighted a thrift store. He directed Glencannon to park at the curb in front of the small establishment. When Glencannon turned off the engine, the sudden silence woke up Tim and Frank.

Frank stretched and looked around. "Where are we?"

"Hutchinson, Kansas," Dwayne announced. "We found a place to get us some work clothes."

Tim yawned. "I want a cowboy hat. I seen a lot of them truckers wearing cowboy hats. So I want one, too."

Dwayne opened his door. "C'mon. Let's see what they got to offer."

The shamus preceded the three across the sidewalk into the store. It was an old building that had obviously been used by several businesses in the past. When they walked through the door they saw it was filled with racks of various styles of clothing. Dwayne also noticed some old furniture off to the side.

A middle-aged lady with a kerchief on her head and wearing an apron greeted them. "Hello there. What can I do for you?"

"Good morning, ma'am," Dwayne said. "We're a construction crew on the way to a job in Colorado and our work clothes got accidently packed away in a tool crate. We're gonna have to buy something to wear 'til it all arrives at the worksite. We don't need nothing fancy."

"All the work clothes are toward the back," the lady said. "Follow me, please."

"D'you got any cowboy hats?" Tim asked.

The lady grimaced at the accent. "We sure do. They're not exactly cowboy hats but they're broad brimmed the same way. Farmers use 'em on hot sunny days. They're made out of straw."

Tim was disappointed. "I want what cowboys wear."

"There's a men's clothing store down the street," the lady informed him. "They have those kind of hats. But they're expensive. Five dollars I think they charge for 'em."

Tim looked at Dwayne. "Let's go there so I can get me a cowboy hat."

"Okay, but let's get some shirts and trousers here first."

The lady took them to the rear wall where some racks of work clothing were located. "You look around and find what you need. There's a changing room over in the corner if you want to try anything on. I'll be up front."

She walked away and Frank Quinn watched her. "Ain't she afraid we'll steal something?"

"You're not in a big city back east, Frank," Dwayne said. "You're out here in the United States of America."

Frank's temper flared. "What the hell d'you mean by that?"

Glencannon gave him a slight push. "Calm down!"

"Goddamn it! *I'm* an American!" Frank grumbled. Then added, "*Irish*-American!"

They began a search through the racks, first concentrating on billed caps. Glencannon found a faded red one that caught his fancy while Frank picked out a green model with the emblem of a leaping deer on the front. The name **JOHN DEERE** was embroidered under the symbol. He was impressed. "Some guy put his name on his cap, huh?"

Dwayne shook his head. "*John Deere* is the name of a farm machinery manufacturer. And I know where you can get a brand new free cap."

"How?"

"When we go to that vehicle sales lot we saw coming in here, they'll give you one if you buy a tractor."

Frank frowned. "What the hell am I gonna do with tractor? I'll just buy this cap for fifty cents."

Glencannon rolled his eyes. "It's a joke, Frank."

"Well, it ain't very goddamn funny!"

After making their choices, they went up to the front. The lady tallied up nine dollars for what they had chosen. Dwayne gave her a ten and told her to keep the change. She was extremely pleased. "This money you spent will help some of the poorer folks around here."

Now Dwayne recognized the store's purpose. "This place is run by a church, ain't it?"

"It certainly is," the lady acknowledged.

Glencannon said, "That's fine. We always like to help those less fortunate than us."

The lady was in agreement. "It's a shame how some folks find themselves in such bad straits."

"Yeah, it sure is," Glencannon replied, not exactly sure what she meant.

The four went out to the car and climbed in. Glencannon started the engine, and pulled away from the curb. He made a u-turn, and headed back up Main Street to the clothing store that sold cowboy hats.

Glencannon and Frank waited in the car while Duane took Tim inside. The proprietor greeted them with a broad smile. "Hello, fellers. What can I do for you this morning?"

Tim spoke up. "I want a cowboy hat."

"I can help you with that," the man said. "Are you interested in a Stetson?"

"No!" Tim snapped. "I said I want a *cowboy* hat."

Dwayne interjected, "Stetson is a brand name of cowboy hats, Tim. But they're kinda expensive." He nodded to the proprietor. "He'll be wearing the hat while he's working. We're on our way to Colorado for a construction job."

"Sure," the man responded. "I got just what you want over here."

They were taken to a counter where several styles of the headgear were displayed. The proprietor picked up a tan colored model and handed it to Tim. "Try this on."

Tim took off his fedora and placed the western hat on his head. He studied his reflection in a mirror on the counter, and showed a wide smile of satisfaction. "This fits perfect. Do I look like a real cowboy, Dwayne?"

"You sure do."

"It's two dollars," the proprietor said. "Plus six cents sales tax."

After Dwayne paid the money, the pair left the store and hurried over to the car. When they got in, Frank gave Tim a close look. "Whoopee! Howdy, partner!"

Tim grinned. "Smile when you say that, stranger."

Glencannon drove down the street, turning into the farm machinery dealership parking lot. He, Tim and Frank stayed in the car while Dwayne got out to look around.

In a few moments a salesman appeared. "Howdy. What can I do you for?"

"I want to buy a panel truck," Dwayne informed him.

"Well...let's see," the salesman said. "We don't handle new models of panel trucks, but we got a coupla used ones."

"Good enough," Dwayne announced.

"Foller me. One was used by a local flower shop that went outta business after the owner died. That was Fred Fenster. His wife Heather didn't want nothing to do with selling flowers so she closed ever'thing down and sold the building and the delivery truck. It's just over yonder."

They walked to a green 1935 Ford model. It had **FENSTER FLOWER SHOP** painted on the sides. The salesman pointed out that the spare tire was mounted on the right side of the vehicle, just behind the passenger door.

"See that?" he said. "Having the spare tire on the *out*side gives you more room on the *in*side. And there's a roof rack on top, so you can strap things up there." He walked around and opened the two back doors. "Take a look at this. Roomy and open without a thing in the cargo compartment."

Dwayne checked it out. "Yeah. That's handy, all right."

"Would you like to take it for a spin?"

"I sure would."

The salesman hurried over to the office and quickly returned with a ring holding the ignition and door keys. Dwayne got in and started the engine. He gunned it a couple of times to listen for sputtering, then put the vehicle into reverse and backed out. He drove past the Nash station wagon where Glencannon, Tim and Frank were standing.

Dwayne got out into the street and headed north where he could give the truck a good run on the highway. As soon as he passed the city limits, he pressed down on the accelerator and got the speed up to sixty-five m.p.h. He glanced in the rearview mirror and was surprised to see the station wagon behind him.

He made a u-turn at a crossroads, then headed back toward town. When he reached the dealership, he came to a halt, waiting for Glencannon to pull up beside him.

Dwayne asked, "Why were you guys following me?"

"We thought you *stole* the panel truck," Glencannon said, "and was making a run for it."

"Jesus Christ!" Dwayne exclaimed in disgust. "Park over there where you was and wait." He drove back to the salesman. He came to a stop and got out.

"How'd you like it?" the man asked.

"It ain't too bad," Dwayne replied. "What're you asking for it?"

"Oh, we'll let 'er go for hunnerd and seventy-five."

Dwayne stepped back and cast a critical glance at the truck. "This vehicle is thirteen years old."

"Yeah. But it's only been drove around town."

"That means there's gunk in the motor since it ain't been taken out on the highway very much. I'll give you a hunnerd."

The salesman crossed his arms across his chest and thought a moment. "Well...I'll take a hunnerd and fifty."

Dwayne walked a slow circle around the truck, kicking the tires and giving it a close inspection. He stopped and stated, "I can't do it. A hunnerd and twenty-five."

Now the salesman sank into a period of quiet contemplation. He finally cleared his throat and announced, "We couldn't give you no warranty on it at that price."

"That's okay," Dwayne assured him.

"We got a deal," the man announced.

They shook hands and headed for the office. Glencannon and his two companions leaned up against the station wagon. "It looks like we got us a panel truck for going out to the truck stop."

Tim liked the idea. "It sure ain't gonna attract as much attention as this woody."

Twenty minutes later, Dwayne walked up. "You guys can take off now. I'm going back to that thrift store to buy a coupla sofas to put in the back of the truck. The furniture will make things more comfortable when we take the girls back and forth to the truck stop."

"Okay," Glencannon said. "I know the way back. State Seventeen to U.S. Eighty-One. Then to U.S. Forty and go west."

"You got it."

Dwayne walked over to the new purchase as Glencannon drove out to Main Street to catch Kansas State Highway 17.

CHAPTER 12

It was late afternoon when Dwayne drove the panel truck past the gatehouse at the Retreat. He continued down the road, going around to the back of the rustic lodge house. When he came to a stop, McCarthy, Glencannon, and Sheehan along with Tim and Frank came out the back door.

"So that's it, hey?" Sheehan remarked.

"Sure is," Dwayne answered. "Let me show you guys something." He got out of the truck and walked around to the back, opening the two doors. The others joined him and looked inside. Two mismatched, worn sofas occupied the space. Both were shoved back against the sides of the truck, facing inward.

Frank Quinn liked what he saw. "That'll be real comfortable for going to and from the truck stop."

"Yeah," Tim agreed. "And we can take breaks and stretch out ever' once in a while when things slow down."

Sheehan laughed. "What's this flower shop sign all about?"

"That's the previous owner," Dwayne explained. "It won't be noticeable in the dark."

Glencannon looked over at Dwayne. "Can I have the keys? I'd like to check the truck out since I'll be doing all the driving in it."

Dwayne obliged him, and the Boston Irishman got in. He pressed down on the starter and the engine quickly kicked over. "I think you got a good one, Dwayne."

"I'm satisfied with it."

"Well," Glencannon said. "I'm gonna run it up and down the highway a couple of times."

As he pulled away from the house, Sheehan and the other two walked toward the back door. Dwayne started to follow, but McCarthy grabbed his arm. "Hold up a minute. I got something to tell you."

"Okay. Let's go up to the room."

They went into the house, climbing the stairs. Dwayne sat down on his bed. "What's going on?"

"It looks like I'll be going back to Boston in a couple of weeks. It's obvious that something is up."

"D'you have any idea what it might be?"

"I've been turning reasons over in my mind. The best I can come up with is that they're gonna expand the operation along Highways Forty and Eighty-One." He paused. "Either that, or there's some goings-on back east."

"Uh oh!"

"Yeah," McCarthy said. "That would mean a gang war."

A strong sense of apprehension swept over Dwayne. "People get killed in gang wars."

"Yes they do, Dwayne."

"Is there any special gang you think will be coming after us?"

"Yeah. The Forzini Family in Boston."

Dwayne was puzzled. "Christ! They must be a pretty big family."

"In this case the name 'family' means 'gang'," McCarthy explained. "It's boss is an evil old guy by the name of Joe Forzini."

"But right now you don't know for sure if this gang wants to take over our prostitution ring, huh?"

"That's right," McCarthy replied. "I'm a natural pessimist and always come up with worse case scenarios. But that's saved my life a couple of times."

"I guess we can't do nothing but wait and see what happens," Dwayne stated. "By the way, what about the two guys at the gatehouse?"

"There's actually three of 'em," McCarthy said. "They stay in a motor lodge west of here. Their names are Tom Fitzgerald, Dave O'Leary and Sean Magee."

"Interesting. Well, I think I'll grab some shuteye and rest up for the visit to the truck stop tonight."

"Okay. I'll see you later."

McCarthy left the room as Dwayne stretched out. He closed his eyes but images of exchanging gunfire with Italian gangsters danced through his mind. It was awhile before he was able to drift off to sleep.

─────

THAT EVENING'S EXCURSION TO THE TRUCK STOP went smoothly. Glencannon, Tim and Frank were pleased with the acceptance of their presence among the big rigs. Before, when wearing their usual clothing, they always received looks of curiosity or double takes from the drivers who caught sight of them. Now the truckers either completely ignored them or acknowledged their presence with friendly nods.

Glencannon suggested they strike up conversations with the drivers, letting them know there were whores available on the lot. "But don't act like pimps," he counseled. "Tell 'em in a friendly man-to-man way. Remember you're supposed to be truckers."

———

LATER, AT MIDNIGHT, DWAYNE ACTED AS AN escort for Fay and Tammy as they approached potential customers among the vehicles. He suggested they concentrate on trucks with plenty of road grime. That was a sign the drivers had been away from home for longer periods of time; thus were hornier.

A little after two a.m., Dwayne went back to the panel truck to take a break. He laid down on a sofa and lit a Lucky Strike, sinking into one of his pensive moods. A lot of people are bored with nothing to do, but when Dwayne was alone, thoughts and ideas boiled up out of his subconscious mind into his conscious to give him plenty to think about. The mental experiences were even entertaining at times.

By now the apprehension he had felt about a possible gang war dissipated as another matter occupied his thoughts. Watching the women at work gave him feelings of shame and disgust. The mood wasn't so much about them as himself. He couldn't deny he was participating in a situation where the unfortunate women practiced demeaning sexual acts with men unknown to them. The fact that addiction to a narcotic was used to force them to submit into that sub-cultural existence made it even worse.

Dwayne thought maybe making the drugs legal like they were decades before was the answer. Prohibition didn't work for liquor and it sure as hell wasn't working for opiates. Drug addicts wouldn't have to pay exorbitant prices for their fixes if they could purchase the narcotics at their neighborhood pharmacy.

The shamus got up from the sofa and stepped down to the ground. He dropped his cigarette butt to the dirt and stomped on it. After a deep breath, he walked back toward the trucks to link up with Fay and Tammy. Both were out of sight, meaning they were servicing customers in the truck cabs.

———

THE RETURN TO THE RETREAT WAS AS ALWAYS. The girls were searched then given the hypodermics and heroin. With that taken care of Dwayne, Glencannon, Tim and Frank went to their respective rooms for a few hours of sleep.

Dwayne did not stay in his quarters. He grabbed his ditty bag of toiletries, a towel and a change of clothes and walked down the hall to the men's bathroom. After turning on the well motor to fill the water heater, he lit the propane stove under the device. The shamus had time for a cigarette before the water was hot.

He filled the bathtub, got in and soaped up. He wasn't as much interested in physical hygiene as scrubbing away the feelings of shame and degradation that clouded his conscience.

He knew it didn't make sense, but somehow he felt a little better.

CHAPTER 13

After a few days passed, Dwayne was able to ease his troubled mind by rationalizing that his undercover assignment was going to put an end to white slavery at this one spot. His fondest hope was that he and Terry McCarthy would gather enough evidence to end the case in record time. As far as the prostitution angle, that was cut and dried. It was the mysterious unknown aspects of the caper that had to be found out.

The nightly routine at the truck stop continued with increasing monotony. The activity began with a drive from the Retreat to U.S. 40 through Salina. Parking was in the same spot in the unlit rear area. At that point, everyone got out of the truck to begin the evening's work. Dwayne and his companions, as always, supervised from a distance while trucker customers were serviced.

That boredom came to an end on the evening Tim Fagin spotted a newly assigned security guard patrolling around the trucks. The Derby gangster quickly alerted the others, and they wasted no time in rounding up the women and getting them back to the panel truck. With that done, Dwayne and his three companions gathered for a discussion.

Duke Glencannon was perplexed. "How in the fuck are we gonna handle this?"

Dwayne, who had worked with private security companies in the past, recognized the seriousness of the situation. If hired guards got wind of prostitution going on at the truck stop, it would result in the local sheriff being notified. And that worthy officer of the law would contact the Kansas Highway Patrol. Although Dwayne and Terry McCarthy would eventually declare their undercover assignment and not be arrested, it would be the end of their mission. That would mean the real perpetrators back east would cease the operation and cover up all the details.

Another bad aspect of a discovery was that Kansas law enforcement would locate the Retreat. The lawmen would quickly raid the site, collaring everyone there. However, the Derbies would all be bailed out and ordered not to leave Kansas. That, of course, would be ignored and the whole group would hightail it back to Boston. The girls, on the other hand, would be denied bail, and that would result in their going through the lengthy hell of detoxification in a county jail while waiting to be charged and put on trial.

"I have an idea," Dwayne announced.

Duke Glencannon, whose respect for the newcomer had increased with every passing day, was relieved by the revelation. "What is it?"

"I know these security firms. They don't pay shit to the poor bastards working for them. I have inside knowledge of a few instances where private guards have been bribed to—shall we say—look the other way."

Glencannon caught on quickly. "Are you gonna try for a payoff, Dwayne?"

"Yeah. But right now we better scram outta here before the guy sees what we're doing."

———

JIMMY SHEEHAN AND TERRY MCCARTHY WERE playing two-handed pinochle at the kitchen table when they heard the panel truck pull up behind the lodge house. Both got up and went to the back door. When they saw everyone getting out of the vehicle, they knew something serious had happened.

"What the hell's going on?" Sheehan demanded to know.

Glencannon let Dwayne do the talking. The shamus stepped forward and announced, "The truck stop now has a security guard watching over the parked rigs."

Sheehan gritted his teeth. "*Goddamn it to hell*! Johnny Cullen is gonna go ape shit when he hears about this."

"Let's calm down," Dwayne said. "I explained to the guys that those security guards are underpaid and under appreciated by their employers. I've worked with them quite a bit in the past. I estimate the guy out there prob'ly gets about twenty-five bucks a week. If we offer him a friendly bribe of fifteen dollars a week, he'll be happy to do a great job of minding the store while giving us a pass."

"Yeah," Sheehan said. "That's a possibility."

"What I think we should do," Dwayne continued, "is to let me and Terry drive out there and talk to the guy." He looked at McCarthy. "Whattaya say, Terry? It'll be like bribing the Kraut cops in our German black market operations after the war."

McCarthy caught on quickly. "Sure!" He glanced over

at Sheehan. "And Dwayne has the ability to handle situations like this."

"Okay. But don't go over twenty-five bucks a week."

Dwayne was feeling cocky. "You're making it easy for us, Jimmy."

Sheehan liked his confidence. "Go for it tomorrow night." He gestured to Duke Glencannon. "Take the girls back up to their rooms and settle them in for the night."

Glencannon went to the office to fetch the heroin and needles. And the rubber gloves.

———

THE NEXT EVENING, WHEN DWAYNE AND TERRY McCarthy drove off to make the bribery attempt, both wore truck driver attire. Dwayne's idea was for them to pose as truckers to make a pitch to the guard as if they were working stiffs. McCarthy borrowed a set of clothing from Glencannon along with Frank Quinn's *John Deere* cap.

After arriving, the pair quickly began a search for the guard. Fifteen minutes of wandering ensued before they caught sight of a large guy wearing a khaki uniform with a peak cap. He carried an eighteen-inch billy club by a leather tong wrapped around his wrist.

"Wow!" McCarthy said under his breath. "That's a real badass dude."

"Yeah!" Dwayne agreed.

They walked slowly toward the man, doing their best to assume expressions of good humor. When they got close enough, the two stopped and stared. The guy was big all right. He was about six-foot, four inches and looked like he packed some two-hundred and twenty pounds of solid muscle on that large body. But he was a kid with a baby face that indicated innocuous naiveté.

Dwayne greeted, "Hey there. How're you doing?"

The guy looked at him with a shy smile. "I'm okay."

"We haven't seen you here before."

"I just started last night."

"I see. Well, my name is Dwayne and this is my pal Terry."

"Glad to know you. My name is Farley. Farley Kuch."

"We're right happy to meet you, Farley," Dwayne said. "I see you're a security guard. What outfit do you work for?"

"I work for the truck stop."

"Then you're not employed by a security company, huh?" Dwayne asked.

"No. I work for the truck stop."

Now McCarthy felt it was time he stepped in. "What's your duties here at the truck stop?"

"Well...I make sure things is peaceful like."

"I bet the pay is pretty good for a lot of responsibility like that, huh."

"I make twenty dollars a week," Farley said. "I wish I could make more. I'm married and my wife is gonna have a baby. But we'll get by, I reckon."

"How old are you?" Terry McCarthy asked.

"I'm nineteen years old."

Dwayne inquired, "Do you live near here, Farley?"

"I live in Connor."

"Where's that?"

"It's down the county road north of here. It's a little bitty place. There wasn't no jobs there, so I'm lucky I got this one. It was either that or move down to Wichita to look for work. But I can't do that because my wife is gonna have a baby."

Dwayne had already figured out Farley was hired more for his physique than his intellect. "It sounds like you could use some extra money."

"I sure could. My wife is gonna have a baby."

"Okay, Farley," Dwayne said. "Us truck drivers have something going here that we really like."

"What is it that you truck drivers really like?"

"Girls come around and get in our trucks with us," Dwayne said.

Farley frowned in puzzlement. "What do the girls do when they come around and get in trucks with you?"

McCarthy interjected, "They let us do what we want with them."

Farley was silent for a moment, then grinned. "Oh, yeah. You fuck 'em, don't you?"

"Yeah," McCarthy replied. "But if the folks who own the truck stop ever found out, they would make us stop. Maybe even call the county sheriff. Or the Highway Patrol. It would get us in a lot of trouble."

Now Dwayne took over, talking Kansan to Kansan. "Now we're wondering if you wouldn't report us if we paid you some money ever' week."

"Money ever' week?"

"Yeah, Farley. We would pay you fifteen dollars a week. Ever' single week."

McCarthy patted his shoulder. "That would give you thirty-five dollars a week total. And you could still do your real job making sure there's no trouble out here. What do you say?"

Farley grinned so wide his eyes almost closed. "Boy howdy! That's what I say!"

Dwayne got out his wallet and pulled out three five dollar bills. "Here you go. Since this is Tuesday, we'll come looking for you ever' Tuesday to give you fifteen bucks."

Farley took the money, tears forming in his eyes. "You fellers don't know what this means to me and Irma. Irma is my wife and she's gonna have a baby. We're living in the backroom of her folks' trailer so now we can get one of our own. There's one for rent in the trailer park where we live. And we can even start saving a little money."

Dwayne and McCarthy shook hands with Security Officer Farley Kuch, then hurried back to the panel truck.

CHAPTER 14

A week passed after striking the deal with Farley Kuch when Dwayne and McCarthy drove over to the telephone exchange. It was time for one of the regularly scheduled calls that McCarthy made to Johnny Cullen for news and instructions.

As usual, Dwayne waited while McCarthy went to an assigned booth for his mandatory communication with the gang leader. After a ten minute conversation, he emerged with some news. "Not much going on except Johnny says there's another girl available from the usual source."

"What's the usual source?" Dwayne asked.

"The woman—or I should say *procurer*—is Babe Robertson. She's an independent madam with a whorehouse in Kansas City and also our source of heroin. I don't know how she is associated with the Derbies. That's something we'll have to find out. Anyhow, when she comes across some girl who would be perfect for our operation we're contacted."

"A drug addict and not too pretty, right?" Dwayne remarked.

"That's it," McCarthy said. "When we get back to the Retreat, I'll let Jimmy know about it. We're supposed to meet her tomorrow."

"Meet her *where* tomorrow?"

"About five miles east of Topeka," McCarthy explained. "It's at the Kozy Korner Motor Cabins."

"Let's see," Dwayne mused. "Topeka is close to a hunnerd and twenty or so miles from the Retreat."

"I'll do the driving over if you want. I know you'll be tired from being out at the truck stop all night."

"Sounds okay to me," Dwayne agreed. "You know exactly where the place is anyway."

————

THE NEXT MORNING MCCARTHY GOT DWAYNE out of bed at eight o'clock. The shamus dressed in a haze of sleepiness, then allowed himself to be ushered down to the kitchen for coffee.

Jimmy Sheehan watched him slurp the brew between bites of a donut. "Instead of the Nash I want you to take the panel truck. I want to keep the station wagon out of sight as much as possible."

"'S'alright with me," Dwayne mumbled.

After a final bite of the pastry, Dwayne stood up. "Let's go, Terry."

The pair left the kitchen and walked out to the truck. Dwayne got in the cargo compartment and laid down on a sofa while McCarthy settled behind the wheel. He stepped down on the starter pedal and accelerator to bring the motor to life, then drove out of the yard past the gatehouse to U.S. 40.

———

BY THE TIME THEY PASSED THROUGH SALINA, Dwayne was in a deep sleep. McCarthy let his companion snooze away as long as possible. They continued to the east side of Topeka, arriving at the Kozy Korner Motor Cabins at ten-thirty. After McCarthy pulled up in front of the office, he glanced back at Dwayne. "Hey, sport, here we are."

Dwayne came awake instantly, sitting up straight and looking around. After treating himself to a satisfying yawn, he opened a rear door and stepped out to walk around to the front of the vehicle. His shamus instincts told him that the Kozy Korner Motor Cabins more than likely dealt in illegal activities. McCarthy joined him and the two walked to the office.

The guy behind the counter was middle-aged and heavily tattooed. *Ex-con, no doubt,* Dwayne thought.

McCarthy spoke up. "We're here to see Babe."

"Cabin Five."

They walked down to the small hut-like structure and knocked on the door. It was opened by a very short heavyset woman dressed in men's clothing. "Hi ya, McCarthy."

"Hi, Babe. This is Dwayne. He's a new guy."

"Hey there, Dwayne," Babe Robertson greeted. "C'mon in, fellahs."

They stepped into the interior and immediately spotted a thin teenage girl with a bad complexion and frizzled red hair. She sat on one of the beds with a dull expression on her haggard face. Dwayne noticed something extremely familiar about her.

Then the girl shifted her eyes to look at him. "Hello,

Dwayne," she said in a subdued one. "Is this where you ran off to?"

"Hi," Dwayne said, still puzzled.

"My daddy said you're in big trouble in Wichita."

"Who's your daddy?"

"My daddy? He's Jessie Pickens as you well know."

Now Dwayne recognized Mary Sue Pickens. He turned to Babe Robertson. "Where'd you pick her up?"

"Mary Sue has been with us for awhile now. She's primed to go to work with your gals."

The realization she'd be working truck stops gave Dwayne an emotional jolt. Mary Sue had obviously become addicted to heroin. The girl's plump body had been ravaged down to skin and bones.

Babe noticed Dwayne's concern. "You know her?"

Dwayne feigned nonchalance. "I actually know her dad. He runs a country western night club south of Wichita."

"She seems to think you're on the lam."

"She's right about that."

Terry McCarthy spoke up. "Dwayne and I were in the army together during the war. I heard about his run-in with the law and invited him up here. Jimmy put him on the payroll."

"Ah!" Babe said with a wide grin. "Welcome to our organization, Dwayne." She reached out and took Mary Sue's hand. "You're gonna be going with these two nice guys."

Dwayne scowled. "She's under heroin right now, ain't she?"

"She sure as hell is," Babe replied. "So you know her dad, huh? Aside from that, what's your relationship with her?"

"Mary Sue is a wild teenager who jumps into the cabs

with truck drivers to go on trips," Dwayne replied. "The girl always catches another ride back home. Then one of 'em pimped her for awhile, and her dad hired me to go find her."

"Well, it looks like that was one case you failed," Babe remarked. She suddenly did a double-take. "What the hell do you mean you was *hired* to find her?"

McCarthy interjected again, "Dwayne is a private eye in Wichita and got caught with his hand in the cookie jar. He's had his license lifted along with a warrant put out for his arrest."

"Well, well," Babe said. "You must be from Kansas, huh?"

"Yeah. I hope things work out so I can eventually go to Boston."

Babe gave out a loud laugh. "I bet you do at that!" She walked over to Mary Sue and picked up a small suitcase beside her on the bed. "Let's go, sweetheart. These nice guys are gonna take you to your new home."

Mary Sue obediently got to her feet. She swayed a bit and walked toward the door. Dwayne and McCarthy walked to her side, each taking an arm and steering her toward the car.

MARY SUE PICKENS' PRESENCE AT THE RETREAT stimulated Dwayne into paying more attention to the women. Over the coming weeks Dwayne studied them; sometimes to the point of getting looks of irritation from the addicts. He noticed now how they displayed slow functioning in their physical actions such as walking and talking. Other mannerisms they shared were agitation and disorientation. And then there was a stunning lack of interest or concern about their lifestyle. It was obvious as long as they got their injections nothing else mattered to them.

During times at the truck stop, after being off the drug for a few hours, they were restless and even short tempered. Duke Glencannon occasionally gave punitive, stinging slaps to those going through that phase. If a particular woman had behaved bad enough to cause trouble, she would be denied a fix after the return to the Retreat. Dwayne witnessed heavy sweating, weeping and running noses of those being denied heroin.

Glencannon knew just how long to make the woman suffer before administering the drug. He always did it while warning them that anymore trouble-making would mean spending a full twenty-four hours of a painful withdrawal.

Terry McCarthy noticed Dwayne's interest and he knew the reason why. "You're worried about that new girl."

"Yeah. She's never had a chance for a good life. Her father doesn't really care about her and the mother is an alcoholic who goes off with men when she's drunk, then ends up calling her husband to come get her."

McCarthy was surprised. "And is that what he does?"

"Ever' single time," Dwayne replied. "His only worry about Mary Sue is that she's gonna get him in trouble with county family services."

McCarthy gave Dwayne a close look. "You're not thinking of doing anything for the girl, are you?"

Dwayne hesitated. "I might."

"You could be headed for trouble."

Dwayne grinned. "That's never slowed me down before."

———

Farley Kuch had become extremely friendly toward Dwayne and the other men when they were at the truck stop. The women, on the other hand, made him nervous and a little embarrassed. Dwayne noticed that when the young security guard was walking his rounds, he would suddenly turn and go the other way if there was a chance of encountering one of them.

On his Tuesday paydays, he would always be waiting in the parking area. When they arrived, he was too shy to ask for the fifteen dollar bribe. Farley would simply greet them with a slight smile and ask how everybody was. Dwayne would quickly hand him three five-dollar bills that the young security guard stuck in his pants pocket. Then, happily grinning, he always left with the same remark. "Thanks. I guess I better get back to work now."

When Mary Sue Pickens first came to the truck stop, she moved quickly into the operation. Dwayne guessed her time with Darrell Bodine had taken away any nervousness she might have about having quick sex with strange men. The other girls had also taken time to make her a little more attractive by teaching her how to put on make-up, fix her hair and even walk and talk.

Tammy the tomboy gave her some sage advice to become a successful whore. "Listen, little girl. You got to be down and dirty in this business. So when you proposition some guy don't just hint around with what you're offering. Give him a come-hither look and say 'Hey, honey, looking for a good time? Fucking, blowjob, or hand job? I do it all.' That'll get 'em ever' time."

Dwayne was uneasy about the situation. It truly hurt him to see the sixteen-year-old turning into a hardcore whoring addict.

CHAPTER 15

Dwayne, Duke Glencannon, and Frank Quinn stood behind the panel truck at one o'clock in the morning at the truck stop. They munched sandwiches and potato chips from the sack lunches Charlie O'Donnell had made for them. The girls rarely ate all their food during the rest periods. One of the symptoms of addiction to opiates was little desire for nourishment. A few nibbles was enough to satisfy their appetites. A respite for them was a short time for smoking a cigarette and catching their breaths between servicing customers.

The sandwich snacking was interrupted when Tim Fagin walked up. He had a worried expression on his face. "You guys ain't gonna believe this shit."

Glencannon groaned. "What now? Has the National Guard showed up?"

"Worser than that, wise guy. I just seen Fat Pauly Cappurio standing in front of the restaurant door."

Dwayne noticed the concern of the others. "Who the hell is Fat Pauly Cap...Cap...whatever?"

"He's a capo in the Forzini Family," Glencannon replied.

"What the hell is a 'capo'?"

"He's like a sergeant," Quinn explained. "An under-boss, sort of."

"I see," Dwayne said. "So he's an important guy in that Boston Mafia gang, right?"

"He sure as hell is," Glencannon said. He looked around at the others. "Is ever'body packing heat?"

Nods of affirmation indicated they were all armed.

"Good," Glencannon remarked. "Fat Pauly sure as hell ain't gonna be alone."

"What're we gonna do?" Dwayne asked, still not sure of what was going on.

"We're gonna sneak through the trucks and get close to the restaurant," Glencannon replied. "Then we're gonna keep our eyes on that son of a bitch as long as we possibly can. If we're lucky, he's just passing through."

"I wouldn't count on that," Frank Quinn said. "The fact he suddenly popped up in the middle of Kansas where we are means he's looking for something."

"Looking for *something*, hell!" Tim exclaimed. "He looking for *us*!"

"Calm down!" Glencannon growled. "C'mon, let's check the situation out."

Dwayne stayed in the rear of the three as they moved through the rows of trucks. The running engines allowed them to speak without being overheard. After ten very careful minutes they reached a point where the front door of the restaurant was in plain sight.

An extremely heavy, swarthy man wearing an expensive pinstripe suit and Charleston hat, stood at the door. He smoked a cigarette, gazing off in the distance. A moment later another individual walked up to him.

They chatted for about a minute, then the slimmer man went into the restaurant. Fat Pauly threw his cigarette down, and walked toward the trucks. He began going down the row that was parked between him and the Derbies.

Glencannon led the way as they carefully kept up with the big man's pace. They now had to keep quiet because of the nearness of the Mafioso. Suddenly Fat Pauly came to a halt.

Farley Kuch the security guard stepped out from behind a truck and confronted him. "Hey, Mister, only truckers is allowed to walk down here."

If Fat Pauly was irritated, he didn't show it. "Oh, yeah? I just wanted to take a look at all these trucks. They're pretty interesting, ain't they?"

"Yeah," Farley said. "But you gotta go back."

Fat Pauly remarked, "I live in the city so I don't get to see trucks like these."

"You gotta go back."

The Mafioso actually smiled. "Sure, pal. I'm always glad to be cooperative, know what I mean?"

"Yeah. I know what you mean."

Fat Pauly turned and made his way back to the restaurant. His companion was waiting for him at the front door. A gray '48 Packard sedan drove up and they got into it. The automobile was driven toward the highway, then turned west.

Glencannon led everyone back to the panel truck. "This is some bad shit, man!"

Dwayne didn't understand. "He didn't give Farley any trouble. And him and his pals are gone."

Frank Quinn was as worried as Glencannon. "The fact that he didn't punch Farley in the face means he didn't *want* any trouble. And why? Because those Forzini bastards know we're around here someplace. They're gonna play it cool until they find us."

"Right," Tim Fagin agreed. "Normally, that fucking goon would've punched Farley out."

"Let's round up the women," Glencannon said. "We're going back to the Retreat. Now!"

———

JIMMY SHEEHAN HEARD THE PANEL TRUCK DRIVE up. He walked out on the back stoop of the lodge house and waited for everyone to get out.

"Now what's the matter?" he demanded to know.

Glencannon replied, "Fat Pauly Cappurio was at the truck stop with a couple of other guys. I'm gonna get the dope kit for the girls, then we can all sit down and discuss the situation."

They went inside the lodge house and Glencannon got the satchel with the heroin and syringes. The others waited while he took care of the task. The tension in the kitchen was apparent because of the lack of conversation.

Terry McCarthy walked through the door. "What's going on?"

"Fat Pauly has showed up at the truck stop," Sheehan replied.

"Goddamn!" McCarty uttered under his breath.

As soon as Glencannon returned, Sheehan expressed an ominous opinion. "Somebody back in Boston spilled their guts."

Frank Quinn agreed. "Maybe they beat it out of one of our guys."

"It don't make no difference how they got it!" Sheehan snapped. "Whether the rat bastard danced over to 'em and ratted us out or got beat up with baseball bats, the Wops know where we are. Maybe not *exactly* where we are, but they'll work their greaser asses off 'til they find us."

Fagin took a deep breath. "There's gonna be a war!"

Sheehan looked at Dwayne. "You're a local guy. Whataya think will happen if there's a showdown here in Kansas?"

Dwayne was thoughtful for a moment. "This isn't like a big city back east where there's a lot of neighborhoods to hide out in. The first time shooting breaks out, the Kansas Highway Patrol is gonna show up and investigate. They can use their airplanes and make aerial photos to check out what's happening on the ground. That means they're gonna find the Retreat in less than a day."

"Shit!" Glencannon exclaimed. "Then we get collared and the Wops can hide out somewhere. They'll only have to wait until we're locked up and bailed out. Since we'll have to get out of Kansas to avoid a trial, they're free to take over the operation."

Jimmy Sheehan looked at Dwayne. "You're the only guy them wops don't know. So you're gonna be our eyes and ears away from the Retreat."

"I'm gonna need Terry with me," Dwayne said. "I don't know all those guys by sight."

"Sure," McCarthy agreed. "We can use Dwayne's car to roam around the area."

Sheehan said, "Just don't show yourselves too much or even the locals will wonder what the hell you're doing."

"I have a disguise kit," Dwayne said. "I got ever'thing from fake moustaches to different clothing."

"Fake moustaches!" Glencannon exclaimed. "You two are gonna look like Groucho Marx."

Dwayne shook his head. "His is painted on. Mine are

quality items. And I got some wigs that look real as long as we're wearing hats."

Terry McCarthy was satisfied. "Dwayne and I are the same size. That gives us dozens of combinations between the clothing, wigs and moustaches."

"I have eye glasses, too," Dwayne added.

Jimmy Sheehan was satisfied. "You guys start out tomorrow morning."

CHAPTER 16

The redness of dawn had faded to a pinkish hue as Dwayne and Terry McCarthy rolled past the gatehouse in the Buick. This was the start of their assigned mission as they traveled down to U.S. 40. In the military it would have been classified as a reconnaissance patrol, but Jimmy Sheehan referred to the activity as a "Wop Hunt." He also wanted them to be looking out for second-hand stores to pick up additional work clothing for the rest of the gang.

Dwayne was dressed in one of his outfits with a battered fedora. McCarthy wore a set of Fred Quinn's used clothing, including the *John Deere* cap. He also had a false moustache. Dwayne's collection of disguises was first rate, with no similarity to cheap costume items for Halloween masquerade parties.

The shamus glanced over at his companion. "You look pretty good in a moustache. Maybe you should grow one."

"Oh, yeah!" McCarthy exclaimed with a laugh. "I'm a regular Clark Gable. Actually I'm not sure if I need it or not. I don't think any of the Forzini family have seen me very often. I was never around during dealings with 'em."

"Better safe than sorry."

When they reached the highway, Dwayne turned west and gunned the engine up to seventy m.p.h. McCarthy cautioned him. "Don't go too fast. We don't want to whiz past any Mafioso in a Packard without noticing them."

"You're right," Dwayne agreed. "These rural types out here drive slow and steady. And I don't want to appear like a city slicker from Wichita to any of the locals. And speaking of disguises and such, we've got to get shoes, too. The footwear didn't matter at the truck stop during the night, but since me and you will be out in daylight, it'd look strange for working stiffs to be wearing oxfords or loafers."

"I guess you got everybody's sizes, right?"

"Right," Dwayne replied. "I've got it all written down in my notebook."

"I just hope they look like country boys in those outfits."

"They might not look like farmers to farmers," Dwayne pointed out, "but gangsters from back east ain't gonna think they're anything else but yokels."

They continued on at forty-five miles an hour. The scenery was made up of the usual Kansas farms off in the distance while most of the vehicles on the highway were local cars and trucks. The exceptions were a few out-of-state autos, but none had Massachusetts plates.

Each time they approached a town, Dwayne pulled into the parking areas of outlying motor lodges to see if a gray Packard was among the tenants' vehicles. They came up empty each time, then continued to the nearest community to see if the elusive automobile might be sitting along a curb.

"Y'know," McCarthy said, "I've been wondering why people wave at us from time to time when we go through these little burghs."

"It's a local custom," Dwayne explained. "A friendly gesture. It's pretty much the same all through the Bible Belt. Know what I mean?"

"Not exactly. Back on the east coast people would think anybody doing that was a fugitive from the loony bin."

"That's because those big city dwellers aren't noted for their friendliness," Dwayne commented. "When I was in the army I learned that most of the guys from large eastern cities were pricks." He paused. "Present company excepted of course."

"Of course," McCarthy replied with a laugh.

Another town loomed on the horizon and once more they checked out the motor courts. Nothing. They continued on through the small business center, carefully glancing around for the Packard. The area showed a marked deficiency of Italian gangsters.

After crossing the town limits, Dwayne increased the speed back to forty-five m.p.h. McCarthy yawned and stretched. "Speaking of back east, y'know what they're beginning to call motor lodges and motor courts?"

"I have no idea."

"Motels," McCarthy stated. "Mo-tels, get it? It's a word that combines motor with hotel."

"Clever," Dwayne remarked without much interest. "And speaking of the east coast one more time, when d'you think you'll be going back?"

"I wouldn't hazard a guess. The fact that the esteemed Forzini Crime Family has sent some envoys out here means my presence might have to be extended."

"I hope that's the case," Dwayne remarked. "I hate to

think of me being on my own in this caper. If things go wrong, there's a good chance I'll need a backup."

McCarthy shrugged. "It's something you'll always have on your mind when you go undercover. It still occurs to me, and I've been on this assignment for eighteen months."

"I've been meaning to ask you," Dwayne said. "Don't you have a family? Wife and kiddies and all that."

"No living relatives, no kids and I'm long divorced."

"You're perfect for the job," Dwayne acknowledged.

———

A HALF HOUR LATER, DWAYNE AND MCCARTHY drove into the town of Oakley at a bit past the noon hour. Suddenly McCarthy called out. "There it is! That fucking Packard! Let's check out the license plate."

Dwayne exclaimed, "Massachusetts! And it's parked in front of a restaurant." He pulled up to the curb and cut the engine. After checking the .45 auto in his shoulder holster, he asked, "Hungry?"

"Starving," McCarthy replied. He loosened the .38 Smith and Wesson revolver in his own holster. "Let's see what's on the menu."

They got out of the car and walked slowly toward the restaurant with McCarthy leading the way inside. Fat Pauly Cappurio and two companions sat in a booth opposite the counter. It was obvious they hadn't been there long since each was munching a hamburger with another on their plates. The trio of heavyset men also had double servings of French fries. The beverage of the day was milkshakes.

Dwayne and McCarthy walked down to the end of the counter where it curved around to face toward the front of the restaurant. They sat down, able to see Fat Pauly assaulting his lunch with gusto. His two companions had their backs to the undercover duo.

The waitress walked up to the pseudo farmers. Dwayne ordered a cup of coffee and a piece of cherry pie while McCarthy settled for coffee and a jelly roll. Dwayne spoke softly, saying, "I hope we can pick up some useful information from their conversation."

McCarthy frowned. "We might hear something if they stop chewing long enough to speak."

As if on cue, Fat Pauly belched, then announced. "I wonder how much longer Joe is gonna make us stay out here."

The man sitting opposite him and closest to the wall was Peachy Russo. He sighed. "'Til we find them Micks."

Legs Spina was the third man. "You guys know sump'n? This area we're in is just like the wide open spaces that Roy Rogers and Gene Autry sing about in the movies."

"There ain't many people though," Peachy announced. He had a second thought. "But that don't make our job any easier."

"That's the rub," Spina stated. "How in hell do we whack somebody out here?"

"Knock it off!" Fat Pauly hissed. "Why don't you just make a sign and walk down the street so ever'body can see why we're gonna do?" He raised his eyes and looked at Dwayne and McCarthy sitting at the end of the counter. The pair assumed blank facial expressions as they stared out the plate glass window into the street.

Dwayne rubbed his mouth with a paper napkin, whispering, "Now we know why they're visiting Kansas. They're the advance party of an invasion."

"Yeah," McCarthy agreed. "And they're also under

orders to kill somebody." He finished his jelly roll and left thirty cents and a five cent tip to cover their lunches. Then he and Dwayne ambled past the Mafioso and out of the restaurant. As they walked down the sidewalk toward the Buick, McCarthy said, "Let's follow 'em as long as it's feasible. Just keep in mind we don't want 'em to take notice of us. Then we can get back to Jimmy."

"Don't forget our shopping chores," Dwayne reminded him.

————

THAT SAME NIGHT IN AN ITALIAN neighborhood of Boston, a meeting of the Forzini Crime Family was in progress in the backroom of the Fogetti Italian Restaurant. The eating establishment had been around ever since its ethnicity went from Jewish to Italian in the late nineteenth century. Other restaurateurs attempted to open businesses in the locale, but none were up to par with the one owned by three generations of the Fogetti family. The food and service were excellent and the business had evolved into a social club with a backroom for cards, drinking Italian wines and chatting with neighbors and kin. A bocce ball court was available out the back door.

The upstairs was where the owners lived for a few years, but during prohibition they purchased a home down the street. The former second floor apartment was now used by the Forzini gang as a headquarters and meeting place.

Joe Forzini and his mobsters were minor league participants in Mafia operations in Boston. Most of their activities were performing errands and assignments for the real godfather Angelo Lundari. This included helping out in crimes such as commercial burglaries and arson. This latter crime was committed at the behest of owners of failing businesses. The purpose was to collect insurance on the commercial properties.

Now and then the Forzini gangsters took people for the proverbial rides or punctuated various warnings with fists and blackjacks to unfortunates who ran afoul of the mob.

The gang was well aware they had no chance of expanding into a powerful organization to match their superiors. This was one thing they had in common with the Derby gang. That outfit was used by large Irish criminal organizations to help out in various unlawful activities. If the Derbies and Forzini family ever joined up for a common cause, they would have an above average chance of giving the other Boston crime cartels a run for their money. But the Irish and Italians had a long history of absolute hatred and loathing for one another that was punctuated with street warfare to wrest control of the minor criminal undertakings in the Boston area.

Joe Forzini, the boss, presided over that evening's proceedings. The gang was seated around a table in a room that had once been the Fogetti parlor. He called the meeting to order in his usual fashion of shouting, "Shaddup!" Everyone quieted down, and Forzini announced. "The first thing we got going is a report from Arrigo."

Arrigo Leone was the gang *consigliere* or advisor, who handled the correspondence and other administrative details of the gang. He had the job because he was a forger and swindler rather than a violent criminal. He also had a college degree in business administration.

The thin, stooped man stood up to address the group. "As you guys know, Fat Pauly, Peachy and Legs are out in

Kansas trying to find out exactly where the Derbies are located."

Joe interjected, "This is the most important thing we've *ever* had going for us. If we can get rid of them Micks, the New York mob will turn to us for the project."

"Right," Leone agreed. "I talked to Fat Pauly on the phone earlier today and he said they haven't been able to find the Derbies. He said he and Peaches and Legs are going back and forth on Highway 40 to all the truck stops, but haven't been able to see any sign of them so far. That concludes my report." He sat back down.

"That's it?" Guido Viola asked, disappointed.

Leone scowled at him. "What do you think?"

Viola knew that it irritated Joe Forzini when anyone showed disrespect to the consigliere. "I didn't mean nothing. I was just disappointed that things ain't going good out there in Oklahoma."

"Kansas!" Joe said. "They're in fucking Kansas. *Not* Oklahoma, understand?" He looked over at Leone. "Thanks for the report, Arrigo. Any questions from anybody?"

Tony Bonvicini, the official loan shark of the family, put his elbows on the table and gazed over at the boss. "C'mon, Joe! When are you gonna tell us who the guy is that's ratting out the Derbies. Don't you trust us?"

"Listen, Tony. Don't get me wrong. I trust all you guys. But the less you know about my source of information, the better the chances for me pertecting his identification. He's the key to us completing our plans to take over the Derbies operation out there in the boondocks."

Freddy Leonardi was pessimistic. "How much more help is that Irish rat bastard gonna be if he don't even know himself where they are?"

Joe replied, "You both know that Johnny Cullen is a

secretive guy, right? And he runs that gang like they was a spy ring. That way one group don't know what the others are doing. So any information he gives out—and it ain't much—is given me that same day by our inside guy. But eventually we'll get the big picture. I'm hoping Pauly and the others can manage to dig up something. This is gonna be our ticket to the big time."

He looked over at Tony Bonvicini the loan shark. "How's your end going?"

"There is one guy who's behind in his vigorish. He's a schoolteacher and stand-up guy. So I won't have to give him a punch-up. A chewing out will get him back on the ball." He shrugged. "That's it. I'll turn in my loan sheet to you by tomorrow afternoon. Ever'thing is in great shape."

"Okay," Joe Forzini said. "Anything else to report or talk about? No? Good!" He gestured to Freddy Leonardi. "Go downstairs and get some menus and a waiter. I hear a stromboli calling my name."

CHAPTER 17

Dwayne Wheeler and Terry McCarthy were gone from the Retreat for two days. When they returned, the Buick's trunk was stuffed with work clothing and shoes along with some additional disguise paraphernalia that Dwayne had purchased at a theatrical store in Topeka. After the shamus parked at the rear stoop of the lodge house, he and McCarthy gathered up everything and carried it into the kitchen.

Jimmy Sheehan watched them dump the stuff on the table without much interest. "I'm glad that's taken care of."

"One other little item occurred that might interest you," McCarthy said. He paused, then stated, "We saw Fat Pauly and two other guys from the Forzini Family in a small town restaurant."

Sheehan sprang to his feet. "Goddamn! What the hell happened?"

"Nothing," Dwayne said. "We saw the Packard in front of a cafe. We went in to check things out."

McCarthy continued the narrative. "They didn't give us a second glance because of the way we were dressed and I was wearing a fake moustache. We sat at a spot at the counter where it was easy to see and hear 'em chatting."

Dwayne laughed. "There wasn't a lot of talk since the fat bastards were stuffing their faces."

Sheehan was somber. "I'm not in any mood for wisecracks."

"Understood," Dwayne stated.

"The main thing," McCarthy said, "is they mentioned whacking somebody."

"Okay," Sheehan acknowledged. He took a deep breath and exhaled very slowly. "There's gonna be a war."

"Does that mean we won't be taking the girls to the truck stop?" McCarthy asked.

"Yeah," Sheehan flatly stated. He looked at the bundle on the table. "I take it these are the clothes we need."

"Yeah," Dwayne answered. "That includes shoes. I also bought some more disguises. Make-up, wigs, moustaches, and fake eyebrows."

"Mmm," Sheehan mused. "No beards?"

"In order to have a realistic looking beard you need sticky stuff and strands of hair."

"You're the expert," Sheehan said. He nodded to McCarthy. "I want you to go to the telephone exchange and phone Johnny. Give him the lowdown and ask for orders, suggestions, or any other goddamn thing he's got to say. Dwayne can take you over there in his car."

"Now?" McCarthy asked.

"*Now!*"

"Speaking of suggestions, I got one," Dwayne said. "Since we're not going to the truck stop, we should use Farley Kuch as our eyes and ears. I say we give him an extra ten bucks. That'll bring his pay up to twenty-five bucks a week. That's more'n the twenty bucks he gets from that cheapskate truck stop operator."

"Do it."

McCarthy stood up. "C'mon, Dwayne, let's get over to those telephones."

Sheehan cautioned them. "Don't go in the fucking restaurant. From now on that telephone exchange and seeing that security kid is all we do over there."

"Gotcha," McCarthy said.

Dwayne and McCarthy got back in the Buick for the drive to the telephone exchange. When they reached the highway, McCarthy said, "I gotta give you the phone number for Johnny Cullen. You might need it someday. And there's another number that's even more important. It's the F.B.I. safehouse in Wichita."

"I know the place," Dwayne said. "It's on Nineteenth Street in Riverside. My girlfriend and I holed up there during the Kansas City mob caper."

———

A HALF HOUR LATER THEY PULLED UP IN FRONT of the telephone exchange. There were several truckers sitting around waiting for return calls from their employers. Dwayne and McCarthy went up to the desk and arranged for the connection to Boston. Dwayne stated he wanted to put in a call to F.B.I. Agent Steve Williams in Wichita.

"What for?" McCarthy asked.

"Just to check in," Dwayne replied. "There could be some new or inte'rsting goings-on."

"Not a bad idea."

Dwayne waited for McCarthy to go back to sit down, before filling out a card for a call to Venus Services in Wichita. With that done, he joined his undercover partner at the rows of chairs to wait. Ten minutes passed, then McCarthy was given a booth number.

Dwayne's call was connected a few moments later. He went into the assigned booth. "Hello. Is this you, Rachel?"

"Yeah," the woman replied. "Hi, Dwayne, it looks like you've risen to new heights in your reputation with Mrs. Davies. She told me to give you her house number when you called."

Dwayne was pleasantly surprised. He scribbled down the information and hung up. He went back to the counter and asked the lady to place the call for him. As he walked past the booth where McCarthy was, he noted that his companion was involved in a serious conversation.

The shamus had a five minute wait before he was informed his call had gone through. He went into the booth. "Hello."

"Hello, Mister Wheeler," said Kathryn Carruthers. "Mrs. Davies is on the other line. I'll put you through."

A moment later, the lady asked, "Is that you, Mister Wheeler?"

"Yes, ma'am."

"Please tell me how your assignment is going."

"Sure," Dwayne said. "First of all I have a question. Are you acquainted with a Babe Robertson?"

Mrs. Davies gasped. "That wicked woman! Yes. I know her and she is evil incarnate!"

"I have to agree. She is indeed involved in truck stop prostitution as well as supplying heroin to keep the girls under control. This is a complicated case, and I'm on top of it. But it's too early to make a report."

"I understand and have complete faith in you, Mister Wheeler. Don't hesitate to contact me at this number when it's convenient for you. Please remember that you're involved in a mission of mercy." She paused, then said, "I saw in the papers that you are in some sort of trouble. Will this be an inconvenience to our agreement?"

"No, ma'am! I guarantee it won't be. It'll all be settled in my favor. I hope you believe me."

"I do indeed believe you, Mister Wheeler. Goodbye."

Dwayne hung up and went back to take a seat and wait.

An entire half hour passed before McCarthy emerged. He gestured to Dwayne to follow him outside to the car. When both were seated, the F.B.I. undercover gave him the gist of his phone conversation with Johnny Cullen.

"The guy went bananas. He can't figure out how the Italians found the area where we're operating."

"Maybe there's a turncoat in the Derbies," Dwayne suggested.

"I don't think so," McCarthy opined. "I don't have a traditional background in the gang like the others since their history goes back a long ways. I'm talking grandfather, fathers, uncles, cousins, etcetera all being in the gang. And most of that history has to do with fighting against Italians in and around Boston. So it would surprise me if there was a snitch in the organization."

"What's the story on the Derbies' neighborhood?"

"The site was settled by English people back in the seventeenth century. The place followed the traditional evolvement of colonial neighborhoods. The wealthy founded it, then moved on as encroachment from newcomers gradually took over as time passed."

"Interesting," Dwayne remarked. "I didn't say much

to Steve Williams. He just said to carry on. What'd you learn from the big guy Johnny Cullen?"

"The same thing Jimmy told us. There's gonna be a war."

CHAPTER 18

All the Derbies, with the exception of Sean Magee, who was manning the gatehouse, were seated around the table in the Retreat's lodge kitchen. Charlie O'Donnell had made sandwiches and provided bottles of beer for the occasion.

Jimmy Sheehan called the meeting to order by restating his own and Johnny Cullen's prediction. "There's gonna be a war."

Everyone's face show signs of grim surprise at the pronouncement. Such statements in the past had been heralds of grisly circumstances. It meant long periods of alert watchfulness, dangerous forays to whack key enemy individuals, and other acts of gang warfare. And woe to any poor bastard that was captured by the other side. Intense interrogation punctuated with brutal beatings followed by being murdered would be the order of the day for those unfortunates.

Sheehan continued, "Terry McCarthy and Dwayne Wheeler spotted Fat Pauly Cappurio and two other Wops by the names of Peachy Russo and Legs Spina."

David O'Leary, one of the gatehouse guards, asked, "What the hell are them three doing out here?"

"I'll get to that," Sheehan said. "Anyhow, Terry and Dwayne saw the sons of bitches in a town west of here on U.S. 40. They were having lunch and talking about whacking somebody. So you can be certain they're gonna try to run us off—or *kill* us off—so they can take over the operation. And getting rid of us will be the first step in their plan."

Duke Glencannon sat his beer down after a swallow from the bottle. "How'd they know we was in Kansas, Jimmy?"

Sheehan replied, "McCarthy talked to Johnny a couple of hours ago, and he didn't know how they knew either. It's a real puzzlement."

"Shit!" Tim Fagin cursed. "Maybe the Banocci Family changed their minds about having us work for 'em out here."

"I'll admit it's possible, but not probable," Jimmy replied. "At one time they prob'ly didn't give a rat's ass whether it was us or the Forzini bunch doing this job. But they chose us, and they'd have to be stupid to make any changes at this stage of the game. Particularly when there's gonna be a second part to the operations."

Charlie O'Donnell set out some more refreshments, saying, "There has to be a snitch that's telling them Forzini Wops what we're up to. That's obvious to me." He paused and looked around the table. "And remember we been doing a hell of a good job. So it's a goddamn stoolie. That's my opinion."

Jimmy Sheehan, who had a lot of respect for the old gangster, nodded. "You're prob'ly right, Charlie."

Dwayne spoke up. "Can't you call the Banocci Family and check things out?"

"You're a new boy, Dwayne," Jimmy said. "If we contact 'em about our troubles, we'd end up fighting Forzinis *and* the Banoccis. This is something we got to deal with ourselves. Get my drift?"

"Gotcha," Dwayne replied.

"I'm gonna divide us into teams," Sheehan said. "As soon as I get ever'thing organized I'll hand out assignments. Bottom line; we're fighting back. That's it for now."

Everyone took final swigs of beer and grabbed sandwiches, then either headed for the stairs to their rooms or went out the back door. Dwayne was about to follow McCarthy upstairs, when Sheehan called him back.

The chief gave him a hard look. "I gotta make something clear to you, Dwayne. You're going to be a hit man in this situation."

A sudden nervous infusion clouded Dwayne's mind for a moment, then he stated, "I've never killed nobody. I've shot at a car driving away after some guys in it killed a bootlegger pal of mine. But that's all."

"Don't worry. I'm gonna send Duke Glencannon and Frank Quinn with you. They've taken care of several problem guys in the past. They'll give you good advice as well as backup."

"Jesus!" Dwayne exclaimed under his breath.

Sheehan gave him a warning look. "You're part of this gang now. You got to prove yourself. If you don't, we can't trust you. I think you can figure what'll happen if you don't pull this off."

"Sure, Jimmy. I just wasn't quite expecting to kill anybody, but I understand and ain't complaining."

"Good," Sheehan acknowledged. "Tonight I want you to go out to the truck stop and get that kid security guard to keep an eye out for any suspicious out-of-towners who ain't truck drivers."

"Okay. It's Tuesday, his regular night for getting paid. I'll tell him exactly what to look for and let him know he'll be getting an extra ten bucks a week."

"Okay. I want somebody to go out there ever' single night to find out what he's seen."

"I'll take care of it."

————

Dwayne pulled the panel truck into a spot at the edge of the truck stop. He was dressed in his working duds as he walked to where the rigs were parked. The rumble of the running engines filled the night as he looked up and down the rows of vehicles. The only people he saw were drivers coming and going to and from the restaurant.

This worried the shamus. It would create a special problem if Farley Kuch had gotten himself fired. Dwayne went over to the rear of the next row, and began moving in the direction of the restaurant. He started to pass by a blue truck then stopped and did a double take. There were words painted in yellow on the door.

DARRELL BODINE
OWNER AND OPERATOR

Dwayne grinned. The son of a bitch evidently wasn't able to find another young girl to pimp, so he had to go back to his regular job. Then for an instant the shamus thought about what might happen if he bumped into the guy. If that occurred, he hoped Bodine wouldn't recognize him. It had been pretty dim at the Nebraska truck stop the night he rescued Mary Sue. It was all for nothing, since she was now worse off as a prostitute again in addition to being a drug addict.

Dwayne continued up the row, looking between each vehicle, until he spotted the big kid coming into view from the direction of the restaurant. The shamus quickened his pace until Farley saw him.

The young guy gave him a happy grin. "Hi! I ain't seen you fellers for a few days."

"We've been busy and it's Tuesday," Dwayne said. He forked over fifteen dollars. "There you go. Now we got another extra job for you to do. It's real easy and pays ten more dollars a week."

"Ten more dollars a week! Boy howdy! That'll give me...uh...let me see—"

Dwayne interrupted. "With the twenty bucks you get from the truck stop owner and us, that's a grand total of forty-five dollars."

"Boy howdy! What do you want me to do?"

"Let's get out of sight," Dwayne said. He led Farley behind a Mack truck, then turned to face him. "We won't be coming out here with the girls for awhile. A small problem has popped up. So what we need you to do is to keep an eye out for any slick looking guys that might show up around here. They'll be in fancy cars and wearing suits or sports jackets."

"City slickers huh?"

"Right," Dwayne replied. "And if possible, get a good look at their license plates to see if they're from Massachusetts."

Farley grimaced, saying, "Massachoopits?"

"Never mind. Give special attention to all out-of-state plates, okay? Write down the numbers. That'll be a big help to us."

"I got it," Farley said. "I look for city slickers in big cars from out of state. I write down their license numbers and give 'em to you guys."

"Exactly, Farley. Don't forget to write down the state names with the numbers."

"I can do that, too."

"See you later," Dwayne said.

He walked back toward the panel truck while a very happy Farley Kuch made his way to the restaurant to begin checking out the customers and automobiles.

CHAPTER 19

Jimmy Sheehan stayed busy preparing his men for the coming war. He organized one hit team—Dwayne, Duke Glencannon and Frank Quinn—with others divided up as security groups to maintain watch on the Retreat's outer perimeter twenty-four hours a day.

Terry McCarthy was appointed as second-in-command since his phone duties gave him access to the gang boss Johnny Cullen in Boston. He asked Sheehan if he could have Dwayne accompany him to the telephone exchange to watch his back in case something untoward happened. Sheehan approved the request.

Meanwhile, the females were made to stay inside except for brief times of sitting on the back stoop by the kitchen door. They felt like they were on a vacation of sorts since they weren't going to the truck stop on a nightly basis. They had to entertain various gang members at all hours, but as long as they got their fixes, they had no complaints.

RIGHT   AFTER   SHEEHAN'S   TACTICAL
announcements, the three-man assassination crew went to
Frank Quinn's room in the lodge house. He retrieved a
leather case from under his bed and opened it. He held up
a small automatic handgun.

Dwayne gave the weapon a close look. "What the hell
kind of pistol is that?"

Duke Glencannon grinned. "It's a mongrel that Frank
designed and machined from a SIG-Sauer."

"Right," Frank said proudly. "It's a .22 caliber chambered for long-rifle hollow points." He reached over to the
case again. "And here's the silencer that fits on it."

"Yeah," Glencannon said. "When you fire it, there's
only small popping sound."

"I get it," Dwayne said. "It fires small caliber rounds,
but since they're hollow-points, they make a hell of a big
exit wound."

"You'll get a chance to shoot it a few times before we
go into action," Frank said. "The guy you whack is gonna
be so close so you won't have to worry about accuracy.
Just point and pull the trigger. Pop! Pop! And he's one
dead motherfucker."

At that point, Dwayne and his two companions began
discussing different scenarios of assassinations. They
conversed about whacking adversaries on the street, in
restaurants, motor lodge rooms and other places,
including throwing the victim in the trunk of a car and
shooting him through the lid. Frank Quinn remembered
doing that a couple of times in a gang war back in the
1930s.

When the gruesome discussion was over, Dwayne
left the room to search out McCarthy. He found him
back in the kitchen sitting at the table peacefully
nursing a beer. Dwayne suggested they take a walk

down to the creek that ran through the small copse on the property.

They were out of the range of hearing from the lodge when Dwayne growled, "Nobody told me I was gonna have to be a fucking hit man!"

"Yeah. We weren't expecting that."

"I'm seriously thinking of discharging myself from this caper and driving as fast as I can back to good ol' Wichita."

"Hold it!" McCarthy cautioned him. "Remember you're under Federal orders on an undercover case. You are required—I say again—*required* to do what it takes to remain on this assignment. You'd make more trouble for yourself by running than if you shot somebody."

"Shit!"

"There is a positive side to this, Dwayne. We know for a fact that Glencannon and Quinn will be a great help for you. In fact, that greatly diminished the danger. Both those guys are experts when it comes to taking people out."

"You mean *murdering* people, goddamn it!"

"Let's not get into semantics. I reiterate; you'll be with a couple of competent guys you can depend on. Nothing bad is going to happen to you."

"How about my fucking conscience? It ain't like I'm defending myself. I'm going to be hunting down human beings and killing them in sneaky ways."

"Let's put this into yet another perspective," McCarthy suggested. "Fat Pauly Cappurio, Peachy Russo, and Legs Spina are cold-blooded murderers. God only knows how many guys they've knocked off. All three of 'em also have tortured people to get information out of them. Afterward they used garrotes to strangle 'em before dumping them at some landfill or another. You'll be ridding the world of cruel villains. They're as evil as the Nazi Gestapo."

"I got a lot of hard thinking to do about this whole goddamn situation!"

McCarthy gazed at him for a long moment. "You're in this thing for the long haul, Dwayne. The Bureau isn't going to let you leave here and return to your happy life in Wichita. You'd be a security risk."

Now Dwayne was both nervous and furious. "*What the hell does that mean*?"

"Well, you might decide to write a book or give an interview about this caper," McCarthy said. "That would reveal a lot about F.B.I. procedures."

"Are you telling me the goddamn F.B.I. would kill me?"

"If they didn't, the Banocci Family sure as hell would."

"I've heard of being between the rock and the hard place, but this is downright unfair! I'll have your fucking Fed'ral Bureau of Investigation hanging over my head for the rest of my life!"

"You know better, Dwayne. If that was the way we operated, we'd never be able to penetrate organized crime. So I suggest you whack who you gotta whack. When it's all said and done, you'll be back in Wichita safe and sound to once again live a normal life."

"I'll still lose a lot of sleep over it."

McCarthy took his arm and steered the unhappy shamus back toward the lodge.

———

TWO DAYS LATER ALL HELL BROKE LOOSE AT THE Retreat. It started on a mid-morning when another all-hands meeting was going on in the kitchen. Wilma, the aggressive whore, burst through the door. "That little broad is dead!"

"Which one?" Sheehan asked.

"Mary Sue," Wilma said. "She overdosed last night."

Sheehan was upset. "Now ain't that just great! We got a stiff on our hands."

Dwayne, still angry and upset about his own predicament, asked, "Are we gonna take her to a landfill?"

"Why?" Sheehan asked. "D'you know of one?"

Dwayne shook his head, regretting his sarcastic remark. "Not really."

Duke Glencannon had a suggestion. "We can wrap her in a blanket and bury her in them trees by the creek."

Dwayne suddenly thought of Jessie and Lorene Pickens. He knew Jessie wouldn't be too upset, but it would set Lorene off on one hell of a bender. That meant getting blind drunk and going off with a man—or men—to some cheap hotel for a few days. Then another slant to the situation occurred to him. If she were buried out by the creek, her parents would never know what happened to her.

He stood up. "I'll go up and check her out."

The shamus ascended the stairs and went down the hall to the rooms occupied by the women. They each had separate quarters, not because of privilege but in order to entertain any members of the gang who demanded their attention.

Dwayne stepped into Mary Sue's room and saw her lying face up. She looked particularly unattractive in death, with half-closed eyes and her lips drawn tightly over her teeth. He took a blanket and worked it under the corpse, then wrapped it around her. He picked the girl up and carried her down to the kitchen.

Sheehan wasn't expecting that. "What the hell are you gonna do?"

"I'm gonna take her out to the woods and bury her like Duke suggested," he said.

Sheehan understood. "That's okay. You knew her and her parents, right?"

Charlie O'Donnell looked over from his stove. "There's a spade in the tool shed."

McCarthy stood up. "I'll give you a hand."

The pair left the lodge house, stopping so McCarthy could grab the spade, then continued across the meadow and into the trees. Dwayne knelt down and laid the dead girl on the ground. He took the spade from McCarthy, and wordlessly began digging.

McCarthy watched him labor at the chore for awhile. "Do you want me to spell you?"

Dwayne shook his head and kept digging. The ground was soft in the trees with little grass or weeds, making the task easy. He dug down until the grave was waist deep. He climbed out and cradled the body, picking it up. After stepping back into the excavation, he gently laid Mary Sue at the bottom.

He glanced at McCarthy. "D'you know any prayers or anything like that?"

"Nope."

"Just as well," Dwayne remarked. He climbed out of the grave to begin shoveling the dirt on top of the dead girl.

CHAPTER 20

There was a short, ancient street in Queens, New York City that jutted out from a main thoroughfare. It was named Barchia Road and was only three blocks long during the nearly two hundred years of its existence. The reason for the name was lost in the distant shadows of time as well as a dearth of written history about the site.

The little neighborhood was hidden from view by an abandoned shoe factory that once provided jobs for the local population. In the latter part of the nineteenth century, the area became known as Little Palermo because of the Sicilian immigrants who eventually settled in the place.

The families in Little Palermo were brought over by the owners of the factory in the 1880s when the business was in full operation. These people were hired in their home country though a special employment agency in New York City that ran a lucrative labor-gathering service in Europe. The glib, multi-linguistic representatives did the recruitment by describing the riches of America available for hardworking employees. These struggling unhappy people were promised free passage across the ocean to those wonderful working conditions and generous salaries. In truth, however, the cost of the voyages would be taken from their wages once they began working at their new jobs. For practical purposes, rather than merciful, deductions were spread out over a full year. After all, the poor wretches needed enough money to buy food.

The management of the factory were several American businessmen who, like others of their ilk, found it profitable to import naive foreign workers for their enterprises. These people not only had no concept of labor unions, they'd never heard of them.

When the Sicilians arrived and were transported to Barchia Road, they discovered the awful truth. The location kept them hidden away from public view as they worked long hours making footwear while earning miserable wages.

The employees never complained about the working conditions after the first few grumblers were fired and forced out of the community. The factory foremen told outrageous lies to those who remained. The gist of these trumped-up stories was that the ingrates would not be able to find jobs, and the American police would imprison them and their families in workhouses. They would labor in those hellholes for the rest of their lives without pay while being given barely enough food to keep them alive.

———

IN THE EARLY TWENTIETH CENTURY, THE SHOE factory went into bankruptcy because of falling sales and inefficiency of management. The owners sold off all the shoemaking machinery and gutted the rest of the interior to sell to scrap merchants. The only thing left was the shell of the building.

The abandoned work force were left in desperate circumstances. They were poorly educated, could not speak English and knew next to nothing about America. In desperation, the husbands and fathers would leave the community daily to seek work for any sort of jobs they could find in other parts of the metropolitan area. There was nothing too hard or humiliating as far as these despairing men were concerned.

Despite this attitude only a small minority of employers wanted to hire non-English speaking foreigners. Eventually, the unemployed Sicilians with hungry families turned to committing crimes such as burglary, shoplifting, and outright robbery in other parts of New York City.

However, in the midst of this hopelessness and misery, a single family by the name of Banocci emerged as the bosses of Barchia Road. The Banoccis were both cunning and highly intelligent. They organized the higgledy-piggledy crime sprees into carefully planned missions. More money came in and some of the families were able to accumulate enough capital to establish businesses in Little Palermo. Within a decade a restaurant, grocery store and saloon appeared. Several people began to raise chickens and pigs while others took advantage of the open spaces to plant vegetable gardens. Life was much better, but far from perfect.

It remained a rather unpleasant place until 1920 when Prohibition became the law of the land in the United States of America. One of the Banoccis, a twenty-one-year-old by the name of Carlo, had developed criminal contacts in various parts of New York City in his short career. When a couple of gangs went into the bootlegging business, they hired Carlo and his compatriots to help them with picking up and delivering the illegal hooch.

Eventually, through hook and crook—including the elimination of competitors by hijackings and murders—Carlo was able to form his own criminal enterprise with trucks and an excellent customer base.

The ambitious young man set up the headquarters of his new business in Little Palermo. The money seemed to roll in faster than it could be counted. It wasn't long before Carlo had politicians, judges and the police in his pocket. Anytime a problem arose, he simply sent one of his "employees" to the right man with the right amount of money in a plain white envelope. This also resulted in getting Little Palermo hooked up to the water, sewage and electrical system of New York City. Getting Barchia Road paved took a little extra effort however.

Meanwhile, Carlo courted and married, eventually having a family of three boys and two girls. He remained adaptable and extremely smart, knowing that in order to keep his operation profitable, he would have to develop a loyal following among the residents of Little Palermo. Thus he used much of his wealth to take care of the local population. He financed the building of houses and apartment buildings to replace the hovels where the families lived. All were rent free. Additionally, if someone was having financial problems, they came to Carlo for advice and loans. He charged no interest and forgave more than half of the transactions.

On many occasions, Carlo called in doctors for the sick, paying the entire medical costs. In a very short time, the grateful people began calling him *il Padrino*—the Godfather. The older males and more prosperous businessmen greeted him as *Don* Carlo, which translated into English as Sir Charles.

There wasn't a single inhabitant on Barchia Road that would refuse a favor or errand asked of them by the Padrino. Liquor was stored in closets, gin was made in bathtubs, and many of the young men of the community became street *soldadi*—soldiers—in Don Carlo's gang.

Thus, during the years 1920 to 1933 when Prohibition was in force, the Banocci Crime Family blossomed into a permanent prosperous organization. Carlo knew that the ridiculous Prohibition laws would not be a permanent part of American life. Accordingly, he began preparing for the expected repeal. He eased into other activities such as bookmaking, loan sharking, prostitution and gambling.

During World War II, the Padrino moved his wife, children, grandchildren and in-laws out of Little Palermo. He, his consigliere Vicenzo Cerro, chief capo Enrico Galo and number one enforcer Dominic Rossi lived in mansions on Long Island. Meanwhile, the junior capos and soldiers resided in the better homes and apartments in Little Palermo.

In 1948 Carlo Banocci still had his headquarters in Little Palermo and made regular appearances on the streets, acknowledging the greetings of the locals, even stopping to chat with them now and then. The neighborhood was now much more sophisticated with an excellent restaurant, a large food market, clothing stores and other commercial enterprises.

And the people still considered Carlo their *padrino*.

———

THE AFTERNOON SUN WAS WARM ON BARCHIA Road as the Padrino and Cerro strolled past the shops, exchanging greetings with the locals. The pair had spent a long morning going over reports sent down from Boston by Johnny Cullen the boss of the Irish Derby mob. The Padrino had chosen that particular gang for a special assignment since it was run efficiently by Cullen. More importantly the gang was located out of New York City and didn't draw any attention from that metropolitan area's law enforcement. The other choice in Boston had been the Forzini Family. Although they were Italian, Consigliere Vicenzo Cerro advised the Padrino not to make any agreements with them.

As Cerro explained, "They're nothing but errand boys for the real Mafia. Johnny Cullen, on the other hand, is a capable leader and has a disciplined organization. They'll be a big help in establishing the beginnings of our expansion." Then he added, "Even way out there in Kansas."

CHAPTER 21

An elaborate roadside restaurant called the Commodore was located on U.S. Highway 5 south of Hartford, Connecticut. It was a rambling one-story building constructed in the early 1900s to serve a very well-to-do clientele. Those people did not go to the restaurant to *eat*; they went there to *dine*.

The Commodore's architecture was in the Tudor tradition of brick and stone masonry with several different dining rooms, each with its own extravagant decor. The *haute cuisine* of the kitchen matched the classic design of the building, and the Commodore enjoyed five-star ratings for decades.

In the early days of prohibition its customer base began falling when fancy speakeasies served banned liquor with their food. The management of the Commodore was unwilling to break the law by providing illegal booze. Unfortunately, this proved costly to the business. Finally, out of desperation, the owners turned to their attorney to arrange payments of bribes to the right people in the local state and county governments so that bootleg liquor and beer could be served without fear of raids by law enforcement.

Thus, the Commodore Restaurant became a sophisticated speakeasy when a newer, richer clientele rediscovered it. These were the *crème-de-la-crème* of the capital city's elite population—judges, politicians, businessmen, and gangsters—who all happily mixed together to party at the establishment.

Long after prohibition was repealed, the Commodore could still boast of a plethora of faithful diners. All were upper crust from more diverse stratums of the local gentry than ever before. The restaurant was also the place where Padrino Carlo Banocci and his consigliere Vicenzo Cerro had face-to-face meetings with Johnny Cullen and Dennis Murphy of the Derby mob. These sessions were held in rooms reserved for private parties, located in the rear of the restaurant. The proprietor, Sheldon Leibowitz, provided a fancy *nosh* for the clandestine events. This Jewish man and Carlo Banocci were fast friends from past social and business associations since the early 1920s.

———

IT WAS ON A MONDAY WHEN THE CHIEF OF THE Derbies Johnny Cullen put in a call to Bradley Darnell, a New York City lawyer. This somewhat shady gentleman acted as an intermediary in the communication activities of the Banocci Crime Family. Johnny wanted to arrange a meeting between him and the Padrino to discuss the projects they shared. Darnell was not a trial lawyer, but had a remarkable expertise for giving sound advice to courtroom attorneys. He also handled sensitive situations during conflicts that erupted between individuals and organizations who required confidentiality in their dealings.

Darnell sensed the tone of impatience in the Irish-American's voice over the phone. After hearing his near desperate request to see the Padrino, the go-between telephoned the crime boss, advising him to meet with Cullen as soon as possible. Don Carlo agreed to have lunch with Cullen on the following Wednesday at the Commodore.

———

ON WEDNESDAY, JOHNNY CULLEN WITH HIS assistant Dennis Murphy showed up early as was mandated by the Padrino's standing orders. They were ushered into the private dining room by Leibowitz himself. The table was set with carafes of wine for the Sicilians and bottles of beer for the Irish. Cheese, crackers, bowls of nuts and smoked oysters were also available.

Within a quarter of an hour, the door opened and Dominic Rossi, the Banoccis' head enforcer, entered the room. Cullen and Murphy knew what to do. They stood up and raised their hands while the burly bodyguard patted them down. When Rossi was satisfied they were unarmed, he went back to the door and gave a wave, indicating all was well.

The Padrino led the way into the dining room with his consigliere Cerro behind him. After an exchange of handshakes and friendly greetings, everyone sat down. The exception was Rossi who stood outside the door to maintain a vigilant lookout.

Cerro poured himself and the Padrino glasses of wine. The two Irishmen had half consumed beer bottles in front of them. Everyone raised their drinks in mutual salute, then the Padrino showed a smile. "So! What is it you wish to discuss with me, Johnny?"

Cullen showed none of the submissiveness or the deference the Sicilians exhibited toward Don Carlo. This didn't mean he lacked a high opinion of the padrino. They shared a mutual respect that included a deep trust. True to form, Johnny cut to the chase.

"I got some disturbing phone calls from my guys out in Kansas."

"This distresses me, Johnny."

"We're pretty pissed off about it, too," Cullen said. "It makes us worry that you ain't satisfied with the way we're handling things."

The Padrino leaned back in his chair, indicating his surprise. "I got no problems with you. What exactly is happening?"

"Three of Joe Forzini's boys have been seen out there. It makes us think you might be thinking of turning the operation over to them."

The Padrino and Cerro exchanged glances. The latter looked at Cullen and shook his head. "We're very pleased with you and your guys, Johnny. And we ain't had no contacts with the Forzini goons for at least five years or so."

The Padrino took a sip of wine and reached for a cracker. "Y'know what I'm thinking, Johnny? I'm thinking somebody in your organization is passing info to the Forzinis."

Dennis Murphy spoke up quickly. "There ain't nobody in our organization that would do that!"

"C'mon!" Cerro argued. "There can be a rat bastard snitch in any bunch. Maybe one of your guys is pissed off about something. An insult. Fighting over a woman. He's owed money. He *owes* money. He don't feel appreciated.

It could be any of a hunnerd things that makes a guy become a turncoat."

"Okay," the Padrino said. "First thing first, Johnny. Don't you worry about nothing, eh? You're a solid guy as far as I'm concerned. Keep up the good work and we'll all be making plenty of dough within a year."

Johnny Cullen smiled with relief. "I'm glad to hear that."

Dennis Murphy had trouble controlling his anger at the insinuation there was a traitor in the Derby gang. "I'm telling you, you're barking up the wrong tree if you think one of our guys is passing information to the Forzini shitheads. They're all assholes, y'know. Ever' goddamn one of 'em. None of our guys got any respect for 'em."

The Padrino gave him a cold look. "Relax. The truth is gonna come out eventually. Maybe sooner. Maybe later." He finished his wine and Cerro refilled his boss' glass. "In the meantime, I want you to whack one of them Forzini guys. And I mean damn quick."

"Not all three of 'em?" Johnny asked.

The Godfather shook his head. "I want the other two to hurry back to Boston so they can tell that shithead Joe Forzini what happened."

"I understand. Good idea."

Cerro added, "You got our complete trust, understand? So do this for Don Carlo as soon as possible."

Johnny nodded his acquiescence, and stood up. "Thanks for the reassurance, Don Carlo. We'll be shoveling off now. So long."

The two Irishmen walked from the room as the Padrino took a drink of wine and looked over at his consigliere. "It's time we got friendly with the Forzini Family, huh? We been rude to 'em. What do you think we make amends by inviting Joe Forzini and Arrigo

Leone to eat with us at Il Siciliano Restaurant on Barchia Street?"

"I think it's a great idea, Padrino," Cerro said. "I think you and me can persuade them to name their fink friend in the Derbies."

"My thought exactly," the Padrino said. He pointed at the table. "Try some of that taleggio cheese over there. It's great. Sheldon has excellent taste in Italian food for a Jew, huh?"

"He sure does!" Cerro agreed.

CHAPTER 22

Dwayne Wheeler, Duke Glencannon and Frank Quinn spent most of the morning firing Quinn's personally designed SIG-Sauer pistol. They took several cantaloupes off Charlie O'Donnell's shelves and went into the woods by the creek for the familiarization practice.

Dwayne didn't enjoy the experience for two reasons. Firstly, the cantaloupes reacted the same as a human head when one of the hollow-point bullets were fired into it. There was a small entrance hole while the exit was splayed out with orange fruit matter as would happen to a human brain. The difference was that there was no blood splattered on the surrounding trees as would happen if the hollow-point had gone into a man's skull.

The second thing bothering the shamus was that they were in sight of the grave where Mary Sue Pickens was buried. No matter how hard he tried, he couldn't help gazing at the small mound of earth. He had yet to figure out how to inform Jesse and Lorene Pickens of their daughter's fate. The main complication was his undercover status. The F.B.I. would forbid him to speak to them on that subject. Ever!

When the hit team finished with the shooting practice, Glencannon and Quinn went to the lodge house kitchen to drink a few cold beers. Dwayne, feeling gloomy, went to his room. He wanted to put his feet up and try to take a nap. He hadn't been sleeping well since Terry McCarthy had given him the talking-to about whacking the Italian guys.

———

THE NEXT DAY WAS TIME FOR THE REGULAR calls back to Johnny Cullen in Boston. Dwayne and McCarthy drove over to the telephone exchange. There wasn't any chitchat during the ride, but the shamus had already made up his mind not to let McCarthy in on his assignment from Mrs. Davies. He knew the F.B.I. agent would be chickenshit enough to make him cancel the caper because of his undercover status.

When they arrived at the exchange, Dwayne told McCarthy he wanted to put in a call to Agent Steve Williams at the Wichita bureau office. McCarthy gave him a sympathetic look. "Dwayne, he's not going to relieve you from making the hit. And he sure as hell isn't going to relieve you from this assignment."

"It's worth a call."

They went inside the building and walked up to the counter. McCarthy filled out a card with the Boston phone number while Dwayne did the same for Wichita. But the number he wrote down was not Williams' office. It was the personal one for Mrs. Belle Davies.

They went back to the chairs to wait for their

summons. A couple of truck drivers were there, talking between themselves. From their conversation, Dwayne assumed they were partners, sharing driving duties with the one tractor they owned. It seemed they were anxious to pick up another trailer to deliver a load before going home.

Dwayne thought: *I wish that was all I had to worry about.*

The lady at the counter sang out, "Wichita call. Booth Three."

Dwayne got up and walked over, entering the booth and closing the door. He turned so he could keep an eye on McCarthy. "Hello. Missus Davies?"

"Yes, Mister Wheeler. How are you today?"

"I'm fine, Ma'am. I wanted to let you know I've infiltrated a prostitution ring operating in a truck stop. But it's gonna take awhile to line up evidence, names and all that. And heroin is definitely a big part of this."

"Very good, Mister Wheeler. It seems you are working with your usual efficiency."

"Thank you, ma'am. I'll keep you posted when I can."

"Please be careful," she cautioned him.

He hung up and stepped from the booth. He looked across the room and could see McCarthy on the phone, taking down notes. Dwayne went back and sat down.

McCarthy emerged from the booth, putting his notebook in his inside jacket pocket. He walked toward the door, signaling Dwayne to follow him. They went directly to the car and within a minute were back on the highway.

"I talked with Johnny Cullen," McCarthy said, gazing closely at Dwayne. "It was good news for you. Sort of. You're only going to have to take out one of the Forzini guys."

"I see."

"What did Williams tell you?" McCarthy asked.

"He told me to stay put and do what I'm told."

McCarthy nodded. "Good advice, my friend. Good advice indeed."

CHAPTER 23

Joe Forzini and his consigliere Arrigo Leone were both in good spirits. At that particular moment, they sat in the Boston gang's office above the Fogetti restaurant. They had just toasted each other with shots of grappa. This jovial gesture was to celebrate unexpected good news for the entire mob.

Earlier that morning Leone had received a phone call from his counterpart in the Banocci Crime Family. Vincenzo Cerro had invited the two of them to drive down to New York City for lunch and a special meeting that same day. The event would be with Padrino Don Carlo and Cerro in the Ristorante Siciliano located on Barchia Street in Little Palermo.

Joe Forzini, seated at his desk, pulled a cigar out of a humidor and pushed it over to Leone. "Y'know what this means, don't you, pal?"

Leone grinned. "You bet your ass I do, Chief. Don Carlo has decided to replace those degenerate Irish mugs in Kansas. And he chose us!" He bit off the end of his cigar. "It's all money in the bank from this point on."

"It's a bonanza!" Joe sung out.

"It's better'n finding gold!"

"The future never looked brighter!"

Leone shouted, "*We're on the fucking gravy train to wealth and power!*"

"I knew them stupid Micks would fuck up," Joe said. "That snitch said it was just a matter of time. Man oh man! It's gonna be the major leagues for us, Arrigo!"

"You know what, Chief? It won't be long before people will be calling you Don Giuseppe."

"No doubt about it," Joe agreed. "We've been working toward this for quite awhile. Once we're established solid, we can start considering a takeover of the Banoccis, eh?"

"You're absolutely right," the consigliere said. "When you put this in the correct perspective, it shows they're looking for help. They're on the ropes. They *need* us!"

Joe chuckled. "Pauly, Legs, and Peachy must have put the fear of God into them Micks. I wonder if they whacked anybody out there."

Leone laughed out loud. "I'm wondering how *many* they whacked."

"Enough to scare the shit out of Johnny Cullen," Joe commented. "As soon as we find out what the big picture is all about, we can settle in and study the entire situation." He became more serious. "This is a complicated undertaking. A complicated *gigantic* undertaking! But we can handle it."

Leone checked his watch. "We better get underway. Guido's got the car parked outside. He said it was all gassed up for us and ready to go."

The pair knocked back two more shots of grappa, then headed for the door.

—————

THE PADRINO AND VINCENZO CERRO STROLLED down Barchia Street in Little Palermo. Enrico Galo, the chief capo, was in front of them, while Dominic Rossi the head enforcer followed. They sauntered along the avenue, exchanging greetings with passersby as well as a couple of shopkeepers standing outside their places of business. The little community hummed with prosperity and contentment. The oldsters appreciated the present prosperity of the town more than the younger people. Those venerables could remember the bad old days.

When the four men arrived at the Ristorante Siciliano, the Padrino, Cerro and Galo walked through the front door. Rossi remained outside on the sidewalk, keeping watch for the invited guests coming down from Boston.

Vito Lazzone, owner of the restaurant, stepped out from behind the cash register and greeted the Padrino. "Everything is prepared, Don Carlo. Ricky Multari will be acting as your waiter."

"Excellent, Vito," the Padrino said. "*Tante grazie.*"

Lazzone escorted the seniors of the crime family toward the back of the dining room to a table with five place settings. The three sat down while Vito poured *Chianti Supremo* into their glasses. The Padrino, consigliere, and chief capo sank into silence as they sipped the wine. The formerly cheerful mood they displayed out on the street had quickly faded away. It had been replaced by one of cold, calculating rage.

Other diners occupied a half dozen tables in the restaurant as would be expected at a typical lunch hour. But there was no talking among those people. Everything appeared normal except for one exception; there was no food visible. These pseudo-diners were locals present at the behest of the Padrino. He offered each twenty-five dollars to come to the restaurant and sit at the tables until being told to leave. They had all refused the money. Don Carlo had shown them and their families much kindness in the past, hence all were delighted to have this chance to do a favor for their benefactor. Similar situations had happened before and each person knew the reason behind it, but said nothing regarding what was going on.

A quarter of an hour passed before the front door opened. Joe Forzini and Arrigo Leone walked in led by Dominic Rossi. The enforcer gestured to the Padrino that the arrivals were not armed, then went back outside. Don Carlo remained seated while Cerro and Galo stood up to the greet the newcomers.

Joe was respectful and humble as he addressed the Padrino. "Don Carlo, I am deeply honored by your generous invitation to join you for lunch. It is a great privilege to break bread with you."

The Padrino, with a show of dignity that would have complimented the Pope, nodded his recognition of the greeting. "Please! Sit down and make yourselves at home."

Ricky Multari, a small unpleasant looking young man who was actually a family soldier, walked up. He passed out five menus, showing a smile with his mouth but not with his eyes. He announced, "The special today is linguini and calamari with the chef's special sauce."

Arrigo Leone ordered the special while his boss Joe Forzini asked for a Pollo Pizzailola. Cerro ordered the "usual" for the Padrino, Galo, and himself. Ricky nodded, then walked off toward the kitchen.

"The kid must be smart," Joe Forzini remarked. "He didn't have to write nothing down."

"Yeah," Galo muttered in a gruff voice. "The kid is smart."

Joe and Arrigo hadn't noticed that the other "diners" were leaving the restaurant one by one. They also didn't see Dominic Rossi step silently inside, walking up behind them. Ricky Multari quickly joined the enforcer.

At that point, Cerro leaned forward, asking, "I guess you guys are wondering why you was invited down here, huh?"

Joe winked at his consigliere. "Yeah. Me and Arrigo discussed that after your phone call."

Arrigo grinned. "We couldn't fathom the reason for this unexpected courtesy."

Cerro glared at the pair. "Who's the fink that told you about the Derbies in Kansas?"

Joe started to stand up, but Rossi put both hands on his shoulders and slammed him back down in his chair. Arrigo, pale and thoroughly frightened, appeared to be going into shock.

Cerro growled, "I ain't gonna repeat myself."

Joe Forzini had trouble calming down. "Uh...uh...this is something...uh...I don't know what you're talking about."

Leone gulped. "Honest! We don't know shit about a snitch."

The Padrino spoke in a low, frightening tone. "Answer the fucking question. Who's the rat fink who told you about what the Derby gang is doing out in Kansas?"

"Kansas?" Forzini said.

"Let's go downstairs," the Padrino stated.

"Can't we stay up here?" Forzini frantically asked.

Galo chuckled. "Are you outta your fucking mind?"

Rossi grabbed the two frightened men by the collars

and yanked them to their feet. He pushed them toward the kitchen and through the swinging doors. The Padrino, Cerro and Galo followed. The diminutive Ricky Multari brought up the rear.

The group went through another door into a short hallway. This took them to a stairway that led down to a basement. Galo used a key to open the small portal to the underground room. He glanced over his shoulder at Forzini and Leone. "We used to hide our hooch down here during Prohibition."

The area was unfinished except for a dirt floor covered by wooden pallets. A single metal chair sat in the center of the room. Galo grinned. "How d'you like it? We fixed it up special for you."

Ricky Multari giggled. "Yeah. Sorry we couldn't find no pitchers to hang on the walls."

Rossi grabbed Arrigo Leone and sat him down. At the same time Galo tied the man's wrists to the chair arms with thick-gauge wire. Ricky walked over to a bench in the corner, coming back with a pair of large tongs.

He giggled again. "These are a blacksmith tool. They're called wolf tongs."

"Okay! Okay!" Joe Forzini cried. "We got information from a guy in the Derby Gang. We'll give you his name. Just let us go."

Leone was close to tears. "I don't know his name. Joe kept that to himself." He looked at his boss. "Huh, Joe?"

"Sure," Forzini said in a quivering voice, having decided to tell the truth. "I'm the only guy who knows. I kept it to myself. I just want outta here. I'll tell you who he is. That's all you want. Right?"

"O'course," the Padrino said. "But we'll keep you down here 'til we check it out. That's only fair, ain't it?"

"Sure, sure," Forzini said. "That's fair, sure. The guy is Dennis Murphy."

Galo smiled an unfriendly smile. "Now you're smart."

Joe Forzini talked fast. "That fucking Murphy called me up awhile back. We met. We talked and made a bargain. I paid him five hunnerd bucks for the info on what you guys got going out there in Kansas."

Galo looked at Rick Multari. "Undo Arrigo's arms."

The kid was disappointed. "Can't I just squeeze one finger with the tongs?"

"If Joe is lying, you can squeeze all the fingers on *both* of 'em."

———

EARLY THE NEXT MORNING AT TWO A.M., THE HIT squad of Dwayne, Duke Glencannon, and Frank Quinn parked in their regular place at the truck stop. They had been out on a patrol of sorts, running up and down U.S. Highways 40 and 81 looking for the three members of the Forzini gang. It had been a frustrating time for all, especially the shamus. His mind buzzed with the thought that when they found the three guys he would be killing one of them.

Now, with the intention of checking in with Farley Kuch, they walked through the trucks looking for the young security guard. They found him up toward the front. As soon as Farley spotted the trio, he rushed toward them.

"Hey! Them guys you're looking for are in the restaurant!"

Glencannon grinned. "Great! Are you sure it's them?"

"Yeah!" Farley exclaimed. "The really fat guy that

wanted to walk down and look at the trucks is in there. I seen him plain as day. He's got two more guys with him."

"Okay," Glencannon said. "Here's what you gotta do. Go into the restaurant and walk up to him. Talk real low and tell him that it's okay for him to look at the trucks for a couple of bucks."

Frank Quinn was confused. "How come he's gotta pay him?"

Glencannon rolled his eyes. "The guy might be suspicious if Farley suddenly says he can check out the trucks, see? If he asks for a couple of bucks, it'll seem more real. Like it's against the rules." He turned to Farley. "If his two pals want to come along, tell 'em no. That'll also make it seem even more like you're doing something you ain't supposed to do."

Now Farley was confused. "But I *am* doing something I ain't supposed to do."

"Okay, yeah. You take him out to the trucks, but don't follow him. Stay up near the restaurant."

"Okay," Farley acknowledged. "I won't follow him and I'll stay up near the restaurant." He paused. "Can I keep the two dollars?"

"Sure," Glencannon said. "Just point him down the same row he walked before."

Farley turned to go back to the restaurant while Dwayne and his two companions hurried down to the parked trucks. They reached a handy spot and stepped back into the darkness between two of the rigs. Dwayne took the special pistol from Frank.

Ten minutes passed before a heavy shuffling of feet on the gravel could be discerned. Frank leaned out carefully for a look. He pulled back, whispering, "It's Fat Pauly!"

Glencannon nodded to Dwayne. "Do what you gotta

do. If me and Frank have to do this job, you're gonna be as bad off as that fat Wop."

Dwayne had already chambered a round and stood waiting. He was surprised he wasn't trembling. But he did swallow hard a couple of times and had to take some deep breaths. As soon as Fat Pauly was abreast of them, both Glencannon and Frank grabbed him, pulling him between the trucks.

"Hey!" the gangster yelled.

Dwayne stepped up and aimed the pistol at his victim.

"Oh, shit!" Fat Pauly said.

Dwayne pulled the trigger with the muzzle inches from the gangster's face. Then he fired twice more.

At the point, Glencannon and Frank dropped the obese victim. Glencannon stooped down and removed everything from the dead man's pockets, including the pistol in his shoulder holster. Then he got to his feet and gave the corpse a final look.

"Let's get the hell out of here!" he ordered.

————

AT FOUR O'CLOCK THAT MORNING, TERRY McCarthy rushed from the room he shared with Dwayne. He ran down the stairs into the kitchen and picked up an empty lunch sack off Charlie O'Donnell's counter, then hurried back up the stairs to the bedroom.

Dwayne lay on his bed, gasping for breath. McCarthy opened the sack and place it over the shamus' mouth and nose. "Breathe deep, Dwayne!"

Dwayne did as he was told, gradually coming out of the attack. "Uh...what happened, Terry?"

"You were hyperventilating. That means carbon dioxide had built up in your blood stream. The paper sack traps the carbon dioxide and lets you inhale it back into your system. Hyperventilation can happen when you go through a traumatic or troubling experience."

Dwayne sat up. "Yeah, I see. You mean an experience like shooting somebody, huh?"

McCarthy nodded. "I don't think we should tell Jimmy Sheehan about this."

CHAPTER 24

The next day was the regularly scheduled trip to the telephone exchange. Jimmy Sheehan decided to have Glencannon drive McCarthy to make the call. They would use Charlie's Ford coupe. Although the vehicle was well-known in the area, it had Kansas license plates.

Sheehan wanted to keep an eye on Dwayne to see how he'd behave after killing a human being for the first time. Some new hitmen didn't react to what they'd done for a period of time following the incident. Even then, it was never very dramatic or worrisome, only a period of irritability. At least that was common for members of a criminal organization. Dwayne's case could be a lot different.

McCarthy and Glencannon left at the regular time, but were back unusually early. When they pulled up behind the lodge house, Glencannon stayed in the car with the motor running. McCarthy hurried into the building. "Jimmy! Hey, Jimmy!"

Sheehan appeared in the door of his office. "What going on, Terry?"

"Johnny Cullen wants to speak to you. Personal and quick!"

"Let's go then."

The three Derby gangsters sat crowded in the front seat for the ride back to the exchange. Sheehan asked some questions, but McCarthy had no answers, except to say, "All Johnny said was he's gotta talk to you right away. It's real important."

Sheehan mused, "I wonder if it's about whacking Fat Pauly?"

Glencannon said, "Jesus! I hope he wasn't planning on calling the hit off."

When they arrived at the destination, McCarthy went through the routine of arranging for the call. When Sheehan's name was announced by the lady behind the counter, he went into the designated booth. McCarthy and Glencannon, both curious and a little worried, watched impatiently as their boss seemed to grow more emotional as the phone conversation went on.

A bit more than twenty minutes passed before Sheehan came out of the booth. He gestured to McCarthy and Glencannon to follow him. When all three were back in the small coupe, he only made one statement.

"Don't ask me nothing!"

———

THE EVENING BEFORE, A DRIVER HAD RUN INTO the truck stop restaurant yelling about a dead fat guy out by the rigs. Peachy Russo and Legs Spino both knew instantly it was Pauly. Peachy nixed Legs' suggestion to look for the security guard in case he had something to do with it. "We gotta get the hell outta here! Right now!"

Both left the booth, went through the door, and sprinted over to the gray Packard. The waitress yelled after them, "Hey, you guys ain't paid your bill!"

A nearby truck driver was surprised. "Damn! You'd think folks that owned a new Packard could afford to pay for their lunch."

Now, after driving north on U.S. 81, Peachy and Legs were in the town of Arlington, Nebraska. Peachy came to a stop in front of a drug store. "Stay here," he said to Legs. "I'm gonna call Joe and tell him what happened."

Legs, who was upset about the hit on Pauly, nodded weakly. Between being extremely tired and frightened as well as far from his home in Boston, he was having a tough time handling the reality of the situation. He remained in the car, staring out the window at the street scene without really seeing anything.

He looked up when Peachy rejoined him. "What'd Joe say?"

"Nobody answered the phone."

"Hey, c'mon!" Legs exclaimed. "There's always somebody there!"

"Well, nobody was there, was they? I let the fucking phone ring a dozen times."

"What're we gonna do, Peachy?"

"This is a nice little burgh. We'll hole up here for awhile and try to reach Joe. If it don't work out, we'll drive like hell back to Boston."

"Good," Legs said. "I hope I never see this fucking Kansas again."

———

JIMMY SHEEHAN IMMEDIATELY CALLED A meeting of the entire gang after the return from the telephone exchange. The exception was Sean Magee who was manning the gatehouse at the entrance to the Retreat. It took fifteen minutes for Tim Fagin to gather everyone up and get them into the kitchen. With they were all present, Jimmy began speaking in a low, serious voice.

"Tomorrow afternoon Dennis Murphy is flying into Kansas City," he announced. "We're supposed to pick him up at the airport. His arrival time is two o'clock." He looked at Dwayne. "How far is Kansas City from here?"

"Kansas or Missouri?" Dwayne asked.

Sheehan was puzzled. "There's two Kansas Cities?"

"Yeah," Dwayne replied. "One is in Kansas and the other is in Missouri. They're joined together at the state line."

Tim Fagin spoke up. "Why don't they call the one in Missouri, Missouri City?"

"Shut up, Tim!" Sheehan yelled. "Goddamn it! Johnny didn't say which one."

"It's prob'ly K.C. Missouri," Dwayne said. "It's got the biggest airport and if that guy is flying in from Boston, that's where he'll land."

"I understand," Jimmy said, then asked again. "How far is it to the Kansas City in Missouri then?"

"A little over a hunnerd and seventy miles. The airport is on the south side of the city."

"Okay. I want you to drive over there to meet Dennis. Duke and Frank will ride along with you. How long do you think it'll take?"

Dwayne did some quick thinking. "We're dealing with around three hunnerd and sixty miles all told including going to the airport. That comes to...I'd say six hours of driving. There's also an hour or so at the airport. If he's coming in at two o'clock, I'd say we better leave around seven to give us plenty of time."

"Good," Sheehan acknowledged. He paused and took a deep breath. "Now! Ever'body listen up good. There's only one way to give you guys the reason behind all this shit. And that's to say it loud and clear." He took another deep breath, then stated, "Dennis ratted us out to the Forzinis."

All eyes opened wide. A couple of beats passed, then Tom Fitzgerald stammered, "Dennis wouldn't—he *wouldn't*—do nothing like that."

"Well, goddamn it!" Sheehan yelled, "according to Johnny he did something *exactly* like that. I don't know why. I don't know when. All I know is that Johnny wants the son of a bitch took care of out here." He glanced at Dwayne once again. "Don't worry. You did your part and proved your worth to us, so we ain't gonna have you whack him. It's more proper that someone who is a friend put a bullet in his skull. That'll be Duke."

Glencannon was obviously not pleased with the assignment. "*Aw fuck!*"

Frank Quinn reached over and patted him on the shoulder. "Nobody is gonna hold it against you, Duke."

"It won't happen right away," Sheehan said. "Johnny wants us to wring him out to get all the information we can before he's offed. That'll be all the who, what and where shit. That'll be my job."

"I have a suggestion," Dwayne said. "After you've interrogated him, why don't you give him a chance to do the job personal. If he's any kind of a man, he'll kill himself to save a friend from having to do it."

Charlie O'Donnell the old gangster spoke up. "I think Dennis'll go for that. He may have been a rat, but I've known him a long time. He ain't no coward."

"All right," Jimmy said. "We'll give him a choice." He looked at the stunned crowd of gangsters. "What the fuck!

Ain't you guys got nothing to do? Get the hell out of here!"

CHAPTER 25

D wayne, Duke Glencannon and Frank Quinn left for the Kansas City airport a few minutes before seven that next morning. Dwayne drove his Buick, not saying much as he tried to gauge the attitudes of his two companions. It was obvious that all the Derbies were enraged about Dennis Murphy's treachery. They were not only angry about what he did, but furious about being put into a situation where one of them would have to kill him.

But there was no other choice. Betraying one's friends and associates to another mob was worse than snitching to law enforcement.

U.S. 40 East would take them directly across the eastern part of the state through K.C. Kansas into K.C. Missouri. Once there, they could look for signs with directions to the airport. Dwayne was glad that Duke and Frank weren't in a talkative mood. The former was on the front seat with him while the latter was in the back, his face stony and grim. Dwayne gave a few surreptitious glances at Duke to see if he could sense any emotion.

There was nothing.

As far as Dwayne was personally concerned, he was still uneasy about having killed Fat Pauly Cappurio The hyperventilation incident proved that. The shamus had never whacked anybody before, and he wondered if he could get used to it if he had to shoot several more people.

When he first looked into the gangster's face in the dim light of the truck stop, he'd sensed the man's fury. But that quickly turned to cold fear as the victim realized he was about to die. At that time Dwayne was frantic with apprehension as he brought the pistol inches from the gangster's face. Then, without so much as a conscious thought, he pulled the trigger three times in a reflex action.

Dwayne tried to comfort himself by remembering his war experiences. He hadn't been in frontline combat, but as a military policeman he was assigned security duties in the rear areas. It was during that time he learned of the outright cruelty the French, Dutch and Belgian people endured under the German occupation. Fat Pauly was the same as those SS soldiers. Cruelty was as natural to him as breathing.

The Nazi Gestapo arrested people who were never seen again, and if the local resistance forces killed German soldiers, at least ten civilian men were executed for each dead Kraut.

The Nazis also conscripted young people as slave labor to be shipped off to industrial centers in Germany. These were prison camps run by vicious guards ready to punish any signs of defiance from the miserable workers. On a day not long after the Allied troops entered Germany, his duties brought him to visit one of the prison factories. He was dismayed by the misery those innocent civilians suffered from the brutal overseers. It was slavery at its worst.

After that, Dwayne felt no pity for the collateral deaths of German women and children. They were getting a dose of what their soldiers had done to people under their occupational policies.

Dwayne wasn't worried that he might go to hell for killing Fat Pauly. The "Thou Shall Not Kill" part of the Ten Commandments made no sense to him. There could be mitigating reasons for taking a life. Jimmy Sheehan had hinted he might be killed himself if he refused to whack the gangster. He had a choice to make and he chose his own life over that of a hoodlum.

At any rate, the shamus didn't believe in life after death. The human race didn't deserve such an indulgence as far as he was concerned, whether it was eternal bliss in heaven or eternal suffering in Hell. That concept also seemed nonsensical to him anyway. Why would Satan make people suffer for sinning when that was exactly what he wanted them to do? Punishing wicked people would be doing God a favor. If there was life after death, the people with Satan would be partying and fornicating in an eternity of blissful carnal pleasure.

Dwayne fished a Lucky Strike out of the pack in his shirt pocket. He held it out for Duke, who took a cigarette. No words were spoken as they sped east to pick up an airline passenger who would be dead by this time the next day.

———

THE TRIO ARRIVED AT THE MID-CONTINENTAL airport at a quarter past noon. With more than a couple of hours to spare, they went into the complex's restaurant for a leisurely lunch. The fact Dwayne could have his favorite mid-day meal of a grilled cheese sandwich, French fries and Orange Crush brightened his mood. The three sat at a counter that offered a good view of several airliners parked on the tarmac.

Frank was curious about the airplanes. "I wonder what kind they are."

Dwayne took a bite of his sandwich and pointed to the aircraft. "That one over there is a C-4 Argonaut. And the one beside it is the Convair CV-240."

Frank saw an aircraft farther away. "What's that one called?"

"It's a Douglas DC-3," Dwayne replied. "The Army Air Corps used 'em to tow gliders and drop paratroopers during the war. They called it the C-47. Were you guys in the service?"

"Sure," Frank replied. "Me and Duke enlisted in the Navy together. We was in the Battle of Midway."

"Right," Duke said. "On the destroyer *U.S.S. Morris.*"

"Wow!" Dwayne exclaimed. "That was when the Jap Navy was defeated, right?"

"You bet your ass," Frank said. "Us Irish guys fought in the war instead of counterfeiting ration stamps or smuggling untaxed cigarettes into the country and other shit. The Mafia done that."

Duke interjected, "A lot of their young guys got drafted though." He glanced over at Dwayne. "How come you know so much about airplanes?"

"Wichita is an aviation town. More commercial aircraft are manufactured there than anyplace else in the world."

"Speaking of Wichita," Frank said, "d'you think you'll ever go back there again?"

The question made him think of Nancy Turner and

the fact he wasn't really a fugitive. He shrugged and replied, "I don't know."

"You stick with us," Duke said. "You'll like Boston when we go back there."

"Yeah," Frank agreed. "There's lots of stuff to see and do." He winked. "Really good-looking broads, too."

After eating they went to the waiting room and settled down. An hour passed before the loudspeaker announced the arrival of Flight 23 from Boston via Chicago. Dwayne, Duke and Frank went outside to the gate to meet Dennis Murphy. The passengers filed down the gangway steps to begin a short walk over to the terminal entrance.

"There the son of a bitch is," Frank said. He nudged Dwayne. "He's the tall guy."

Dennis Murphy was easy to see. He was six-foot four with a thin build. The most remarkable thing about him was his dapper clothing that was obviously tailor-made and expensive.

As he neared the gate, Duke called out, "Dennis!"

The guy looked around, then beamed a smile. "Hey, Duke!"

Murphy shook hands with Frank and Duke, giving Dwayne a gaze of curiosity. "Hiya."

"Howdy," Dwayne replied.

"This is the new guy," Duke said. "Dwayne Wheeler."

"Johnny told me about him," Murphy said cheerfully. "I guess we've got quite a ride ahead of us, huh?"

Dwayne trailed after them as they entered the terminal and headed for the front doors. He wondered if Murphy would notice that Duke and Frank were more than just a little subdued. Murphy, on the other hand, seemed happy about a get-together with his old pals.

———

The state of New Jersey has gotten a bum rap over the years. People in New York City poke fun at the state's people as well as its reputation for a trashy appearance. But New Jersey has many spots of great natural beauty that measure up to any of America's national parks. The beaches, forests and open country make it a vacation paradise. And that includes the wetlands that also serve as wildlife sanctuaries.

In early 1948 two objects, weighed down with cement blocks, were added to the watery, muddy depths of a particular marshy area. These were the quickly decomposing corpses of *Messieurs* Joe Forzini and Arrigo Leone.

R.I.P.

CHAPTER 26

D wayne turned off the highway and headed down the dirt road toward the Retreat. He was waved through the gatehouse and continued toward the lodge, pulling around to the back. He braked to a stop and turned off the ignition. He let out an unintentional loud sigh, thinking of the fate awaiting Dennis Murphy.

The trip back from the Kansas City airport had left the four travelers stiff. Everyone stretched as they got out of the car, and Dennis Murphy walked around to fetch his suitcase from the trunk. Frank Quinn and Duke Glencannon exchanged glances as the shamus stepped back out of the way.

Glencannon pointed to the lodge. "There's the door, Dennis. It opens into the kitchen."

Murphy grinned. "I hope there's some cold beer in there." He went up the steps with Glencannon and Quinn following. The moment he entered the building, his two companions seized his arms, forcing him to drop his suitcase.

"Hey!" Murphy exclaimed. "What the fuck's going on?"

Terry McCarthy, Jimmy Sheehan, and Tim Fagin entered from the hall door. Jimmy Sheehan quickly frisked Murphy, then stepped back. "The game's over, Dennis."

Murphy paled. "Uh...what game? What're you talking about?"

"We know you told Joe Forzini all about this operation," Sheehan said.

"I never did no such fucking thing!"

Sheehan nodded to Frank and Glencannon who frog-marched Murphy across the kitchen, then flung him into the storeroom. Tim pulled the door shut and locked it. Sheehan turned to McCarthy. "Have Dwayne drive you over to the telephone exchange. Give Johnny a call and tell him we got Dennis and are ready to deal with him."

McCarthy went outside to join Dwayne at the Buick.

THE UNIDENTIFIED BODY OF FAT PAULY Cappurio had been picked up by the Saline County Sheriff. A quick identification was impossible since they could find nothing in his pockets. Even his watch and rings were missing. Taking a photo of his face wouldn't have done any good either. The victim's features had been badly ripped up by three bullet holes and the back of his head was completely gone. The corpse did not resemble any locals the sheriff and his deputies knew. They called in the Kansas Bureau of Investigation for help with the identification.

That law enforcement organization was also stymied by the situation. Their only alternative was to turn to the

F.B.I. The Topeka office sent a lab technician down to handle the situation. The man used a hypodermic needle to inject paraffin into the dead man's fingertips to make the digits easier to print. The results were mailed off to the F.B.I. laboratory in Washington, using second class mail. After all, the victim didn't seem to fit any wanted felons in the active files.

A "John Doe" death certificate was filled out by the county coroner, and a local funeral home took the body for cold storage in their basement morgue.

———

DENNIS MURPHY SAT ON THE FLOOR OF THE dark storeroom, leaning against the far wall. Each time footsteps could be heard outside the door, he shuddered with nervous anticipation for it to open. Somehow the gang learned he had revealed sensitive information to the Forzini mob. The frightened man knew the long-established penalty for disobeying that most important dictum of all criminal codes.

The traitor's thoughts turned to his wife and four kids. He had made the deal with Joe Forzini to get enough money to take them away from Boston and out to the West Coast. He wanted to escape from the underworld, but that was impossible as long as he was in Boston. Organized crime groups do not provide honorable discharges for discontented associates. Anyone with inside information about a gang's activities was a serious security risk.

After being paid off by Joe Forzini, Murphy spent evenings at home on the telephone. He wanted to have a job waiting for him upon arrival in the west. He called information in Los Angeles to get the number of an employment agency. The three hours' time difference between the coasts, gave him ample time to pursue his search.

During the war Dennis Murphy had been an aircraft mechanic in the 8th Air Force in England. The unit made countless bombing runs into Germany and many times the pilots brought their flak-battered B-17 bombers limping back from the raids. Over time Murphy had developed into a skilled mechanic in repairing and replacing damaged engines. He eventually worked his way up to the rank of master sergeant, earning letters of commendation and medals of merit. Not surprisingly, it hadn't taken the California employment agency long to find him a job with Trans-Global Air Freight at the company's hub terminal in Los Angeles.

But it was all for nothing now.

The door to the lodge storeroom opened. Terry McCarthy, Jimmy Sheehan, Duke Glencannon, and Tim Fagin walked in. Murphy raised his watery eyes and looked up into Jimmy Sheehan's face.

Sheehan's voice was low and controlled. "We got some questions to ask you, Dennis. There's a few things Johnny wants to know. And, take it from me, you'll find things a lot easier if you tell the truth."

Murphy exhaled a sardonic chuckle. "No belly shots, huh?

Sheehan ignored the remark and began his interrogation. "Who'd you squeal to?"

"Joe Forzini."

"Was he the only one?"

Murphy nodded. "He told me he wasn't going to let nobody else know about it. Not even his own guys."

"What made you do it?"

"I wanted money to move me and Molly and the kids to California."

Frank Quinn interjected, "Why the fuck did you want to do that? You was making big bucks, Dennis!"

"I wanted a normal life with my family," Dennis replied. "A safe normal life where there wasn't no worries about prison or getting whacked."

Sheehan asked, "What kind of work was you looking for?"

"I got a job with an air freight company as an airplane mechanic. That's what I done in the Army Air Corps. I didn't want to be in the rackets no more."

"You made a real serious commitment a long time ago when you joined the Derby Gang," Sheehan pointed out. "You swore a solemn oath and knew you'd never be cut loose." He stared his hatred at the turncoat. "You brung yourself to a sad end, Dennis."

"I understand." He paused. "Can you get a priest for me to confess to?"

Tim Fagin snorted, "Are you outta your fucking mind?"

A flash of defiance flared up in the condemned man. "I got a right to the sacraments."

"Sure," Sheehan stated. "And just what the hell do you think that priest is gonna do after he leaves here?"

"A priest ain't gonna violate the sanctity of the church!"

"It won't violate any religious laws to tell the law about *this* place," Glencannon countered. "He's gonna figure out we ain't exactly running a kindergarten out here."

"You really fucked up," Frank Quinn added. "We're right in the middle of a big operation and you chose the worst time to rat us out."

"Okay," Murphy conceded. "How'd you find out about me?"

Sheehan's voice was cold. "All I'm gonna say is that Carlo Banocci told us. You ain't gonna want to know how he found out and what he did about it."

"That's right," Glencannon interjected. "How'd you like for us to turn you over to the Banocci Family to deal with you? They'd take three or four days to kill you."

Murphy remained silent.

"So here's what we're offering you, Dennis," Sheehan said. "We'll take you some place and hand you a heater. You can put a bullet in your brain to save one of us from having to do it."

"Are you crazy?" Murphy sobbed. "I ain't gonna get the last rites…and then commit suicide…that'll send me to hell as sure as…as…as anything." He desperately looked at Terry McCarthy. "You and me have always been pals since you joined the gang. Wouldn't it be enough to promise I won't tell nobody else ever about this project?"

McCarthy shook his head. "You damn near messed up a big operation, Dennis. That's something that can't be forgiven."

"Goddamn it!" Murphy cried. "I got a wife and kids!"

Sheehan gestured to Duke Glencannon and Frank Quinn. They pulled Murphy to his feet and held him while Sheehan tied the man's hands behind his back. The four left the storeroom and walked across the kitchen to the outside door while Dwayne Wheeler watched.

The execution party went down the steps of the back stoop and walked across the open field toward the woods by the creek. Dennis Murphy had eased into shallow shock, walking like an automaton. When they entered the woods they continued through the trees until reaching the grave of Mary Sue Pickens. Old Charlie O'Donnell had dug another one beside it the day before. Glencannon and

Quinn walked the condemned man up to the edge of the excavation.

Murphy, his thoughts on his wife and kids, began to sob.

Sheehan, in the rear, immediately brought up Frank's special pistol and fired a bullet into the back of Denny's Murphy's head. Glencannon and Frank pushed the victim forward to fall face first into his eternal resting place.

"Wow!" Frank exclaimed. "That hollow point really fucked up his face. There's an eyeball on the edge of the grave. Look!"

"*Yuck*" Glencannon uttered and nudged it into the grave with the tip of his shoe.

Sheehan glanced down at the dead man and delivered a *coup de grâce* final shot. "I'll have Charlie come out and cover him up."

CHAPTER 27

The evening trips to the truck stop began again on the same day that Dennis Murphy paid the price of his betrayal. Although it meant the women would be going back to work, they appreciated the release from the cabin fever that had developed during the long days and nights in the lodge.

Security guard Farley Kuch was glad to see the group again. "Hey, ever'body," he called out, walking up to the panel truck. "How've you fellers been?"

"Great," Dwayne answered, opening the doors to let the women and Tim Fagin out.

Duke Glencannon appeared and gave a friendly grin to Farley. "Well! There you are, buddy. We're kind of curious about what happened after the fat guy was kilt."

"There was a lot of to-do," Farley replied. It hadn't dawned on the slow-thinking kid that they had been the killers. "The Highway Patrol and a bunch of fellers in suits showed up. They was real excited."

"I bet they were," Glencannon agreed. "Did they question you?"

"Yeah. And do you know what I told 'em?"

Dwayne chimed in, "What did you tell 'em, Farley?"

"I told 'em that fat feller had been here before. And he wanted to go down and look at the trucks and I told him he couldn't do it so he didn't. Then, on the night he was shot, I told 'em the fat guy showed up again and wanted to go look at the trucks and I told him he couldn't. But I guess as soon as I turned my back he went anyhow."

"Way to go!" Glencannon exclaimed. He was glad to see the kid had been smart enough to keep quiet about giving Fat Pauly permission to walk around the trucks.

Farley showed a wide grin. It wasn't often he received a compliment.

"We owe you some money, Farley," Dwayne said, pulling out his wallet. He handed him five ten-dollar bills. "You get a bonus for doing a first rate job for us."

"Boy howdy!"

Glencannon looked over at the women. "Get your asses to work."

———

ON A SUNDAY MORNING IN WICHITA, NANCY Turner, Holly and Maggie had just settled down in their kitchen for breakfast. Holly spread some peach preserves on a piece of toast and took a bite. She chewed thoughtfully for a few moments, then asked, "When is Dwayne coming back?"

"It's hard to tell, honey," Nancy replied. "He's a detective and he don't have reg'lar hours like other folks."

"I miss him," Holly said.

"Me, too," Nancy commented. "But we'll see him soon."

Holly finished off the toast and asked, "How's come

we don't go to church? All the other kids in school go to church."

Maggie looked at her granddaughter. "We never got in the habit, honey. Your grandpa worked all over Texas and Oklahoma and we never settled down. After you was born it was the same old moving around like restless meadowlarks. Maybe now that we're settled in Wichita we might think on it."

"Didn't we even go to church before my daddy died?"

Maggie and Nancy exchanged glances, then Nancy said, "No. We've never gone to church."

The meal continued with small talk until the food were consumed. Holly asked to be excused from the table, then carried her plate and flatware to the kitchen counter. The girl left the kitchen to listen to the radio.

Nancy poured a couple of cups of coffee. "One of these days we're gonna have to tell Holly about her daddy."

"Why? We've already told her he died in a car accident."

"How much longer can we stick to that story? The day's coming when she's gonna wonder why her last name is Turner instead of something else."

Maggie shrugged. "By then she'll know you and her daddy wasn't married. She'll understand."

"D'you think she'll understand I hardly knew that no good son of a bitch? That I met him in a honky-tonk in South Tulsa and went off to a motel with him?"

"We don't have to tell her *everything*!" Maggie exclaimed. She took a sip of coffee. "What about Dwayne? I just hope that trouble he's in ain't too serious."

"He said it was a misunderstanding that'll take some time to clear up."

"I'm sure it'll all turn out just fine," Maggie assured

her. She paused a moment. "D'you think this thing between you two is gonna last?"

"I didn't for awhile. But he did take me to dinner and came over here before he left Wichita."

"Those could be good signs," her mother opined. "If he didn't care nothing about you, he'd've just took off without so much as a quick goodbye."

"I've taken that into consideration," Nancy admitted. "As a matter of fact, if he wants us to sleep together when he comes back, I'll give him one more chance. If he ain't declared any decent intent after that, I'll break off from him for good."

"Are you in love with him, honey?"

Nancy shrugged. "It depends on how I feel about him. If he does the right thing, I'll let myself love him. If he don't, I'll hate the sight of the man."

Maggie showed a sad smile. "If that happens, it'll break your heart."

"Mmmf! I just hope he don't get me pregnant."

CHAPTER 28

It was a few minutes before midnight when Peachy Russo and Legs Spina drove into the Derby gang's neighborhood in Boston. After Fat Pauly's death they had spent a week in a small Nebraska town, making numerous phone calls to Joe Forzini. The fact that no one seemed to be present at the mob's headquarters above the Fogetti Restaurant did nothing to soothe their discomfiture.

Peachy finally reached a conclusion that there was nothing left for them to do but return to Boston if they wanted to find out what was going on. Thus, on a cool early morning, the two Mafioso began a grueling cross- country trip. They decided to take turns of continuous driving in order to get back to their hometown as fast as possible.

———

Now, numb with fatigue and worry after the thirty-five plus hour journey, Peachy and Spina pulled up in front of the Fogetti Restaurant. They quickly scrambled out of the car, hurrying around to the back to the building. After stumbling up the outside flight of steps leading to the second floor, Peachy banged on the door.

Freddy Leonardi, dressed in pajamas, answered the impatient summons after several minutes. "Hey!" he exclaimed, his sleepy mind suddenly coming wide awake. "What're you guys doing here?"

Peachy ignored the question. "We called about a hunnerd times from back there in Kansas."

"We was in *Nebraska*!" Legs corrected him.

"Whatever," Peachy said. He turned back to Freddy. "How come you didn't answer the fucking phone?"

"Joe told me not to."

Legs glared at him. "Where the hell is Joe?"

"I don't know for sure exactly," Freddy said with a shrug. "Him and Arrigo have been gone for days now. I ain't heard shit from 'em."

"So where'd they go?"

"They was invited down to New York by Don Carlo Banocci."

Both Peachy and Legs were surprised. The former asked, "What about?"

Freddy was becoming annoyed. "How the fuck should I know? I ain't a consigliere."

Peachy shared his irritation. "Well, Freddy, didn't they say nothing to you? I mean what'd they do, just waltz down to New York without a goddamn word?"

"Joe told me to stay here 'til him and Arrigo got back," Freddy said. "He hinted that things was gonna change for the best around here." He did a double-take. "Hey! Where's Fat Pauly? Did you leave him back in Kansas or wherever you was?"

"I guess you could say that," Peachy remarked in a voice dripping with sarcasm.

Legs said, "He got whacked."

Freddy paled. "You guys was supposed to sneak around and make some hits on them Irish bastards."

"Before you can put a hit on anybody, you gotta find 'em," Peachy commented defensively. "And it's obvious as hell that they found us first."

"Man!" Freddy said. "That's a tough break all right. Poor Fat Pauly. By the way, Guido got tired of waiting around and said to call him if he was needed. Tony comes in ever'day."

Peachy was growing tired of the inane and crude tête-à-tête going on. "It sounds like you ain't heard nothing from Joe since he went to New York."

"Not a word," Freddy remarked. "I was starting to get worried, but they seemed real happy about going down there."

Peachy sighed. "We better wait 'til morning to think things over. I'm tired as hell and I'm going home." He glanced at Legs. "I'll drop you off at your house."

They left abruptly and Freddy Leonardi stood motionless for a moment, then went back to the bedroom and found his girlfriend Rosa sitting up on the bed.

She frowned. "What's going on?"

"Fat Pauly got whacked back in Kansas."

"Gee!" Rosa exclaimed under her breath. "Maybe a cowboy shot him, huh?"

"Yeah," Freddy snorted sardonically. "I think he got kilt at the O.K. Corral like in the fucking movies."

———

DWAYNE WHEELER AND TERRY McCARTHY walked into the telephone exchange in what was becoming countless visits. They went to the counter and, as always, filled out request cards for calls. McCarthy had to make his regular report to Johnny Cullen and Dwayne took his time filling out a request form for a call to the F.B.I. agent Steve Williams. This wasn't exactly necessary but Dwayne knew he had to speak to Williams now and then to cover the calls to Mrs. Davies.

Dwayne had only a ten minute wait when he was directed to a booth. "Hey, Steve," he greeted.

"Hello, Dwayne. What's going on?"

"Same old stuff," Dwayne answered.

"Terry is on a call back to Boston, and I'm just checking in to see if you got any new information or maybe some instructions."

Williams replied. "Nope. Nothing to pass on to you. How's it going?"

"We're hanging in there, waiting for things to happen." He decided this would be an awkward time to bring up the deaths of Fat Pauly and Dennis Murphy. It could develop into a long monotonous discussion that would have to include Terry McCarthy.

"Okay, Dwayne. Keep up the good work."

"Will do and I'll call again later."

Dwayne crossed the room to take a seat, noting that McCarthy was involved in another serious conversation with the gang's boss. Twenty minutes passed before McCarthy exited the booth and walked over to Dwayne. The shamus was expecting him to make a remark or ask a question regarding Steve Williams, but he had important news to report instead.

"We're going to start dry runs pretty soon."

Dwayne was puzzled. "What kind of dry runs?"

"I don't know yet," McCarthy stated. "But when they start we'll learn the real reason for all these activities in the middle of Kansas."

CHAPTER 29

The next morning Peachy Russo and Legs Spina made an early appearance in the office above the Fogetti Restaurant. The instant they walked in, Peachy went directly to Joe Forzini's desk and began going through the drawers.

Legs watched him for a few moments. "What the hell are you doing, Peachy? You shouldn't be looking into Joe's stuff."

"I'm trying to find the phone number of the Banocci mob in New York," he replied pawing through numerous papers.

"You'll need it to call, huh?"

Peachy looked up with a scornful expression on his face. "Yeah! I think having the right number might be helpful." He discovered a notepad. "Ah! Here it is! Don Carlo's name and his number under it." Peachy grabbed the phone and quickly dialed "O" to speak to an operator.

After a couple of rings, a bright feminine voice announced, "Operator."

"Hello," Peachy said. "I want to place a long distance call."

"One moment please."

When the long distance operator came on, Peachy gave her the number on the notepad and requested the call to be station-to-station. Then he hung up and sat down behind the desk to wait for the notification the party had been reached.

Suddenly loud talking and laughing could be heard out on the stairs. The door opened and Freddy Leonardi, his girl Rosa and Tony Bonvicini walked into the office. They had just had breakfast in the downstairs restaurant. They instantly stopped and stared at Peachy sitting in Joe's chair.

"What's going on?" Freddy inquired.

"I've put in a long distance call," Peachy explained. "It's to the Bonoccis in New York. I'm gonna see if they know where Joe is."

"Don't forget Arrigo," Freddy reminded him. He glanced at Rosa. "Get lost. The bedroom."

"How come?" she asked.

"We're conducting business here," Freddy said. "You gonna go or d'you want a smack on the nose?"

She left the office just as the phone rang. Peachy grabbed the receiver. "Hello."

A voice replied, "Hello. Who's this?"

"Peachy Russo. From Boston."

"Hey, this is Enrico Galo. How are you, Peachy?"

"Okay. Listen, I hear that Joe and Arrigo went down there to see you guys."

The chief capo sounded downright cheerful. "Yeah! Sure! We had a real nice time."

"I'm glad to hear that," Peachy said. "We ain't seen

'em around here. Did they say where they was going after they left?"

"They sure didn't," Galo said pleasantly. "We had a nice time. Good lunch, y'know. Lots of laughs. Ice cream for dessert. Then it was over and we all said goodbye. It was a very nice time for ever'body."

"Okay," Peachy said, then hung up. He was silent for several moments.

"So?" Freddy asked.

"They're dead."

"Did Galo say so?"

"He didn't have to," Peachy replied. "The son of a bitch was cheerful as hell about them coming down for lunch. He made it sound like a fucking tea party."

"Those goddamn *Sicis*!" Freddy growled

Legs walked over to the sofa and sat down dejectedly. "I know what happened. The Sicilians wanted to find out who the Irish rat was that gave Joe the information about what was going on out in Kansas."

Tony Bonvicini complained, "Joe never even told *us* who it was."

"Well," Peachy growled. "You can bet your ass he told them Sicilians."

"God!" Legs exclaimed. "Arrigo didn't know who it was either. I hope them New York pricks sweated Joe first so they didn't get worked over."

"It was their tough luck they went down to New York," Freddy stated. He looked at Peachy. "What're we gonna do?"

Peachy was thoughtful for a moment. "I'm taking Joe's place. Any objections?"

"It's okay by me," Freddy announced.

Legs and Tony nodded their heads in agreement.

Peachy picked up the phone. "I'm gonna call the Lundari Family."

———

IT WAS TWO A.M. AS DWAYNE STROLLED DOWN a line of parked semis at the truck stop. The night had been busier than usual and it was hard to keep tabs on the women. He walked through the trucks twice without seeing even one of them. Finally, he spotted Carla stepping down from a running board.

The shamus walked up to her. "Looks like you're doing a load of work, huh?"

"You ain't kidding," Carla acknowledged. "I missed my break."

"Go on back to the panel truck and take a load off your feet."

Carla chuckled. "You mean off my ass."

Dwayne went back to his patrol and ran into Farley Kuch up near the front of the parking lot. "Hey, Farley. How're you doing?"

"Perty good, Dwayne. What's up with you?"

"I'm having trouble keeping tabs on the girls."

"Yeah," Farley said. "I noticed they was getting in and out of a lot of trucks." He hesitated. "Something's come up, Dwayne. My Uncle Orville is lining me up with a job down in Wichita."

Dwayne was pleased by the news. "That's great, Farley. What kind of work is it?"

"It's at Boeing. He's got me a welding apprenticeship in the department where he works. I'll be making real good money."

"You sure will. And you'll have a good career ahead of you."

"I'll be leaving in two weeks. My wife is gonna have a baby and she wants it borned here in our home town. So I'll be going down to Wichita without her. I'm gonna be staying with Uncle Orville and Aunt Lucille."

"Well, that'll give you time to find a place for you and her and your baby to live."

"We're gonna live in Planeview. Uncle Orville already put down the deposit for the first and last month's rent."

Planeview was a town built on the southeast side of Wichita to house aircraft workers during the war. It was still in use in 1948 but many of the people living there didn't work for the Boeing Aircraft Manufacturing Company. It was the low rent that attracted them.

Farley said, "I really appreciate what you fellers done for me. I asked my boss if he was gonna hire another security guard but he said he wasn't 'cause it was just another expense and that fat feller got shot dead anyway."

"Okay. Thanks for the info, Farley," Dwayne said. "Well! I got to look around and see how the girls are doing. See you later so's we can pay you off."

Dwayne walked back down another row of trucks when he heard a scream. It was definitely feminine and he rushed toward the source. He ended up near the extreme west end of the parking lot and saw a man hitting one of the girls.

"Hey! What's going on?"

The guy was a trucker and had just slapped Wilma hard across the face. He growled at Dwayne. "You go mind your own business, bud."

"Sure," Dwayne said with a grin. "Having some fun, huh?"

The guy grinned back. "I just got started."

Dwayne put his hand in his front trouser pocket and slipped into his brass knuckles. He pulled it out and slammed it into the trucker's chest. Dwayne hadn't hit him with much force, just enough to make him stumble back and feel the metal protrusions of the device.

The guy wheezed. "What the...hell...did you...do that...for?"

"Is that your truck behind you?"

"Uh...yeah."

"Then get up there in the cab, put it in gear and drive out of here. This is the truck stop where that guy got shot and killed awhile back. If you want to be the second dumb dead bastard, go ahead and really piss me off."

The guy reached up for the door handle of his truck and glared at Dwayne. "You're her...pimp, ain't...you?" he gasped, still trying to catch his breath.

Dwayne ignored the question. "You really want a work-over, don't you?"

The trucker wasted no time in driving away.

Dwayne got his flashlight and shined it on Wilma's face. There wasn't much damage other than a red spot where she'd been struck by the man's open hand. But it would eventually start swelling.

"How're you feeling, Wilma?"

"Scared. This is the first time anything bad has happened to me here. Most of the truck drivers are actually pretty nice."

Dwayne could see she was shaken up. "Let me walk you over to the panel truck. You can take a few deep breaths and calm your nerves."

Wilma slipped her arm through his as they walked slowly through the semis. She gave him a fond look. "You're a real neat guy, Dwayne. All us girls like you."

"Is that a fact?"

"Yes because you're always nice to us." They went a bit farther then she said. "Dwayne, if you want to be with a woman I'd like to be the one. It's true that the other three girls want the same thing. We noticed you never come to our rooms." She smiled. "But remember I asked first, okay?"

"Sure."

Dwayne knew that the other men made regular visits to the women. Terry McCarthy was the exception. He figured the F.B.I. agent was too straitlaced to have sex with a whore. But the shamus had begun feeling horny. Wilma's invitation had sparked that desire to a higher level. The last time he had sex had been weeks before with Nancy.

He and Wilma continued on their way to the panel truck.

CHAPTER 30

B ack in 1948, fifteen miles in a northerly direction
from Boston, there were numerous acres of empty
pastureland called Broadview Meadows. To casual
observers it seemed strange that the locale had been left
alone in the postwar building boom. Housing tracts were
going up everywhere in the country where there was space
to build. The fact that no developers had moved onto
Broadview Meadows to begin construction was a puzzle.
Most people assumed the present owner or owners simply
had no interest in selling any of the valuable property.

The real reason behind this inexplicable situation was
a gang boss by the name of Angelo Lundari. Lundari was
the second chief to rule over that organization that was
now referred to by his name. The man that formed the
original group was Marcelo Maggiore. Lundari was his
consigliere during those early days. Like most criminals
before Prohibition they were minor street offenders. But
once illegal liquor became a good source of income,
Maggiore and Lundari entered the lucrative profession of
bootlegging. They had grown up together and enjoyed a

sincere and trusting friendship. Unfortunately for the mob, but not law abiding people, Maggiore suffered a fatal stroke toward the end of the Prohibition era and Lundari took over the gang.

Lundari was never considered a godfather but as time passed he began to be addressed as Don Angelo out of respect. Back in the late 1920s, he had built a manor house on Broadview Meadows from the millions of dollars he made during prohibition. And he didn't have the slightest intention of selling the property.

Lundari had interests in many unlawful activities ranging from labor unions, houses of prostitution, gambling dens, bookie joints, and narcotics among others. He also had influence with certain important personages all over Massachusetts among members of the legislative, judicial and law enforcement echelons of the commonwealth.

Consequently, any aggressive real estate developer who attempted legal shenanigans such as seeking declarations of imminent domain to build on Broadview Meadows was discouraged by red tape and stonewalling. If those methods didn't deter a persistent builder, sabotage of his place of business did. There were only three stubborn individuals who went too far and ended up with threats on their lives. They wisely withdrew their applications.

———

PEACHY RUSSO AND LEGS SPINA SAT IN THE BACK of the limousine that had picked them up at their neighborhood headquarters. They were on their way to a unique and most important meeting. Peachy had called Lundari's residence the day before and patiently explained he wanted to speak to somebody about the activity in Kansas regarding the Derby Gang. The guy that took the call was sarcastic and told Peachy he would pass the information on, but not to expect a return call.

Peachy had been dismayed by the snub. His whole life had taken a nosedive after the deaths of the Forzini family's top cadre and his pal Fat Pauly Cappurio. Neither Freddy Leonardi, Tony Bonvicini or Guido Viola had the right connections or knowhow to continue their mob activities. Joe Forzini was a strong believer in a micromanagement style for running his organization. His absence caused a collective mood of hopelessness among the gang who had no idea of the ins and outs of the organization's operations.

A half hour after Peachy's call, the phone rang and it was the same guy. But this time he was more polite. He stated that Don Angelo wanted to speak to Peachy and one other guy of his choice from the gang. A car would be sent for them. That made Peachy and Legs both happy but also extremely nervous. If, for some reason, things went bad, they could end up like Joe and Arrigo. It was plausible this could happen because they were being given a ride. This meant the Lundari family wouldn't have to get rid of their car after whacking them.

THE LIMO TURNED OFF THE MAIN ROAD ONTO A lane leading to the Lundari manor house. The place was actually a village with small buildings clustered around the large mansion. The driver went up a circular driveway to the front door and came to a stop.

"Awright. You're here," he announced.

Peachy and Legs got out of the car in time to see a

man step out on the portico. He led them through the door where another guy skillfully patted them down. With that done, the first man gestured that they were to follow him. The pair was taken across a foyer, up a wide spiral staircase, down a hall, across a wide ballroom, into a shorter hall to a pair of portals nine feet high.

Their escort knocked on the tall, heavy doors. A dapper, but tough-looking man in a tailor-made suit appeared, showing a pleasant demeanor toward the visitors. "Come in, gentlemen. I am Ralph Costiero, Don Angelo's consigliere."

Peachy spoke up. "I'm Peachy Russo and this is my associate Mister Legs Spina."

They were led to two chairs set in front of a massive teakwood desk. A middle-aged man sat behind it. Costiero quickly explained that the pair were from the now defunct Forzini mob. He introduced them, indicating that the older man was Don Angelo of the Lundari family. The Don said nothing, only nodding toward them with obvious interest.

"Sit down, gentlemen," Costiero invited. "Don Angelo has given me a list of questions he would like for you to answer, if it pleases you."

"Sure," Peachy said. "It pleases us."

"Yeah," Legs added. "I'm very pleased, too."

Costiero stood by the desk with the list in his hand. "Why was you in Kansas?"

Peachy did the talking. "We was sent there by our boss Joe Forzini to find out what the Derby Gang was doing out there."

"Who is *we*?"

"Me and Legs here and Fat Pauly Cappurio." He paused, then continued with some hesitation. "Fat Pauly was shot and killed by the Derbies. We was supposed to make a hit, too, but that didn't work out."

"We'll get back to that later," Costiero said. "Did you discover the reason why they was way out in Kansas?"

"Sort of," Peachy said. "They was running whores at a truck stop at night. The women would go to the parked trucks to proposition the drivers. I called Joe Forzini our boss and told him about that and he figured that was not all he would need to know. He said there was something more the gang had going on and we was supposed to stay there until we found out what it was."

"Where did he get the idea things was more than they appeared?"

"A snitch in the Derbies was telling him all about it," Peachy explained. "And he said the whole situation was for a special set-up out there in the middle of the country. But the guy didn't know what it was."

Costiero glanced at Don Angelo who motioned him to continue. He turned back to Peachy. "Do you know who the snitch was?"

Peachy shook his head. "Joe kept it to himself. He didn't even tell his consigliere. That was Arrigo Leone. Anyhow, it was me and Legs and Fat Pauly who scoped out the truck stop whore racket."

Don Angelo cleared his throat, and the consigliere walked over to him. He bent down and the don whispered in his ear. Costiero stood up and walked back around the desk. "What was that area in Kansas like?"

"Well," Peachy said. "There wasn't much to see really. U.S. Highways 40 and 81 crossed there. One ran east and west and the other north and south. It was a real busy intersection since it connected the highways from all directions. Lots of traffic ran through the spot. Especially trucks."

"Where did the Derbies stay in Kansas?"

"We figgered out two or three of 'em was at a motor court," Peachy informed him. "As for the rest—" He shrugged. "—who knows? And we didn't even learn how many of 'em there was. But we know for sure it was them that whacked Fat Pauly. It couldn't have been nobody else 'cause they done it at the truck stop."

Don Carlo signaled to his consigliere once more. Another session of whispering followed, then Costiero returned to face Peachy and Legs. "Don Angelo has found all this most interesting. He would like to stay in touch with you."

Peachy hesitated, then blurted out, "We're cut off from ever'thing now. Our boss and the consigliere are dead. There's five of us left and we don't have any good way of making money. It looks like we're gonna have to work the streets. Maybe rob a bank."

Costiero wiggled a finger at him. "Don't do that. Don Angelo figured you was having some difficulties. He wants to put all of you on our payroll. You guys'll be paid fifty bucks a week. If you run into any financial problems let us know. Don Angelo wants you to lay low and don't call no attention to yourselves."

The faces of Peachy and Legs brightened. Peachy gazed appreciatively at the crime boss. "Thank you, Don Angelo. We are at your service and will be honored to do what we can for you."

"Follow me, gentlemen," Ralph Costiero said. "I'll take you back to the car."

Both Peachy and Legs bowed respectfully, then turned and followed the consigliere.

———

DWAYNE WHEELER STARED OUT THE WINDOW where the mid-day sunrays came in to light up Wilma's room. After getting back from the truck stop the night before she had gotten a fix and once more invited him to visit her. By then her previous invitation to provide him with sex had made him horny, and he had a man's need to scratch that eternal sexual itch.

Wilma was not an attractive woman. She had nice hair, but her face was long and her eyes large and sunken. Her body was thin and bony but her legs indicated she had once had a nice figure. She had lost what good looks she might have had from the addiction to heroin.

Dwayne had used two condoms during intercourse and when they had sex for a third time, she performed fellatio on him. After that they talked a bit and he learned she had once been a high school teacher. Her downfall came from a handsome man she had gone off with during a summer vacation. They went to a city she wouldn't identify and she had her first experience with heroin. Addiction came quickly and she never returned to her teaching job. Eventually, the boyfriend talked her into entertaining men to pay for their mutual habit. She ended her story at that point.

Dwayne really didn't have to hear anymore. He was sure her boyfriend ultimately sold her to a pimp. And it was probably Babe Robertson.

When the shamus started to leave her, she begged him to stay and cuddle. Although he was sexually satiated and tired, there was something in her request that touched him. Wilma was a lonely woman, a dope addict, and a whore. She craved affection anywhere she could find it. He got back in the bed, and she laid her head on his shoulder.

After a little less than an hour it was nearly noon and

Dwayne noticed she was in a deep sleep. He got up, dressed, and went down to the kitchen for some coffee and pastry. Jimmy Sheehan greeted him with a grin. "Did you get your ashes hauled?"

"Yeah," Dwayne answered, pouring a cup of coffee. He grabbed a cinnamon roll and sat down at the table.

"We all noticed that Wilma seems to like you," Sheehan remarked. "That's something about whores, y'know. Ever' once in awhile they want one guy that only comes to them for sex. For them it's like having a love affair."

"I suppose," Dwayne said. He wanted to change the subject. "It looks like some big happenings are coming up, huh?"

"Yeah. But we're gonna keep taking the girls out to the truck stop until we're told to knock it off."

Dwayne dunked the roll into the coffee. "I'm anxious to find out exactly what we're doing here."

"Me, too," Sheehan replied. "I've been wondering who the hell is behind all these goings-on for quite awhile."

Dwayne sipped from the cup, thinking of Wichita and Nancy Turner.

CHAPTER 31

The United States Road Atlas lay open on the page that showed the entire continental U.S. It was on a table in Don Angelo Lundari's office where the boss and his chief assistants, Ralph Costiero the consigliere and Fabio Lazzoni the chief capo, gazed down at the chart.

"Ah! You see," Don Angelo declared, pointing at the map. "There is U.S. Highway 40. It runs from Baltimore in the east all the way to—" He bent down for a better view. "—San Francisco."

Costiero took a closer look. "It seems to be the longest highway going east and west."

Don Angelo continued studying the map. "And look here. U.S. 81 is north and south, going from Pembina, North Dakota on the Canadian border all the way down to Laredo, Texas on the Mexican border. And it's the longest route that goes right down the middle of the United States."

"And again, it offers easy access to other parts of the country," Costiero remarked.

"Look!" Lazzoni exclaimed. "Them two highways

cross at Salina, Kansas just like them guys from the Forzini family told us."

"Exactly," Don Angelo said. "The way I figure it, the Derby Gang is working for a big organization or maybe several organizations that want to smuggle goods into the United States."

Lazzoni nodded in agreement. "Since it goes straight from Canada to Mexico you can move a lot of goods over dirt roads and paths through trees and across fields. That's a hell of a lot easier than trying to sneak through customs inspectors in a port city."

Don Angelo was thoughtful for a few moments and his two companions immediately shut up to let the boss ponder the situation. After five minutes he had figured it out. "They ain't gonna bring in nothing from the north. It'll all come in from the south."

Costiero shook his head. "I don't know about that."

"Me either," Lazzoni agreed.

Don Angelo grinned at them, then pointed to the Gulf of Mexico. "Look at that Texas coastline. There's gotta be a hunnerd places to bring stuff in. And a hunnerd places to fan out and travel to U.S. 81. Then you go north to U.S. 40 where you can split off either east or west for direct routes to contacts in those directions."

"Yeah," Costiero acknowledged. "And that's exactly what they're gonna do. And they'll be in areas with lots of cities and towns."

"Wait a minute!" Lazzoni exclaimed. "There's a lot of ports on the east and west coast that's being used now. How's come they're doing it this way?"

"The answer to that just occurred to me," Don Angelo said. "They got a big plan to take all the activity away from the western and eastern coast ports. U.S. Customs are a real stumbling block in them places. So it's safer if they set up some completely different directions for their operations. And you can bet your bottom fucking dollar they'll have some kind of a center up there in Kansas to ship their loot in all directions by truck."

"This is gonna cut deep into our operations, Don Angelo!" Lazzoni exclaimed.

"Yeah, Fabio," the Don agreed. "Now we got to come up with a plan."

Costiero was pessimistic. "It'll take us a long time to set up a similar system."

Don Angelo grinned again. "We ain't gonna set a new one up. We're gonna take this one over from the Derby Gang." He glanced up at Costiero. "Call up them two guys from the Forzini bunch. We'll need 'em to get the ball rolling."

———

DWAYNE HAD BEEN NEGLECTING HIS BUICK SINCE arriving at the Retreat and when Charlie O'Donnell announced a grocery run into Salina, the shamus asked him to pick up some cans of 30-weight motor oil.

When Charlie returned from his shopping trip, Dwayne drove his auto under a carport and began changing the oil, checking the radiator and the generator and fan belts. When he finished with this preliminary maintenance he was satisfied. The shamus would get a proper tune-up in Salina the first chance he got. He headed for the lodge to take a break.

When he got to the top of the stairs he encountered Wilma waiting for him. "Can we talk?" she asked in a whisper.

Her cautious demeanor confused him. "What about?"

Wilma was obviously nervous. "We can't carry on a private conversation out here. Come with me to my room, okay?"

"I was gonna take a nap," he said. "And, besides, I ain't horny right now."

"Please, Dwayne!"

Now he was aware that she was badly frightened about something or someone. A combination of curiosity and concern made him follow after her. They went into Wilma's room and the woman closed the door, turning to face him.

"I'm taking a big chance right now," she said. "And I hope I can trust you."

Dwayne sat down on the chair beside her bed. "Let's talk then."

Wilma remained standing, her nervousness obviously increasing. "It's like I told you before. You're a nice guy, Dwayne. All us girls think so. You've never spoken an insulting or threatening word to any of us."

He pulled out a pack of Lucky Strikes and gave her one, taking another. After lighting both, he cleared his throat. "Okay. Keep talking."

"I know you're a new member of the gang, so I'm hoping like hell you I can trust you for a big favor.

"Sure. If I can swing it," he replied. "What d'you need?"

"I want out, Dwayne. I want to quit heroin and get back to a normal life. I want...I want...you to help me."

"You mean *sneak* you outta here?"

"Yes! Oh, yes! And take me someplace where I can get the help I need."

He gazed at her for a long moment. There was nothing more he would rather do than get the addicted woman away from the Derbies. In truth, he would like to take all of them far from the Retreat and that horrible truck stop. But there was one big difficulty. Wilma would have to go without a fix for several days if he could get her away. He was aware of the dangerous symptoms of withdrawal. As if that wasn't enough, he still had the undercover assignment to consider.

"I have extra heroin and needles that'll last me awhile," Wilma said. "I've been squirreling them away for several months now, waiting for a man like you to come along." She sat down on the bed. "Do you know somewhere to take me to get off the drug? A hospital or something?"

He shook his head. "I'm afraid not. And believe me, I'd like nothing better than to help you. But there's no—" He stopped, suddenly remembering Mrs. Davies in Wichita. "Wait! I *do* know somewhere. And it involves a nice lady."

"Oh, Dwayne!"

Now the shamus stood up. "This is real iffy, Wilma. It's gonna take time under the best of circumstances. I can't make any promises except one—" He paused. "I'll do my damnedest to pull it off."

"That's good enough for me."

"Just make sure you keep this to yourself. One slip and we're both gonna be in deep shit."

"I am well aware of that."

"I'll be touch with you as soon as I can," Dwayne promised. He impulsively leaned over and kissed her on the cheek. He left the room, and tears welled up in Wilma's eyes.

———

THE NEXT DAY WAS SCHEDULED FOR A CALL TO Johnny Cullen in Boston. Dwayne and McCarthy drove over to the telephone exchange to take care of the weekly chore. There wasn't any chitchat during the ride, but the shamus had already made up his mind not to let McCarthy in on the plans to rescue Wilma. He knew the F.B.I. agent would be chickenshit enough to thwart the scheme if it threatened their undercover assignment.

When the pair arrived at the exchange, Dwayne told McCarthy he wanted to put in a call to Agent Steve Williams. "I want to see if he has any special information. We ain't been in contact with him for a hell of a long time."

"Good idea."

When they went inside, McCarthy filled out a card with the Boston phone number while Dwayne did the same for Wichita. But the number he wrote down was not Williams' office. It was the personal one of Mrs. Belle Davies.

They went back to the chairs to wait for their summons. The two sat in silence, each occupied by individual thoughts. A few minutes passed, then the lady at the counter sang out, "Wichita call. Booth Three."

Dwayne got up and walked across the room, entering the booth and closing the door. He turned so he could keep an eye on McCarthy. "Hello. Missus Davies?"

"Yes, Mister Wheeler. How are you today?"

"I'm fine, ma'am. I have a serious question to ask you. It's about one of the prostitutes here who has asked me to sneak her away. She wants to get clean of heroin and return to a normal life."

"I see," Mrs. Davies replied. "I presume you need to know my ability to assist you."

"Yes, ma'am."

"Our organization is not only prepared for such events, but has participated in quite a few of them. When is this to occur?"

"I don't know for sure," Dwayne replied. "You've given me the information I need for the present. I'll be in touch as soon as I have something positive to report. Thank you so much. Goodbye."

He hung up and stepped from the booth. He looked across the room and could see McCarthy on the phone. Dwayne went back and sat down. He lit a cigarette, his mind concentrating on the best way to rescue Wilma.

Ten minutes passed and McCarthy emerged from the booth, putting his notebook in his inside jacket pocket. He walked toward the door, signaling Dwayne to follow him. They went directly to the car and within a minute were back on the highway.

"Did Williams have any pertinent information?" McCarthy inquired

"Nope. He just said for us to keep at it."

"That's what we'll do, Dwayne. That's *exactly* what we'll do." He looked over at his companion, noting a slight sign of edginess.

CHAPTER 32

D wayne and McCarthy had a quick lunch of sandwiches after returning from the telephone exchange. Jimmy Sheehan sat with them, drinking a Guinness Stout. Dwayne didn't take part in the conversation between his companions, and when he finished eating, he quickly excused himself and went up to his room.

Sheehan watched him leave. "Dwayne seems out of sorts."

"He is," McCarthy said. "I notice he was a little fidgety and distracted when we were at the exchange."

Sheehan nodded his understanding. "Yeah. I bet it's about whacking Fat Pauly, ain't it?"

"I'm sure it is."

"Well, I hope the situation don't turn out to be a problem," Sheehan said. "Dwayne's a good man. It'd be a shame if he lost his edge."

"Y'know," McCarthy said, "I think he needs a break. What d'you think if he and I took a few days off? We could hop in the Nash station wagon and drive around a bit. Maybe even make a run to Wichita."

"I thought he was wanted down there."

"That's true, but Wichita's a city of a hundred thousand or so and there's not an all-points bulletin out for him. Dwayne'll know the places to go where he wouldn't get caught. Besides we won't be in his Buick."

"Okay," Sheehan said. "I'll have Dave O'Leary take his place at the truck stop. The other two gatekeepers can pull a few extra hours. It won't hurt 'em none."

"I'll go upstairs and ask if he's interested in a little trip."

McCarthy went up to the room he shared with Dwayne and entered it to see him on the bed, leaning back against the headboard. McCarthy grinned. "It looks like you're deep in thought."

Dwayne shook his head. "Nope. Just resting." He'd actually been doing some heavy rumination about Wilma's escape. And it was becoming more and more frustrating.

"Listen up," McCarthy said. "You and I are going down to Wichita in the Nash for bit of vacation time. Jimmy said he'd get one of the gatekeepers to take your place at the truck stop for a few nights. And I need a chance to talk with Steve Williams and get some Bureau matters cleared up."

Dwayne immediately brightened up as he considered a visit to Nancy Turner. Carnal thoughts of getting her to go to his apartment popped into his mind. Since he wasn't a real fugitive, the place wouldn't be watched. "Yeah! I need to get away for awhile."

"Great!" McCarthy said. "We can stay in that safehouse on Nineteenth Street. I'll go down and let Jimmy know what's going on."

Dwayne got off the bed and began happily packing for the trip.

———

PEACHY RUSSO AND LEGS SPINA SAT IN FRONT OF Don Angelo's desk in the Lundari Broadview Meadows mansion. Besides the boss, Ralph Costiero and Fabio Lazzoni were present. The two ex-members of the defunct Forzini mob waited to see what was wanted of them. Both were hoping it was a chance to take part in making a big score in the local crime scene.

"Okay," Don Angelo said. "I got a few questions about this Kansas thing, see? It has interested me a great deal, so I called you guys up here to have a serious discussion about it."

"Sure, Don Angelo," Peachy said agreeably. "But I gotta be truthful with you. Me and Legs don't know a hell of a lot about what was going on out there."

"We understand," Costiero remarked. "Just do your best."

"The first thing I need to know," Don Angelo said, "was there any indication of a smuggling operation?"

Peachy was confused by the question. "Nothing like that. All we know was that they was running a prostitution operation at a truck stop."

"Yeah," Legs said. "Joe never mentioned anything about smuggling. We was really sent down there to try to scope things out."

"Do you know where the Derbies was staying over there?" Don Angelo inquired.

"We had no idea," Peachy explained. "We was really in the dark."

"Understood," Don Angelo stated. "Did you see any guys anywhere who looked like they was strangers in the area."

"No."

Lazzoni turned his attention to Legs. "Did *you* see anybody that looked differ'nt from the other people."

"No," Legs replied. "Ever'body I seen was dressed like the other yokels. A lot of their clothes are out of style. And that includes the new stuff in store windows for sale."

"The farmers dressed a little differ'nt," Peachy added. "They wore what they called bib overalls with ball caps and denim shirts."

Ralph Costiero opined, "Maybe the Derbies was dressed the same way, huh?"

"I ain't sure about that," Peachy admitted. "Fat Pauly wasn't when he got whacked."

Don Angelo was silent for a few minutes, then announced, "Awright! Here's what's going down. I've already decided that you two, along with Fabio, are gonna go back to Kansas. I had Ralph check out the best way to get out there. You'll go by train to Kansas City. You rent a car and drive back to the junction of U.S. Highway 40 and U.S. Highway 81. Start from that location. I want you to look around for anything that is differ'nt from everything else. Get my drift? If you see a man or car or truck or something that don't seem to belong, I want you to check it out. And don't ignore anybody that looks local if they're acting differ'nt from the others."

"When do we leave?" Peachy asked.

"As soon as possible," Don Angelo replied. "I'll have you driven back to your neighborhood so's you can pack. Do it quick 'cause I want you to come straight back here."

"Let's get down to your stomping grounds, guys," Lazzoni said. "I'll go with you."

The three left the office as Costiero picked up the phone to dial for railroad schedule information.

IT WAS TEN O'CLOCK IN THE MORNING WHEN Terry McCarthy pulled the Nash up to the curb in front of the Wheeler, Kelly, Hagny Building in downtown Wichita. McCarthy got out and Dwayne slid across the seat to the steering wheel. Since the shamus was a "civilian" undercover agent, he would not be made privy to any conversation between McCarthy and Steve Williams.

"Give us a call in a couple of hours," McCarthy said. "We should be finished by then."

"Will do," Dwayne replied. He drove away with the intention of contacting Nancy Turner. He knew he couldn't go inside the Beachcomber Tavern since the owner Bret Underwood might decide to play the good citizen by informing the police a fugitive was in his place of business. Both McCarthy and Williams would go nuts if they had to straighten out a mess like that.

Dwayne went south on Market Street to a Bay Petroleum filling station he was familiar with. There was a payphone at the north edge of the site that would serve his purpose. He parked beside it and got out. After feeding in a nickel and dialing, he was reward with hearing Nancy's voice.

"Beachcomber Tavern."

"Hey," Dwayne said. "It's me."

Her voice dropped to a whisper. "Oh, my God! Where are you?"

"I'm in Wichita. For awhile anyhow."

"Is everything all right?"

"Sure, but it ain't over with," Dwayne informed her. "But I'll be here in Wichita for a short stay." He paused, then asked, "Would you like to go to a movie tonight?"

"A movie?"

"Yeah. You know what I mean. We'll go over to my—"

She quickly interrupted. "Dwayne, you know I won't sleep with you until we get our relationship straightened out."

Shit! he thought. "Well, okay. I tell you what. I can pick you up after you get off work and we'll go to the Continental Grill for some hamburgers and milkshakes to take back to your house. I'll meet you down the block from the Beachcomber."

He hung up and began trying to figure out how he could get rid of McCarthy until later in the evening. The solution leaped into his mind unbidden. He slipped another five cents into the phone and dialed Steve Williams office.

"F.B.I.," said the receptionist.

"Hi. This is Dwayne Wheeler. I have to talk to McCarthy."

"Wait a moment, please," she replied.

McCarthy's voice came over the receiver. "What's up, Dwayne?"

"Is it all right if I don't go to the safehouse until later this evening?"

"What's going on?" McCarthy asked with a suspicious tone in his voice.

"I want to see a lady friend. We'll be going to her house after I pick her up when she gets off work."

McCarthy knew that Dwayne was an experienced and skillful detective who could avoid being sighted. Besides, seeing a girlfriend would be good for his morale. "Sure. Williams can drive me to the safehouse. I'll see you later."

———

DWAYNE DECIDED TO SPEND THE DAY DRIVING around Wichita checking out old land marks he knew. This was something he hadn't done for a couple of years. The short absence from the city stimulated his sentimental side to contemplate bygone days.

He began by driving eastward on Kellogg Street, turning south on Green. He drove slowly until coming to a stop in front of the house where he had lived with his parents before his dad was run over and killed. A strong sensation of melancholia stirred his emotions as he gazed at the residence.

It was a rental and he could remember times when his parents fell behind in making the monthly payments. But Mr. Cooper the landlord always gave them time to catch up.

But when his dad was killed, there was no income at all. After three months he and his mother were evicted. The memory of that awful event now made it unbearable to look at the house. He quickly put the station wagon into gear and headed down to Lincoln, turning right.

It was a short distance to the George Washington Boulevard and Grove Street intersection. He pulled up to the curb out of traffic in front of a building bearing the sign **SUNDRG STORE**. It had originally been the **SUNDRUG STORE**, but the owner was ordered by the Sedgwick County Attorney's office to remove the word **DRUG** from the sign. This was because he didn't deal in prescription medicine. His business had a soda fountain, notions counter, a trio of pinball machines, and a magazine rack. The owner shrugged, then simply took the **U** out of the sign to obey the directive.

Dwayne grinned to himself. This was typical of a Wichita businessman who felt harassed by the local government. Obviously, everyone who mentioned the business still said, "The Sundrug Store."

The shamus gazed across the street at the open field to the south that bordered the Schweiter edition where a lot of his boyhood friends had lived. He and his pals played pick-up baseball and football games at the site after school and on Saturdays

Dwayne went up Grove Street back to Kellogg for a drive out of Wichita to spend the afternoon with Tommy Brady at his farm near Augusta. The pair enjoyed several hours in quiet conversation, sipping the thick, pungent brew that Tommy called coffee.

WHEN DWAYNE RETURNED TO WICHITA, HE STILL had some time to kill. He parked the Nash on McLean Avenue along the Big Arkansas River at a place in view of Lawrence Stadium. This is where the minor league Wichita Indians played baseball. He used to make extra money hawking popcorn and peanuts during games.

Dwayne stayed at the location for awhile, reading a *Look* magazine he'd purchased at a newsstand. He yawned, put the publication down and checked his watch, noting it was fifteen to five. Time to pick up Nancy.

She was already waiting for him a block down from the tavern. When he honked, she didn't recognize the car. She ignored the vehicle and turned away. He tapped the horn again. Nancy glared in his direction, then recognized him.

"Where did you get this car?" she asked, getting in.

"It belongs to some associates of mine," he replied. "How've you been?"

"Worried about you," she said.

"Everything's under control, but I have to leave tomorrow morning."

"Where are you staying?"

"I'm afraid I can't say."

"I knew it!" she exclaimed. "You're on a caper, aren't you?"

"Yes I am," he said. "Well, shall we pick up some goodies at the Continental so we can have a nice supper with Holly and Maggie?"

"That's a wonderful idea!"

———

DWAYNE WAS PLEASED AT THE LOVING reception he received from Holly when he and Nancy walked through the front door. She hugged him so tight around the waist that he almost dropped the carry-out paper sack.

Holly exclaimed, "What a nice surprise!"

He handed the food to Nancy, and knelt down so he could hug Holly. He kissed her on the cheek and she returned the favor. "Well," he said. "I have to leave tomorrow but I won't be gone too much longer."

Maggie came up and also embraced him. "D'you have to leave so soon?"

"I'm afraid so."

"I hope ever'thing is okay for you."

"Ever'thing's fine," he assured her.

They were interrupted by Nancy calling out that the food was on the table. The three walked over and sat down to the hamburgers, French fries and strawberry milkshakes.

After eating, they went to the living room for an evening that included listening to *Fibber McGee and*

Molly and *The Great Gildersleeve*, on the radio. By then it was Holly's bedtime and Dwayne knew he had better head over to the safehouse. After a good night kiss for Holly and a farewell to Maggie, Dwayne went outside to the car with Nancy by his side.

The couple embraced and Nancy as apologetic. "I'm sorry I didn't go to your apartment, Dwayne. But I explained my reasons for not sleeping with you."

"It's okay," he said, holding back his irritation. He kissed her quickly, not wanting to be aroused by a lingering cuddle. "I'll be back as soon as I can."

Nancy watched him get in the car and waved as he drove off.

CHAPTER 33

The first time going back to the truck stop after his return, Dwayne strolled alone among the parked vehicles. He needed some solitude to concentrate on developing a plan to rescue Wilma. He was lost so deeply in thought that the rumble of numerous chugging diesel engines was blocked out of his conscious mind.

The first scheme that occurred to him was to have Wilma feign illness to avoid going to work, then he would sneak her out of the lodge to a rendezvous spot out on the highway. Problem: The ruse might result in Jimmy Sheehan taking a special interest in the woman. That meant she wouldn't be able to leave her room without attracting attention.

Or Wilma could sneak out of the truck stop during working hours and hide somewhere among the vehicles and wait for somebody from Mrs. Davies' organization to pick her up. Problem: It wouldn't take much time for Duke Glencannon or Frank Quinn to note she had dropped out of sight. They would immediately begin searching for her. That would cut down the time of making the pick-up and create a critical condition without much chance of succeeding.

Perhaps after returning from the truck stop and going through Glencannon's inspection she could sneak out of the lodge and hide in the trunk of the Buick. It would be easy for him to drive her to a prearranged appointment that Mrs. Davies arranged. Problem: Wilma would have to receive her after-work injection and be too high for quick reactions that might be necessary if something untoward popped up. And if she declined the heroin, it would raise suspicions as well as make her go into withdrawal symptoms during the linkup.

It would also mean Dwayne couldn't return to the gang without being suspected of aiding the escape. Terry McCarthy as an F.B.I. agent would be infuriated about a rift in the undercover assignment and see that the Bureau punished him in some fashion. It would not be difficult for them to come up with serious charges. He had no doubt that the Bureau was aware of several things in his past that could send him to prison for several years.

Back to the cerebral drawing board.

———

PEACHY RUSSO DROVE THE CAR WESTWARD ON U.S. Highway 40 with Fabio Lazzoni on the front seat beside him. Legs Spina relaxed in the back. The 1941 Oldsmobile sedan had been picked up at a rental agency shortly after their arrival at the Kansas City, Missouri, depot. Now the rising sun behind them had lifted into full view at that early morning hour.

Legs was thoroughly bored by the passing prairie landscape. Fabio, on the other hand, was fascinated. "Christ! You can see forever around here. Nothing is in the way."

"It gets to you after awhile though," Peachy said.

Fabio glanced at the speedometer. "Hey! Slow down. We don't want to get any attention from the local cops."

Legs chuckled from the backseat. "There ain't no speed limits in Kansas."

"No shit?" Fabio exclaimed.

"That's right," Peachy said. "D'you want to see how fast we can get this Olds going?"

Fabio shook his head. "Naw. We might have a wreck. That'd screw up our job and really piss off Don Angelo." He chuckled mirthlessly. "In a case like that, we'd be better off killed in the accident."

"Okay," Peachy said. "I'll hold her around seventy."

"I don't want to go that fast," Fabio stated. "Go a steady sixty."

BUSINESS WAS SLOW IN WICHITA'S Beachcomber Tavern after the initial rush of businessmen having their morning eye-openers. Nancy Turner finished rinsing and drying the last glass and putting it on the shelf with its companions. She completed her chores by wiping up the spills under the spout of the coffee urn.

Her boss Bret Underwood had gone around the bar with a copy of that morning's *Wichita Eagle* to dabble at the crossword puzzle. He settled on a stool and took a preliminary look at the challenge he faced. "Uh oh! This is gonna be a tough one today."

"You always say that," Nancy remarked. "And you always finish 'em up."

Bret chuckled. "You don't notice the number of times I have to erase entries." He started the puzzle, then looked up. "Have you heard anything about Dwayne?"

Nancy shook her head, not wanting to reveal he had been in Wichita. "The last I heard from him was on the day he left. He said it might take some time to clear things up and he didn't want me to worry."

"Well...I hope ever'thing turns out okay for him," Bret said. He began filling in the blocks of the puzzle, and quickly became lost in the procedure.

Nancy got herself a cup of coffee and sipped it while leaning against the ice cabinet where the bottles of beer were kept. It hadn't been long after Dwayne left that she experienced an unpleasant feeling of shame for not going to bed with him. Her feminine instincts screamed that he needed comforting and affection because of his present predicament. She had really let him down.

Dwayne had shown no anger or disappointment at any time since her declarations, but she knew he had been upset. Perhaps she was demanding too much. Deep in her heart she felt he was worth holding on to. In reality, Dwayne was paying the price for her unhappy experiences with other men.

"Oh, well," she said. "A gal's got to kiss a lot of frogs before she finds her prince."

Bret looked up from the puzzle. "What'd you say?"

"Nothing. Just thinking out loud."

———

AS SOON AS THE THREE BOSTON HOODS HAD gotten close to Salina, Fabio Lazzoni gave Peachy some puzzling instructions to pull off the highway and go into the town proper. Since they had to get gas anyway, Peachy did as directed. He turned south onto College Street then right on Iron Avenue, going to the nearest Conoco station.

While a teenage kid filled the gas tank, Fabio got out and spoke to him. It was a quick exchange as the chief capo got directions to the Saline County Courthouse. He got back in the car and waited patiently while the young attendant cleaned the windshield.

Fabio looked over at his traveling companions, asking, "Did you guys ever notice that the name of the town is Salina—ending with an *a*—and is in the county of Saline —ending with an *e*?"

"I never noticed that," Peachy replied.

"Me either," Legs added, "One of them names has got to be wrong, huh?"

Peachy laughed. "Maybe they had too much invested in signs to change 'em."

The windshield was finished and Peachy started the Olds' engine. Minutes later, he pulled up to the curb in front of the courthouse. Legs was curious. "What're you gonna do here, Fabio? Courthouses make me nervous as hell."

"I got some business, that's all. I'll fill you guys in on it as soon as I get back. Wait here."

Fabio left the car and walked up the steps into the building. He scanned the directory in the lobby, then went to the zoning department down the hall. A lady behind the counter left her desk to speak to him. "What can I do for you, sir?"

Fabio produced a business card that identified him by a pseudonym with the title of commercial real estate investor. She studied the I.D. "You're from Massachusetts, huh?"

"Right," Fabio said. "My company is interested in establishing a project in this vicinity if it proves feasible."

"That's very interesting."

"I would like to purchase a county map, if I may,"

Fabio said. "And any aerial photos that might be available."

"Yes, sir," the lady said. "We have packets prepared. Excuse me." She walked to a nearby filing cabinet and retrieved a heavy 10x14 cardboard envelope. She returned and placed it on the counter. "That will be three dollars, sir. Do you think you'll be doing business here in Saline County?"

"That is what my company has sent me to investigate," Fabio answered. He paid the fee, and went back to the car. When he joined his traveling companions, he instructed Peachy to find the nearest motor court.

"We've got a lot of work to do," he announced.

CHAPTER 34

On the evening of the same day that Peachy, Fabio and Legs had arrived in Kansas, Dwayne was back at the truck stop, ambling slowly among the vehicles. He once again mulled over how to keep his promise to Wilma. At this point he was beginning to feel there was no way of getting the woman into the care of Mrs. Davies' organization.

Dwayne's train of thought was interrupted by the sounds of an angry man and woman quarreling somewhere nearby. He hurried toward the disturbance and saw Wilma and a truck driver involved in what seemed a serious disagreement. They were next to a semi that obviously belonged to the male.

"What's going on?" the shamus asked.

The driver, thinking Dwayne was also a trucker because of the way he was dressed, growled, "Hey, buddy, this whore short-changed me. I gave her a twenty and she only gave me back five bucks. I got ten more owed me." He glared at Wilma. "And I'm damn well gonna get it."

Wilma was adamant. "You gave me a ten!"

Dwayne knew it was Wilma who was not telling the truth. "Go on, girly. Give the guy the ten you owe him. You don't want any trouble, do you? Us truckers stick together."

Wilma had no choice but to obey. She glared at the man. "You're taking advantage of this situation." But she handed over a ten dollar bill.

The guy grabbed it from her hand, then stepped up on the running board and got back into in his vehicle. He leaned out the side window and nodded to Dwayne. "Thanks a lot, buddy."

"You're welcome, pal," Dwayne said. He took Wilma by the arm and pulled her back as the driver put the truck into gear and rolled away toward the highway.

He turned to her. "You was cheating him, right?"

Wilma shrugged. "Right. This was the first time I've worked this close to the highway. I thought I could get away with it."

Dwayne took a look around and heard the noise of a passing vehicle. He walked to the outside line of trucks and could see U.S. 40. He noticed there wasn't much traffic at that time of night. The shamus took out his flashlight and stepped off the cement parking lot, going down to a ditch along the highway. He looked to the east and could see a couple of cottonwood trees amid some thick brush. The shamus walked over to check the layout of the spot, and realized he had discovered an excellent hiding place.

He went back to Wilma and took her hand. "Come with me."

The woman allowed herself to be led down to the ditch, then over to the trees and bushes. She looked around. "So?"

"Y'know," Dwayne said, "a smart gal could hide inside them bushes and wait for a car to come along. Then walk over to the car and get in it for a ride out of here."

Wilma was speechless for a moment. "D'you really think it can be done?"

"I'm sure I can come up with something," Dwayne promised. "But first I got to make a phone call to set up a meeting. That won't happen 'til the next time I drive Terry over to the telephone exchange."

Wilma clamped her hand on his arm. "God, Dwayne! Make it work!"

He nodded. "Let's get back to the parking lot."

Dwayne helped her up from the ditch to the trucks. Wilma went off to look for customers while Dwayne renewed his wandering with his mind racing on how to make the final arrangements for the woman's escape.

———

THE NEXT MORNING FABIO LAZZONI AND HIS two companions returned to the motor court after eating breakfast. Fabio sat down at the room's desk. He wasted no time turning his attention to the county map and aerial photos. "Gather 'round, boys."

Peachy and Legs each stood on one side of the capo. Legs asked, "Is that what you got at the courthouse, Fabio?"

"Right. Now look at this map. Here's where we are now. Show me that side road you've mentioned."

Peachy shrugged. "It's just a country lane. There's a lot of 'em."

"I'm a natural manhunter," Fabio said. "Too bad I ain't a cop. I got a hunch about that road."

Peachy looked at the map and pointed. "It's right there."

"Okay," Fabio said. He took the aerial photos and thumbed through them. "Here we go. Here's a picture of that same spot." He studied it a bit. "Aha!"

"What do you mean, 'aha'?" Legs asked.

"There's some buildings off to the side three or four miles from the turn-off," Fabio said. He flipped the photo over to check the date. "This shot was made about a year ago. So you can be damn sure it's still pretty much the same out there."

"What's that?" Peachy asked, eyeing a large structure. "A barn?"

"No, it ain't a barn," Fabio informed him. "This is some kind of set-up. Maybe a hunting or fishing lodge and there's carports and a couple of small buildings around it. And a fence with a gatehouse." He lit a cigarette. "That'd be a good place to hole up. See how far it's off that road? And there's a driveway that goes to the lodge." He peered closer. "It seems to be abandoned."

"So nobody's staying there, huh?" Peachy asked.

"At least not a year ago," Fabio said. "And it seems the best place to settle in to run a whore racket at that truck stop."

"Shit!" Peachy exclaimed. "We never thought them Micks would be staying out in the countryside somewhere."

"It's just as well," Fabio opined. "You'd have a hell of a time getting inside the place by driving to it. It appears to me the best approach would be from here—" He pointed to a spot on the other side of a creek and wooded area. "—and sneak up in a roundabout way." He replaced the photos and maps into the cardboard envelope. "I think we better drive past there and take a quick look."

"Then what?" Peachy asked.

"I'll put in a call to Don Angelo and see how he wants to handle this," Fabio answered. "You can bet he'll come up with a way to settle this problem once and for all."

CHAPTER 35

Dwayne Wheeler and Terry McCarthy walked into the telephone exchange as was normal for this oft-repeated routine. They went to the counter and, as always, filled out telephone cards. McCarthy had to make his regular report to Johnny Cullen while Dwayne took his time, composing a card to speak to F.B.I. Agent Steve Williams in Wichita. McCarthy finished his application first, going over to the chairs to wait.

Dwayne, speaking softly, asked for another card. This second one was for Mrs. Davies. If McCarthy learned he hadn't called Williams when he said he did, the F.B.I. man would start a fuss that could prevent Wilma's escape. This would include a demand to know who else he was talking to. If McCarthy and Williams ever found out his working agreement with Mrs. Davies, they would raise unholy hell and forbid him to contact her again.

Dwayne's request went through first and he hurried over to his assigned booth. In less than a minute the phone rang and Dwayne picked up the receiver. "Hey, Steve," he greeted.

"Hello, Dwayne. What's going on?"

"Same old stuff," Dwayne answered. "Terry is on another call and he wanted me to check in with you."

"Okay. I don't have a thing to pass on."

"That's too bad. We're getting anxious. So we'll be patient. Thanks. I'll call again later."

"Right," Williams acknowledged. "Just hang in there. That's all you can do at this stage of the case."

The lady had sent the second call to the same booth. Now he had to stay alert and keep an eye out to make sure that McCarthy didn't come over and want to speak to Williams. The phone rang again to be answered by Miss Carruthers.

"Hi," the shamus said. "It's me, Dwayne Wheeler. I need to speak with Missus Davies. It's really important."

"I'll transfer you to the lady," the secretary said.

A quick moment later Mrs. Davies answered. "What can I do for you, Mister Wheeler?"

"It's about that woman who wants to get outta here," Dwayne said. "I got a plan worked out."

"I'm listening."

"Her name is Wilma and she works in the evenings in a truck stop east of Salina," Dwayne begun. "I can set things up so's she can be picked up around two a.m. Is that a problem?"

"I can't say one way or the other. Please continue."

"You have to drive up north on U.S.81 to U.S. 40 and turn east," Dwayne began. "There's a tall neon sign reading Acme Truckers Service that sticks up above the place. You can see it over a small patch of trees and brush."

"Speak slower please," Mrs. Davies requested. "I am writing this down."

"Sure," Dwayne said. He began articulating in a slow, regular rhythm. "She will be hiding in those trees and brush. It's all next to the highway. I'll be with her if possible. When you stop, give a little honk and she'll come out and get in your car. Then off you go."

"*I* won't be driving, Mister Wheeler. But there will be someone available for the job."

"I understand. Now I got to tell you that although Wilma is addicted to heroin, she won't be high or nothing like that since she's supposed to be having sex with drivers. She ain't supposed to get an injection 'til after she gets back to the lodge. That's the building where she's staying. But Wilma is bringing needles and smack with her to keep from going into withdrawal after she's picked up and driven away."

"Our people will also be equipped to avoid that problem," Mrs. Davies assured him.

"Unfortunately, none of the other women are in on this," Dwayne admitted. "Frankly, they're damaged goods. I hope you'll think it's worth the effort to get the one that wants to run away."

"We will be most happy to help even if it is only one."

"I'm glad to hear that, Missus Davies. I'll call again when a definite date can be set."

"I'll be waiting," she replied. "And I see you know some of the slang names for heroin. Smack indeed!"

"Yes, ma'am. I'm turning into a reg'lar street person."

Dwayne left the booth and crossed the room to take a seat, noting that McCarthy was still carrying on his call. Another twenty minutes passed before McCarthy exited the booth and walked over to Dwayne. "Johnny Cullen says it won't be long until we're up to full speed."

Dwayne was puzzled. "What's he mean by 'full speed'?"

"I don't know yet," McCarthy stated. "But when it

starts we'll learn the real reason for all these activities in the middle of Kansas."

Dwayne felt a flash of uneasiness. Now he would have to get Wilma away quicker than he'd planned.

———————

THE TRIO OF BOSTON HOODS WERE IN THE rented Oldsmobile as Peachy Russo drove east on Highway 40. Fabio Lazzoni was on the passenger side while an excited Legs Spina was in the back, leaning forward, resting his hands on the front seat.

"There it is, Peachy!" Legs exclaimed, pointing through the windshield at the turn-off they were searching for.

"Gotcha!" Peachy said. He turned off the highway onto the road.

"Awright," Fabio said. "Just take it easy. Remember that we want to look like we're gonna visit some farmer pals down the road, okay? The map and photos showed some farm houses over there."

"Gotcha!" Peachy repeated.

"Don't either of you look to the left," Fabio cautioned. "If there's somebody in that gatehouse, he'll get suspicious if we all seem to be looking for something. I can stay out of sight on this side of Peachy and get a good gander at the joint."

"Gotcha!" This time it was Legs speaking.

They continued down the road per Fabio's instructions, and Peachy slowed down a tiny bit. Fabio looked past the driver at the gatehouse, then turned to the front as they passed.

"What'd you see, Fabio?" Peachy asked.

"There was a guy on duty there. That means they got a lot of security going for 'em."

"What's our next step?" Legs inquired.

"I'll have to call Don Angelo and make a report," Fabio answered. He got the map out of the cardboard envelope. "I gotta figure out a roundabout way to get outta here. I don't want to go past that gatehouse again."

Peachy continued driving, waiting for directions to get back to Highway 40.

CHAPTER 36

Don Angelo Lundari received a special delivery package from Fabio Lazzoni that was mailed from Salina, Kansas. Fabio had returned to the Saline County Courthouse to purchase another copy of the aerial photographs and maps to send back east for the boss to study. He also included a roadmap with Kansas on one side and the United States on the other.

The special delivery had included a written description of the physical features of the lodge headquarters of the Derby Gang. Don Angelo and his consigliere Ralph Costiero studied the material like military staff officers. Their immediate impression was that attacking the lodge was impossible. It was nothing like their usual hits in urban areas where their victims were walking down a street, eating in a restaurant, getting a haircut or doing something in places where it was easy to fire at least three shots into the doomed quarry.

"Damn!" Costiero exclaimed. "In order to get up close to that main building we'd have to cross a wide open area."

"And before reaching the place we'd have to wade a creek and scramble through that bunch of trees there," Don Angelo pointed out.

They turned their collective attention to discussing what the Derby Gang might be doing out in the hinterlands. Neither had come across similar circumstances during their criminal careers. The first impression they perceived was one of pure puzzlement.

Some of the confusion disappeared after they learned the Derbies planned to set up prostitution activities all along the two highways of U.S. 40 and 81. But that didn't make much sense either. Don Angelo declared, "That's too much trouble and expense for that kind of racket! There's gotta be a lot more to this."

After a bit of additional study, it occurred to the pair that the Derby Gang was making a permanent move from Boston to the middle of Kansas. Costiero opined, "Another dead end. The only thing they could do out there would be getting some kind of weird kick-backs from farmers or cowboys!"

Their fourth and final speculation was that the first three impressions showed the futility of trying to figure out what was going on with the Irish mobsters. After a few silent moments, Don Angelo sank into a deep spell of cerebral deliberation. He leaned back in his chair, closed his eyes, appearing to have drifted off into a deep slumber.

Costiero recognized this practice of the boss, and wisely relaxed into silence to wait and see what the result of this contemplation might be. Ten minutes passed, and Don Angelo's eyes popped open. He reached out for his phone. He handed it to Costiero, ordering, "Call my cousin Tony."

Costiero spoke into the handset. "I want to place a person-to-person long distance call to Corpus Christi,

Texas. I want to speak to Tony Lundari." After giving the number, he put the handset back on the cradle.

Ralph Costiero had a lot of respect and admiration for Angelo and Tony. Both were smart and shared a strong bond between them. In most gang scenarios they would have been mortal enemies, meaning one would whack the other in order to take over the mob. Instead, Tony the younger, gracefully stepped aside and remained as second-in-command.

Eventually, Tony developed his own contacts and left Boston, ending up in Corpus Christi after a few years of criminal activity in various locations. Now he was running several rackets on the docks in the Texas port. Through a ruthless campaign that included knocking off a trio of interlopers, he worked himself into big bucks through the longshoremen's union and getting kickbacks from trucking companies that operated out of the harbor.

Once comfortably settled into that routine of outlawry, he turned his attention to smuggling untaxed cigarettes and liquor through a hidden harbor on the coast of the Gulf of Mexico. Tony avoided contact with law enforcement with clever cover-ups as he maintained a low profile in the illegal operations. This was an innate talent he had nurtured in order to remain virtually unknown.

Ten minutes later the phone rang. Don Angelo answered it. "Hello? Yeah, it's me. Just a minute let me put you on the speaker." He punched the button. "Okay. Ralph is here with us."

"Hi, ya, Ralph," came Tony's voice over the phone. "So what're you guys up to?"

Don Angelo had to be careful about what he was about to say. There was always the chance of phone taps; either by law enforcement or rival gangs. "I've been thinking on going into the international fashion market to sell several clothing lines to American retailers. New York and Boston don't fit into my plans. I'm just starting out and need to know the most economical location where I can bring in the goods. I was thinking of the Texas seaboard."

"Sure," Tony said, understanding his cousin had some clandestine operation in mind. "There's smaller harbors that can be used more economically than here in Corpus Christi." He paused. "But...uh...I can't quite recall any in particular. Maybe if you came down here, I could be more helpful."

"Okay. I'll send Ralph," Don Angelo said. "Keep this under your hat, Tony. The international fashion business is a hundred percent cut-throat competition. And I'm just a run-of-the-mill guy trying to establish a profitable business."

"Sure. I understand. I'll be looking forward to seeing Ralph."

Don Angelo hung up. "There's one more thing we gotta learn. Who is bringing in the stuff for the Derby Gang to peddle?"

Ralph was thoughtful for a moment. "That's a puzzler all right. It could be some foreign outfit. Most likely European."

"Well, that ain't important right how. Whoever it is will have to use our organization after we take over from the Micks. Naturally we'll negotiate a better deal for us than what the Derbies now have."

"Naturally," Ralph agreed. "I think we're taking the right steps."

DWAYNE CHECKED HIS WATCH, NOTING IT WAS 1:45 a.m. This was fifteen minutes before H-Hour when the car arranged through Mrs. Belle Davies was scheduled to pick up Wilma. It was time to take the woman to the edge of the parking area.

Wilma was ready when he walked up to her. It was easy to see that she was in a good mood. Dwayne grinned. "All set to head for your new life?"

Wilma nodded. "I sure am. And thank you so much, Dwayne. This couldn't have happened without you."

"I was happy to help," he replied. "Too bad none of the other gals want to change their lives."

"They're lost souls," Wilma said. "They'll end up dying early in squalor and misery in some alleyway."

Dwayne reached in his pocket and pulled out a roll of bills. "Here's some money that I—"

She interrupted him with a light laugh. "I have a hundred dollars."

Dwayne was surprised. "Where the hell did you get that much money?"

"I saved it up."

"How could you save it up with Duke searching you gals after each trip out here?"

"He always checked my ass and pussy," Wilma replied. "But he never looked inside my shoes. That's where I hid the extra money."

"My God! Are any of the other girls doing that?"

"No," Wilma said. "They think of getting fixes, not of trying to save money to run away."

"Well, well. Wonders never cease," Dwayne stated. He took her arm. "C'mon. We better get over there."

After another look around, he led her out of the parking area to the ditch that led to the trees. They went into the small patch of foliage where they could easily see the highway. There was little traffic as would be expected at that early morning hour.

After several minutes, the sound of an approaching car engine slowing down could be distinctly heard. Dwayne gazed out from the cover just as it came to a stop. He took Wilma's hand and led her up to the vehicle.

"Are you from Missus Davies?" he asked.

A lady stepped out. "Yes! I take it this is our new friend." She gazed at Wilma. "How are you, dear?"

"I'm fine," Wilma smiled.

"Don't worry if you start feeling sick. I'm a nurse and can take care of you until we get you back to our little hideaway."

Wilma quickly turned and kissed Dwayne on the cheek, then got into the car. The door closed and the driver made a quick U-turn to head back south.

Dwayne watched it disappear, then walked back along the ditch to return to the parking area.

———

DWAYNE MADE SURE HE GOT BACK TO THE PANEL truck at 4 a.m. A couple of minutes later Duke Glencannon showed up with Fay. They were followed by Frank Quinn and Tim Fagin. It was a full ten minutes before Tammy and Carla made an appearance.

Duke checked his watch. "I guess Wilma has a late customer."

After fifteen minutes he walked up to a place where he could get a good look at the parking area. "Goddamn it! Where the hell could she be?"

"Me and Tim'll take a look," Frank said. "I hope she ain't been beat up or nothing."

The two disappeared into the midst of the semis.

Meanwhile, Carla and Tammy got into the back of the truck to settle down on the sofas. Dwayne and Duke lit cigarettes and stood at the cargo compartment's entrance. The other three women inside were getting fidgety as their need for fixes began acting up.

When Frank and Tim returned they were worried. "She ain't nowhere to be seen," Tim announced.

Duke started to curse, then stopped. He had just experienced a disturbing thought. "Maybe one of them truckers killed her. If so, the killer'd prob'ly drag her someplace to a corner in the parking lot."

"Uh oh!" Frank exclaimed. "That means the law will come swarming when she's found."

"Yeah!" Dwayne agreed. "We sure as hell don't want to get caught in here."

No other words were needed as the four men got into the panel truck for a quick ride back to the Retreat.

CHAPTER 37

Ralph Costiero had a long, tiring four-day rail trip from Boston, Massachusetts to Corpus Christi, Texas. He had to change trains three times which precluded him from getting a sleeping berth. That meant miserable hours of sitting up while napping fitfully with a small pillow given him by a porter.

When Ralph arrived at the Texas depot, he stepped wearily down from the passenger car and stood transfixed for several long moments. The other arriving travelers stepped around him as they headed for the interior of the station.

The consigliere took a deep breath, gripped his suitcase a bit harder, and began looking for a payphone. He was stopped when a huge cowboy suddenly appeared in front of him. The guy had the look of a veteran prize fighter who had experienced a long and painful career.

"Are you Ralph?" the stranger asked in a husky voice.

"Yeah."

"I'm here to pick you up and take you to Boss Tony. C'mon."

Ralph, relieved by this surprise welcome, expected him to take his bag, but the big guy simply strode off without looking back. The consigliere had to hurry to catch up with the taciturn greeter. They went outside to the curb where a light blue Cadillac sedan was parked.

"Get in," the cowboy stated.

Ralph got into the back while his escort settled into the front on the passenger 's side. There was a driver— evidently also a cowboy—who was a short lightweight with a mean, frowning expression on his face.

As they drove off, Ralph noticed that most of the men on the street were wearing western attire. This was obviously the accepted style in that part of the world. He started to make some innocent inquiries, but changed his mind as his two companions remained silent.

The drive was a long one that traveled due south out of the city. Ralph caught a quick glimpse of the harbor in the distance, then settled back to check out what else he might see in this strange place where Don Angelo's orders had sent him.

The roads grew simpler and bumpier as the diminutive driver steered the Cadillac through the flat countryside. They came to a barbed-wire fence and the auto was braked to a halt. The big cowboy got out and opened a wooden gate. After the car was driven through the gap, he closed the barrier and got back into the front seat.

A sprawling ranch house appeared after five minutes of travel, and the trip ended at a veranda on the front of the building. The big cowboy got out and waited until Ralph joined him, holding onto the suitcase.

Ralph followed the guy through the front door and down a hall. His escort stopped at an open interior entrance. He nodded his head sideways, indicating Ralph was supposed to go through the entry. Ralph stepped in and came to an abrupt halt.

Tony Lundari sat at a big desk. He stood up with his hand stretched out. "It's good to see you again, Ralph."

Ralph stood in wide-eyed surprise at his old friend. Tony wore western-style clothing, headlined by a navy blue shirt with red and yellow floral embroidery across the front, collar and cuffs. He sported a bolo tie with a silver slide that had a large turquoise stone inlaid in the center. Somehow Tony seemed taller, and when he walked around the desk Ralph noticed the cowboy boots.

"Hi, ya, Tony. It looks like you've gone native, huh?"

"You bet! I prefer this type garb now." He raised a foot displaying a colorful boot. "These cost a hunnerd bucks."

The big cowboy stood silently in the entranceway, waiting for a dismissal or some further instructions regarding the visitor.

Tony looked over at him. "Tell Conchita to serve lunch, Red."

Still mute, the cowboy turned and strode off to carry out the order.

Tony turned his attention back to Ralph. "I bet you can use a drink. A shot of tequila will set you up just right."

"I've heard of tequila, but never tried it."

"It's an underrated liquor," Tony said, walking over to a sideboard holding various bottles of alcoholic beverages. "It's distilled only in Mexico and it's made out of a plant called the blue agave. It's a cactus or something, I reckon."

"You *reckon*?" Ralph said. "You're even beginning to talk like a cowboy."

"I like it here in Texas," Tony stated as he poured them each a shot of the fiery liquor. "And I've managed to fit in right well. He handed a glass to Ralph and raised his own. "*Salud, dinero y amor!*"

"What's that mean?"

"That's Spanish, Ralph. It means health, money, and love."

They raised their shot glasses in the toast, then downed the libations. "Whew!" Ralph said. "This has a kick all right. I don't think I'd want to get drunk on it." He paused. "Are those two guys who picked me up cowboys?"

"No," Tony replied. "The big one is my number one guy. His name is Red Glover and is one tough *hombre*. He's also a good shot."

"What about the smaller guy?"

"Dale Wickham is his name. He races stockcars when he ain't working for me. Naturally he's an expert when it comes to driving."

"Interesting," Ralph commented. "By the way, I could use another shot."

"Happy to oblige, pardner!" Tony said. "Tequila is actually supposed to be drunk in a routine with salt and lemon. I'll teach you that later."

"That's interesting."

They knocked back a couple of more rounds, then a third. Ralph walked over to his suitcase and knelt down to open it. After pulling out a 10x14 cardboard envelope, he stood up. "I got some stuff here to show you."

"Okay," Tony said. "Let's go to the dining room. I'll look at it after we eat."

"You're gonna be surprised by what I brought with me."

"So are you, Ralph. I'm gonna treat you to some *real* Mexican food. Then we can go out on the patio and you can fill me in what you and Angelo have got going."

————

DWAYNE AND TERRY MCCARTHY ALONG WITH Jimmy Sheehan and Tim Fagin sat around the kitchen table in the lodge. They weren't in a talkative mood as they drank from bottles of beer that Charlie O'Donnell had set out for them.

Tim worked absentmindedly at peeling the label off his bottle between swallows. "It's a shame we don't have Farley Kuch working for us now. He could've been a damn good source of information on whatever happened to Wilma."

"He's a good kid," Dwayne remarked. "I'm glad he's got that welding job in Wichita. He'll get along fine."

"Piss on his welding job," Sheehan muttered. "There's prob'ly gonna be plenty of instances in the future when we could use him."

"Duke and Frank won't have no trouble with what's going on today," Dwayne opined.

Duke Glencannon and Frank Quinn had been dispatched to the truck stop restaurant to see if there was any information regarding Wilma's disappearance. They were dressed in their truck driver disguises and had been chosen for the task since they had only rarely been inside the eating establishment.

Charlie finished fixing some grilled cheese sandwiches —an art form he had learned from Dwayne—and set them on the table. "I hope you guys don't want no potato chips. I ain't been able to get to the store yet."

"That's all right," Sheehan said. "None of us are really hungry right now."

"I'm not surprised you're worried," Charlie said. "It took the wind out of me to hear that woman had disappeared. None of 'em seemed like runners."

"Well," Dwayne said, picking up a sandwich, "if she's taken off and disappeared on her own, that's okay. It'd be worse if she'd got killed and left in the truck park somewhere. That would bring the law into the caper as soon as the body was discovered." He wanted to downplay her disappearance. "I think some trucker with smack and a hypodermic talked her into going with him."

The sound of the panel truck driving up outside stopped all conversation. At the sound of two doors being slammed, everyone waited in worried anticipation. Duke Glencannon led the way through the door with Frank Quinn right behind him.

"Relax," Glencannon announced. "Nobody knows nothing about Wilma. There wasn't no cops there and none of the small talk we heard mentioned any dead bodies being found. Then me and Frank walked all around the parking area and even looked in the bushes by the highway. No sign of her."

"Well," Sheehan said, "I guess we can turn our minds to other matters now."

"Yeah," Glencannon said. "We'll prob'ly never learn what happened to her."

Dwayne finished off his grilled cheese sandwich wishing he'd had some French fries with it.

———

THE AFTERNOON SUN SPREAD A PLEASANT warmth over Tony Lundari's patio. He and Ralph Costiero sat at a small table with an umbrella for shade, drinking *Dos Equis* brand beer from south of the border. Tony looked at his old pal and grinned. "How'd you like that Mexican lunch?"

"It was good," Ralph replied. "I think we got some

Mexican restaurants in Boston but I never went to any. I think I'll try one out when I get home." He took a sip of his beer. "I notice you spoke to the maid in Spanish. It sounds a lot like Italian."

"The languages are pretty close," Tony explained. "If I don't know a word in Spanish I say it in Italian. I always get understood that way when I'm talking to Mexicans." He gave Ralph a calculated look. "So tell me what's going on with you and Angelo."

"Let me start at the beginning," Ralph said. He slid the cardboard envelope over to him. "Take a gander at that."

Tony opened the container and pulled out the photos, county maps and the roadmap. "What's all this?"

"That's where everything is going down. Make note of the road map. Notice how U.S. Highways 40 and 81 cross there in Kansas. Now turn it over to the side that shows the entire U.S. Look at the state of Kansas and see where it's located."

"Mmm," Tony mused. "That's damn near the exact center of the country."

"Yeah," Ralph said, settling in for a long period of explaining. "You remember the Derby Gang, right?"

"Right."

Ralph started from the beginning, patiently and completely explaining how Peachy Russo and Legs Spina from the Forzini mob called and asked to see Angelo. He went through everything the pair knew about the Derbies' activities. He included their trip to discover where the Irish gang was staying way out in Kansas. He also included Pauly Cappurio getting whacked and the sudden disappearances of Joe Forzini and Arrigo Leone in New York City while visiting Carlo Banocci.

"So what'd Angelo do after hearing all this?" Tony inquired.

"He sent Fabio with Peachy and Legs to Kansas to see what they could dig up. Fabio bought the aerial photos and maps at the local courthouse." Ralph elaborated on the deserted church camp, and how Fabio figured that was where the Derbies were staying. "The main thing they're doing right now is running a prostitution racket at a truck stop near that town of Salina. See?"

"Yep."

"Angelo don't think the whore racket is permanent," Ralph continued. "It's prob'ly for temporary finances until they can start the real operation behind all this."

"What might that be?"

"Angelo senses a smuggling operation bringing up stuff from the south on U.S. 81 to that area where U.S. 40 is. From there they can head east and west to deliver the goods to wherever it's gotta go."

"I understand," Tony said. "That junction offers easy and fast transportation on good highways to all parts of the country. And Angelo figures them Micks want to avoid big ports to bring in whatever it is they're gonna be smuggling. So the Texas coast south of Corpus Christi is a good place to bring it all ashore. Right?"

Ralph grinned. "You and Angelo still think alike."

"I have some contacts down in Kennedy County," Tony informed him. "There's a little harbor where I have my untaxed cigarettes and liquor brought ashore. The county has a population of only three hundred or so people on nearly five hundred square miles. And more important, its entire east side is on the Gulf of Mexico."

Ralph settled back to see what he would say next.

Tony chuckled. "This is gonna be great. And I'm

looking forward to working with Angelo again." He stood up. "Let's settle you in. Then we can go on a fishing trip. That's a cover, o'course. I'm gonna take you to my landing place so's you can check it out."

CHAPTER 38

L ife at the Retreat suddenly exploded into a riot of activity after Dwayne and McCarthy returned from the most recent trip to the telephone exchange. They brought back the electrifying news that gang boss Johnny Cullen would be flying to Kansas City to visit them. He was scheduled to arrive the next day, and was bringing along Enrico Galo who was the chief capo of the Banocci crime family.

"So a Banocci big shot is traveling with him," Sheehan remarked. "Did they give you the reasons they was coming out to Kansas?"

"Nope," McCarthy replied. "I tried to find out, but Johnny told me he didn't want to elaborate over the telephone. All he said something big was about to go down. I personally think we're about to find out the real reason why we're out here on the prairie."

During the time at the exchange when McCarthy had been talking to Johnny Cullen, Dwayne called Mrs. Davies and learned that Wilma was safe and sound in a secluded place in Sedgwick County. She had come through the detoxification process with flying colors. Now they were concentrating on giving her nourishment and counseling to assist her in returning to the real world.

Dwayne was glad that Wilma was doing well. Helping her escape the degradation of her former life dulled the constant uneasiness he experienced about killing Pauly Cappurio. He was also happy there was a real probability that the undercover caper would soon be over. When he and McCarthy learned enough about the overall plan, they would be pulled out by the F.B.I. to help build a case against the east coast hoods.

———

NOW, IN THE LODGE KITCHEN, SHEEHAN LIT A cigar and exhaled smoke with a big Irish grin on his face. He glanced at McCarthy. "I want you and Dwayne to go over to Kansas City in the morning to pick up Johnny and especially Galo. He's real close to Carlo Banocci so we can consider him a very important player in all this whatever-it-is."

"Well!" Dwayne said. "It'll be a big day tomorrow then. I better make sure the station wagon's gas tank is filled."

He left the kitchen and went outside to tend to the task. He saw Carla sitting on a bench by the carports smoking a cigarette. She had a worried expression on her face. "Did you find out anything about Wilma?"

"It's obvious she ain't been hurt or nothing," Dwayne replied. "It looks like she went off with a trucker. He prob'ly had some smack with him."

"That could be good or bad," Carla surmised, dropping her cigarette to the ground and stepping down on it. She glanced up at Dwayne with a look of affection. "Since

Wilma is gone I'll take her place if you want any loving. I can really give you a good time, Dwayne."

"I'll keep that in mind."

He walked over to the station wagon with the hope that the next sex he had would be with Nancy.

And soon.

———

TONY LUNDARI WAS THE PROUD OWNER OF A 1937 Chris Craft runabout motorboat. It was designed for speed, not comfort, and it served his purpose for conducting his business interests along the shores of the Gulf of Mexico. The craft, with an inboard motor, was speedy enough to outrun even a Coast Guard cutter.

Now, traveling southward along the Texas shoreline, he and Ralph Costiero sat in the rear cockpit while Dale Wickham did the piloting. Red Glover, sitting beside his friend, held a Winchester carbine to provide protection if necessary. Everyone wore western style clothing, and that included Ralph. He had borrowed an outfit from Tony that included a pair of cowboy boots.

Wickham carefully piloted the sleek boat, making sure he stayed out of the surf. Even under fair weather it was possible to run aground because of the underwater sand that shifted unpredictably. Those conditions could sometimes create currents that swirled and created undertows.

Their destination that day was Arenosa Lagoon, where the harbor Tony used was located. This waterway went a bit more than two miles inland from the Gulf. It was salt water at the entrance, but deeper into the interior a series of springs fed fresh water into the inlet. This feature kept the incursion of salt water from penetrating no more than half a mile into the lagoon's core.

Ralph studied the shoreline. "Jesus! It's really barren and threatening out there."

"It's not quite as bad as it looks," Tony said. "At least the rattlesnakes and Gila monsters like it."

"What kind of monsters?" Ralph exclaimed in alarm.

"They're lizards," Tony explained. "Poisonous but not particularly vicious as long as you give 'em a wide berth. When they bite, they chew the venom into their prey."

"God!" Ralph said. "It sounds horrible. And you can get bit by rattlesnakes out there, too, huh?"

"Rattlesnakes don't actually bite," Tony informed him. "I learned they extend their fangs and stab their victims. The venom helps to soften their prey to make 'em easier to digest, so you can imagine what it does to your skin and muscle if they strike you."

Wickham called out, "The Arenosa is coming up."

That also piqued Ralph's curiosity. "What's an Arenosa?"

"It's the name of the lagoon we're gonna visit," Tony said. "It actually means 'sandy' in Spanish. It's a shallow waterway about a couple of miles long to the docking area."

Wickham turned the boat into the channel entrance. It was fifty plus yards wide, but quickly narrowed to twenty or so. Wickham slowed down to maintain a steady course in the middle of the lagoon.

As the boat moved inland, sparse vegetation on the banks became visible, thickening quickly as they penetrated farther into the lagoon. Tony explained, "We're into the fresh water now. The brush gets pretty thick and tall the farther we go."

The lagoon spread out as they reached the end. A small village of crude huts and a narrow dock twenty yards long was at the water's edge. "This is where contraband is brought in," Tony said. "Look over there at the barges lined up along the shore. Obviously ships couldn't come in here, so the barges go out to them and bring in the loads."

"That makes sense," Ralph said. "Is this a village? I can see women and kids."

"Yeah," Tony said. "Those people make their livings from the smuggling activities. The stuff is unloaded on that dock and wheeled on dollies over to a couple of trucks parked behind the houses. It's got to be done that way because the vehicles are too heavy for the pier. Then the goods are driven out to a camp farther inland where there's a warehouse to store them until they can be transferred to the receivers."

Wickham skillfully brought the boat up to the rickety pier as Red Glover climbed out on the bow and picked up a line. He jumped out onto the dock to loop it around a cleat. Tony tossed him a line from the stern to be attached to another.

A voice sounded from the front of the dock. "Tony!"

A muscular Mexican of middle age walked up to them. "I ain't seen you for awhile. You got a load coming in?"

"No," Tony replied. "We're just dropping by for a visit." He indicated Ralph. "This is an old friend of mine, Beto. Ralph, this is Beto Valverde. He's the head man around here."

Beto was obviously what is termed a bad ass. He was muscular and short, well-balanced on his feet like a boxer and had a threatening demeanor about him. But he smiled at Tony. "Well if you ain't got a load is there anything else I can do for you today?"

"We're just out looking around," Tony replied. "Anything exciting going on?"

"*Seguro*," Beto answered in a Spanish language affirmative. "A couple of guys have shown up to do business here. They told me they're gonna have small loads but a lot of 'em. And it'll be over a long period of time. I was hired to help 'em out with my crew."

Tony had a reaction of discomfort. "What kind of business?"

"The same as yours, Tony. Ships will come in, barges will go out and trucks will haul it all away."

"Tell me more about them two guys."

Normally Beto would have refused the request, but he did a lot of business with Tony and they were also very good friends. "They're not exactly Gringos. As a matter of fact, they're a lot like you guys."

Tony and Ralph exchanged glances, knowing he was referring to Italians. "I'd like to see them guys," Tony said. "But not in person. Get my drift?"

"Sure," Beto said. "If it turns out you don't like 'em, I'll be on your side. We're old *compañeros*. We can go over to Miron Hill and you can take a good look at 'em from a distance without them seeing you."

Tony turned to Red. "Get my binoculars off the boat." He turned his attention back to Beto. "How about giving me and my boys a ride over there?"

"I can do that."

Miron Hill was the only rise in the flat terrain for miles. It offered good views both out to the Gulf and inland. The camp with its warehouse was in a direct western line a half mile from the spot.

Red came back with the binoculars in a heavy leather case. Tony slipped it over his shoulders and Beto led everyone off the dock over to a building with a crude hand-lettered sign that read **CANTINA DEL GOLFO**. Because of the lack of electricity in the primitive community, the saloon served warm drinks. Now and then ice was hauled in for *fiestas* to celebrate various Mexican holidays.

Beto's ancient but well maintained combination Model A and T Ford—made up of parts from two different automobiles—was parked behind the rustic saloon. It was used mainly for errands and shopping trips into the small town of Sarita. When community gasoline supplies were low, an army surplus thousand-gallon tank trailer was towed by truck to the same town to be filled.

The four men got into Beto's mobile contraption as their Mexican host worked the crank to get it started. With that done, he got behind the wheel and drove out onto the hard-packed terrain that led to their destination.

When they arrived, Beto, Red and Dale stayed with the car while Tony and Ralph went the short distance to the apex of the hill. They laid down to avoid being spotted from the warehouse. Tony reached into the case and pulled out his huge binoculars and put them to his eyes. He fidgeted with the focusing drive.

"Let's see," Tony said as much to himself as to Ralph. "There's some Mexicans...more Mexicans...a truck...it's a Studebaker...about two tons I figure...warehouse...and two guys...white... and..." Suddenly he stopped talking. A quick moment later he handed the binoculars to Ralph. "Take a look at the two guys standing between the truck and the warehouse. Then tell me what you see."

Ralph did as he was told, changing the focus for his own eyes. He gazed through the instrument for ten seconds then hollered. "Holy shit! I see Dominic Rossi and Ricky Multari! From the fucking Banocci gang!"

CHAPTER 39

The entire Derby contingent was already seated around the lodge kitchen table when Johnny Cullen walked in with Enrico Galo. They had just arrived on the site after the ride from the Kansas City airport with Dwayne and McCarthy.

Cullen and Jimmy Sheehan shared manly handshakes and exuberant pats on the shoulders as was proper when Irish buddies get together after a long time apart.

"Glad to see you," Cullen said. He nodded enthusiastically to the others. "Hey, big team!"

A chorus of welcoming shouts answered his greeting. Dwayne and McCarthy carried Cullen and Galo's luggage into Jimmy Sheehan's large bedroom. He would move upstairs into Wilma's vacant room while the two visitors were there.

Johnny Cullen didn't waste a minute of time, nodding toward Galo. "You guys know this gentleman with me, right?"

"Sure," Glencannon said. "How're you doing, Enrico? Still the chief capo?"

"Yeah. I'm doing okay."

Cullen said, "The Banocci family are gonna be partners with us in this great plan I'm about to reveal to you."

Galo took a chair off to one side since he wasn't really a member of the Derby Gang. Cullen, although an old man of sixty-seven years, was energetic and obviously enthusiastic about the reasons behind the surprise visit. He looked over the men seated in the kitchen.

"Okay. I know exactly what you guys are thinking. You're thinking why the hell in the name of our sacred Saint Patrick have we been made to be pimps? Well that part's over with. Babe Robertson will be here tomorrow to pick up the four whores and take 'em away."

"There's only three of 'em, Johnny," Sheehan said. "One ran off. And we'd gotten another, but she croaked from an overdose."

"Oh, yeah?" Cullen remarked. "That'll be a surprise for Babe, huh? Anyhow, you ain't gonna be pimping no more. Me and the Banocci family have been working close to eighteen months to set up a foolproof operation to import certain special goods into the country."

Tim Fagin raised his hand. "What kind of special goods, Johnny?"

"Heroin and cocaine," Cullen replied. "But first I want to give you the big picture on what's going on."

That pronouncement caught the rapt attention of his audience. They sat up straighter and leaned forward.

Johnny Cullen launched into his spiel. "As you guys know, the Feds have been putting a lot of pressure on organized crime back east. Several guys were deported and others given tough sentences in prison. Some of the poor bastards have even gone over to the desert in Nevada to try and set up a gambling operation. That's how desperate they are, and this has worried me."

Terry McCarthy, as an F.B.I. agent, found that interesting. "Where in the hell are they going to find a satisfactory place for that scheme?"

"It's a little hick town name of Las Vegas," Cullen answered, then went on with his discourse. "So one bright day I contacted my colleague and pal Carlo Banocci to discuss this disturbing fucking situation. This conference was also attended by Enrico and Vicenzo Cerro who is Carlo's consigliere."

Everyone automatically turned their eyes on Galo who sat with his arms crossed over his chest. He showed a wide smile of satisfaction.

"Me and Carlo had a long talk," Cullen continued, "and we considered the fact that several organizations have decided to move to the west coast to set up operations. The organizations out there are small and, while profitable, aren't anything to brag about. Me and Carlo decided we couldn't take over any large territories out there, so why not create a plan to cooperate with 'em? However, we didn't want to work under them organizations. See what I mean? We decided we wanted to provide a service for which they would pay us handsomely." He looked at Galo. "Right, Enrico?"

"You bet, Johnny."

"We was working on this plan straight through for a couple of weeks," Cullen went on, "and we came up the idea of working in the middle of the country to truck the narcotics on Highways 81 and 40. We knew it was gonna be expensive, so we decided to use whores at truck stops to earn a few bucks, see? We got ahold of our lady associate Babe Robertson and the rest is history."

McCarthy thought the information was a little sketchy for an undercover agent, and he asked, "What's gonna link all this up, Johnny?"

"I'm glad you asked that, Terry," Cullen responded. "We got a spot to bring the dope ashore off the Gulf of Mexico. That's down in Texas. We're gonna bring it up here to be picked up and delivered to the west coast at San Francisco, California on Highway 40. The customs officials there ain't gonna know nothing about this set-up, see? We'll have warehouses located inland—hear what I said—*inland*? That's the icing on this cake."

Galo interjected. "We'll use the Coast Highway there to take the goods to Los Angeles where the big money is. That means we'll be the best suppliers of dope available. That's a damn good selling point."

"Right," Cullen said. "The stuff will be small loads but lots of 'em. So, to keep things smoothly, the Bonoccis are gonna bring the goods by truck on Highway 81. But they're not gonna drop it off for you all the way up here. It'll be done where Texas and Oklahoma come together."

Dwayne spoke up. "Have you got any place picked out in that area?"

"No. We're gonna be working on that while me and Enrico are here."

"I know a perfect spot," Dwayne said. "I did a lot of work for a bootlegger in Wichita. We'd go down to the Texas line and get his liquor there from his Dallas supplier."

"Ah!" Cullen exclaimed. "You just solved that problem for us."

"Yeah," Sheehan said. "Dwayne's turned out to be real valuable. He gave us good advice."

"Great," Cullen said. "D'you have any more suggestions right now?"

"Yeah," Dwayne replied. "The best thing about that spot is that it's real close to U.S. 81 near the Red River. That means a straight shot from here to there."

"I like that!" Cullen said. "It'll be real handy."

"The river separates Oklahoma and Texas," Dwayne continued. "The highway runs through the town of Terral, Oklahoma. You turn east off the highway onto a country road and turn south at a spot I know. It'll take you to close to the river in an out-of-the-way place. It's got a lot of gullies. That's where we picked up our bootleg liquor."

Galo was also pleased. "Then it's a safe place to do our business, huh?"

"You bet," Dwayne promised. "Bootleggers from both Kansas and Oklahoma have been using that spot for years. They refer to it as Whiskey Junction. And, just in case your inter'sted, Oklahoma is a dry state."

This confused Cullen. "Hey! Prohibition was repealed."

"Yeah," Dwayne replied. "But Oklahoma voted to stay dry. So the local law and Okie bootleggers still have certain agreements."

"That's another good point," Cullen said with a wide grin.

Jimmy Sheehan was worried about one thing. "We ain't got very good communications, Johnny. We can't have a phone here so we have to use one at a telephone exchange."

"Not to worry," Cullen assured him. "We'll have to use telephones to coordinate things for a little while between here and Texas. That'll be okay for these practice operations. We're gonna set up a spot close to San Antonio similar to this. Right now we're using a motor court where we got a room permanently rented. It's got a phone. When the reg'lar runs start we'll have a coupla shortwave radios. One will be here and the other in San Antonio. Thanks to—" He pointed to Dwayne. "—our new member here, we can get started right away. We can set up a dummy run to check things out like the time it'll take and what sorts of towns we'll be driving through."

Terry McCarthy sat dumbfounded. The longer he knew Dwayne Wheeler, the more he thought the shamus should be in prison. The F.B.I. agent thought Dwayne's black market activities in Germany were bad enough, but now he realized his partner in this undercover caper happily wandered back and forth between the law and outlawry with nary a care.

McCarthy's F.B.I. straight-arrow mind shuddered.

CHAPTER 40

A few days following the visit to Arenosa Lagoon, Red Glover and Dale Wickham picked up two more visitors from the Corpus Christi depot. These gentlemen were Luigi Pegna and Fabio Lazzoni from the Lundari Gang. Fabio had been called back from Kansas along with Peachy Russo and Legs Spina. That pair had returned to their old headquarters in the room above the Fogetti restaurant to wait for the next summons requiring their criminal expertise.

The visitors were immediately taken into Tony Lundari's presence at the ranch house. Fabio, the chief capo for Don Angelo, was confused by the way his old pals Tony and Ralph were dressed. "What the fuck are you guys up to? Playing cowboys or something?"

"We'll talk about western vogue later," Tony said. "But you ain't in Boston anymore, and you better get used to outfits like these."

It was then that the newcomers noticed a Mexican seated in an easy chair sipping a glass of pure tequila. Tony pointed to him. "That guy is Beto Valverde. He's the crew boss on all the operations at the harbor where I do my business."

Fabio asked, "What harbor?" He was irritable from the long train trip.

"It's south of here on the Gulf Coast," Tony said. "It fits into the plan Angelo set up with me. Me and him had several long phone calls, and I learned he had figured out what all that shit in Kansas was about."

"Now *that* interests me," Fabio stated.

"By the way," Tony said, "Angelo was pleased that you sent him them aerial photos and maps. And he figures the Derby Gang and the Banocci New Yorkers are getting ready to run a smuggling operation from south of here on the Gulf of Mexico to the center of Kansas."

Fabio was pleased by the revelation. "So that's it! I'm finally glad to find out what them Mick bastards are doing."

"Right," Tony said. "And they was using whores to finance themselves until they could start the racket."

"Wait a minute," Fabio said. "How come Don Angelo thinks the Banocci gang is in on this?"

"Because two members of the Forzinis visited him after they found out that Joe Forzini and Arrigo Leone was bumped off by the Banoccis."

"This is getting confusing," Luigi Pegna complained.

Tony felt a snap of irritation. "Don Angelo learned there's a snitch in the Derbies. And the guy told Joe Forzini all about the Kansas angle. Carlo Banocci had Joe Forzini and Arrigo whacked after they sent three guys up to—"

Fabio interrupted again. "Peachy Russo, Legs Spina and Fat Pauly Cappurio were them guys. And the Derbies bumped off Fat Pauly."

"Shut up!" Tony yelled. "I'm doing the talking here!

You knuckleheads keep any comments you wanna make 'til later! You got that?"

They all nodded affirmatively.

"Okay," Tony continued. "Don Angelo wants us to take over the smuggling gig from the Banoccis. They're the ones running the whole thing and the Derbies are working for them."

Luigi pointed to Beto Valverde. "And he's in on it, too, right?"

Tony gritted his teeth and spoke in a low, threatening tone. "One more interruption and that somebody in this *room* is gonna get whacked!" With that, he glared everyone into silence. "Okay! Me and Ralph went to the harbor. By the way it's a place called the Arenosa Lagoon. While we was there Beto told us about two guys who were setting up an operation. Me and Ralph checked it out and spotted Dominic Rossi and Ricky Multari at the warehouse where the goods are gonna be landed. I guess all you guys know they're in the Banocci mob. That's where they'll load the trucks and drive 'em up to Kansas. So now we know something that Carlo Banocci don't know."

The group leaned forward, eyes and ears wide open.

Tony nodded to Beto Valverde. "Tell 'em what you know, Beto."

Beto got to his feet. "What I found out was that they wanted make an *ensayo*—a rehearsal—to check out their plan. So them two guys is gonna drive an empty truck up to the Texas and Oklahoma line on Highway 81 to see how things will work out meeting them other guys. I'll go along to find out the exact spot."

Luigi Pegna was confused once again. "How come you're going with 'em?"

"Because me and my guys will be doing all the driving when ever'thing is ready to roll."

Tony took over again. "Once the deliveries are firmed up, we're gonna whack them two Sicilians. Beto and some of his boys can take 'em out to the Gulf of Mexico and send 'em to the bottom to feed the fishes. Then Ralph, Luigi, and Fabio are gonna get in the truck and go to the rendezvous. I got some .32 caliber Beretta automatics with silencers. Them three will be enough to let the Micks walk up to 'em with grins on their faces. They'll open fire on 'em. No noise. No big disturbance."

"That's all well and good," Fabio said. "But what about the Derbies up in Kansas?"

Tony's patience finally gave out. "*Listen to me goddamn it!* I'm beginning to realize that some of you guys ain't exactly the brightest bulbs in the chandelier! So I'm gonna make this easy for you dickheads. There's gonna be two trips we gotta make! A *practice* run to check things out! Then an *actual* run for the showdown with the Derbies. So just shut your fucking yaps and do what you're told when you're told to do it!"

He gave his audience a wide-eyed glare, then walked out of the room.

———

THE THREE REMAINING WOMEN AT THE LODGE had packed their bags and moved out of their rooms, going down to the kitchen. Babe Robertson would be showing up to take them back to the whorehouse in Kansas City since they were no longer needed as financial support by the Derbies. The females sat quietly around the table, smoking and drinking coffee.

They had been kept busy the night before when eight of the Derbies visited their rooms. The men took advantage of the feminine presence since it would be awhile before they would come in contact with women again. The only exceptions were Dwayne, McCarthy and oldsters Charlie O'Donnell and Johnny Cullen. Enrico Galo of the Banocci Gang also had no interest in what he considered some very unattractive females. Of course he wasn't long out of New York City.

———

BABE ROBERTSON AND HER HULKING bodyguard Buddy arrived at a bit past noon to pick up the prostitutes. The first thing Babe saw when she walked into the kitchen was that two of the girls was missing. "Where's Wilma and Mary Sue?" she asked.

Jimmy Sheehan shrugged. "The girl died from an overdose and Wilma disappeared from the truck stop. We don't think she was hurt or killed. More'n likely she ran away with a truck driver."

Babe chortled. "I'll bet the son of a bitch had some smack, huh? Well, our Wilma has prob'ly been dropped off in some town by now. Too bad about the kid." She motioned to the three women. "Let's go! I ain't got all day."

Buddy held the door open as Babe led the whores out to her car. Dwayne followed behind them, stopping on the stoop. He watched them get into Babe's Cadillac, feeling terribly sorry for them.

"Poor miserable, lost frails."

Dwayne went back inside to begin a task given him by Johnny Cullen. He had to figure out a time table to reach the exchange point in the early evening. The route itself was simple. Go south on United States Highway 81 until the Red River comes into sight. From there it was only a short jaunt to Whiskey Junction where the unloading and loading of smuggled goods would be made.

A piece of cake.

CHAPTER 41

The evening after Babe Robertson had taken the three women away, Dwayne and McCarthy were called into Jimmy Sheehan's office. When they made the mandated appearance, Sheehan and Johnny Cullen were waiting for them at what was strictly a Derby Gang conference. The Banocci chief capo Enrico Galo had gone for a walk around the grounds.

"Okay, guys," Cullen said. "A phone call has to be made to San Antonio to speak with the Banocci guys and set up the date for the trial meet. That'll be day after tomorrow between one and two o'clock in the afternoon. You'll be speaking with Dominic Rossi to set up the times and locations."

"Right," Sheehan said. He looked at Dwayne. "What've you got worked out?"

"Okay," Dwayne replied, pulling a small notebook out of his shirt pocket. "Here's the distances and times as I figure 'em. From here to the meeting place by the Red River is 354 miles. That should take about six to seven hours to get there from here."

"Not bad," Cullen said. "I wonder if them two Sicilians have worked that out for their part of the trip."

"I thought about that, too," Dwayne said. "They're gonna have 330 miles going from San Antonio to the Red River. That's about the same amount of time."

Sheehan actually smiled and looked over at Cullen. "Dwayne can be trusted to always make extra effort."

"Yeah," Cullen agreed He swung his eyes over to McCarthy. "Be sure and tell 'em that over the phone. The length of the trip might not have occurred to them."

"Will do," McCarthy replied. "They'd also find it handy to know the distance and hours from the Gulf Coast to San Antonio."

"I looked into that, too," Dwayne remarked. "That mileage is 168. That's a little less than two hours. So when we're in full operations, it'll prob'ly take them 9 hours to go the total of 498 miles from the Gulf to San Antonio and up to the Red River. All these estimates are based on an average of 55 miles an hour. That includes going through towns and cities as well as lunch and piss breaks."

"Tell 'em that, too," Cullen said. He turned his attention back to Dwayne. "I want a copy of them time and distance notes."

"I made extra," Dwayne said, handing over a copy of his figures.

Cullen grinned at him. "I bet you got a lot of Irish blood in you."

"Maybe so," Dwayne remarked. "A couple of the guys here have told me they know of a Wheeler family in South Boston." He continued, "When we're in the town of Terral, we'll go south a short distance to where we turn off eastward at a country road. We'll take that for a short jaunt where we can change the goods over to our truck."

"Sounds easy," Sheehan remarked. "You told us you

used that area for bootlegging pickups and deliveries. Is there any chance they'll be there?"

Dwayne shook his head. "The Okies always get their deliveries around the midnight hour."

Sheehan said, "There's another matter we gotta tend to. I'm talking about getting a truck."

"We can go to that place in Hutchinson where I bought the panel truck," Dwayne suggested. "They have a good choice of vehicles."

"You attend to that after the phone call tomorrow," Sheehan instructed him. "How much money are you gonna need?"

"We want a good'un. So let's spend six or seven hunnerd dollars. We can get a pretty good deal on a 1940 or '41 model."

"Buy a new '48 model," Cullen said. "I can give you two grand in cash."

"That'll be enough."

"Now here's something else important," Cullen said. "I want you two to stay out of sight of them Banocci guys. Me and Jimmy talked this over and think it'd be a good idea if the two of you didn't show your faces. That way if any bad shit went down, you wouldn't have to lay low since nobody in the Banocci family would recognize you."

"Mmm," McCarthy mused. "Enrico has obviously seen us since he came here with Johnny."

"One guy wouldn't be that big a threat," Cullen explained. "And we're all gonna be packing heat."

Dwayne's basic lessons learned during that caper had been how organized crime worked. Their dealings and so called agreements weren't always on the up-and-up. And that included pacts that might have begun with a lot of trust among the people involved ended in someone getting killed.

"Now I have a suggestion, Johnny," McCarthy said. "I think you should go with us to the telephone exchange in case there's a need to answer questions or issue orders."

"Okay," Cullen acquiesced. "I'd like to have a look around the countryside anyhow. This is all new for me. Hey! And I'm gonna go with you to buy the truck, too." He stood up. "If there's nothing else, I think I'll go out and join Enrico on his walk."

━━━

THE NEXT MORNING DWAYNE, MCCARTHY AND Cullen arrived at the telephone exchange in the Nash station wagon a little before seven o'clock. Dwayne and Cullen took seats while McCarthy went up to the counter to fill out a call request. When that had been completed, he walked back to join his companions. He had a worried expression on his face.

"The lady up there was surprised I wasn't calling Boston like always," he muttered. "I guess Dwayne and I have been recognized."

"It's a risk, I admit," Cullen remarked. "But after we get our shortwave radio net set up, you won't be coming over here anymore. After a month or so, they'll prob'ly forget all about you."

A couple of minutes later, the lady announced, "The call to San Antonio is ready in booth four."

McCarthy and Cullen with Dwayne's figures in his hand, walked up to the phone's location and the elderly boss slipped inside.

Dwayne gazed at McCarthy standing by the open door in case he was needed for anything. They exchanged glances and nods as Johnny Cullen talked to the Banocci guy. The conversation was over in ten minutes and

Dwayne joined them as they went outside to the station wagon.

"Is everything set up?" Dwayne asked.

"Yeah," Cullen replied. "Tomorrow at two in the afternoon. And I made him copy down them numbers you worked out."

"Okay then," McCarthy said. "Let's go over to Hutchinson and buy us a truck."

"A *brand new* truck," Cullen reminded him.

LATER THAT AFTERNOON TWO VEHICLES DROVE up and parked behind the lodge. The first was the Nash being driven by McCarthy and the second was a brand new 1948 Chevrolet stake bed with a canvas cover over the back. Dwayne was driving the truck while Johnny Cullen sat beside him, enjoying a ride in something bigger than a limousine.

"This countryside makes me feel like I'm in a bigger world," the boss remarked. "And this is the first time I've seen tractors on the road ahead of me."

"It's even worst during the harvest," Dwayne said. "That's when the combines are moving from field to field. You can get held up anywhere from twenty to forty minutes or so."

"I hope that don't screw up our deliveries."

Dwayne shook his head. "I got it figured into my estimates for the summer runs."

He killed the motor and the two stepped down from the truck to follow McCarthy into the lodge.

Chapter 42

Johnny Cullen wanted to arrive at the rendezvous point at least an hour early. This would allow Dwayne and McCarthy enough time to walk the short distance to the nearby gullies where they could remain out of sight of the Banocci guys. As they headed for U.S. 81 Dwayne drove the new Dodge truck with Terry McCarthy beside him and Johnny Cullen riding shotgun.

Duke Glencannon, Frank Quinn, Tim Fagin and Enrico Galo sat back in the cargo compartment under the canvas cover, unable to enjoy the passing scenery of Kansas and Oklahoma. One of the sofas from the panel truck had been pulled out and put in the new vehicle to ease the discomfort of the trip for them.

When they were five miles outside of Terral, Oklahoma Dwayne slowed down and made a left turn that brought him onto a narrow dirt road. He pointed to the south, saying, "That's Texas over there."

"By all the blessed saints!" Cullen exclaimed. "I never thought I'd ever see Texas."

"That's it all right," Dwayne said. "The biggest state in America." He chuckled. "And every Texan you meet will remind you of that."

A stand of cottonwoods came into view a half mile ahead and Dwayne made a right turn on a track that led through the trees. He came to a stop at a clearing.

"This is it?" McCarthy asked.

"Sure is," Dwayne replied. "Welcome to Whiskey Junction. This is where the Okie bootleggers pick up their loads from the Fort Worth suppliers."

"Look at all the tire tracks," McCarthy said. "Doesn't that make it easier for the law to catch the bootleggers?"

"Let me put it this way," Dwayne stated. "There are certain agreements in affect regarding liquor around here. The bootleggers don't make trouble and the lawmen don't make arrests." He got out of the cab and called out, "Okay, guys. We're here."

Glencannon, Frank, Tim and Galo scrambled through the canvas opening and jumped to the ground. Glencannon looked around. "This place is really hid, ain't it?"

Yeah," Dwayne agreed. "Actually the trees are part of a pattern of groves for windbreaks. The farmers out here learned to do that from government farm agents a little more'n ten years ago during the Dust Bowl. You stop the wind, you stop the topsoil from being blown away."

Tim Fagin walked into some bushes to urinate, then jumped back. "Jesus Christ! Look at that big fucking snake!"

A serpent, as startled as the Irishman, was coiled with its rattle whirring. Dwayne came over and cautioned Tim. "Step back real slow without any quick moves."

Tim did as he was told. After he backed off three

steps, the reptile whipped around and fled into the brush. "What kind of snake is that?"

"It's a prairie diamond back rattlesnake," Dwayne replied. "It's poisonous by the way, so you're lucky you didn't get bit." He turned to the others. "Be careful where you walk, guys. There's lots of those critters out here."

"God!" Tim exclaimed. "Why don't the people just start killing them off to get rid of the horrible bastards?"

"They're beneficial to the wheat farmers," Dwayne said. "Them and the bull snakes keep the rat population down."

"Shit!" Frank Quinn exclaimed. "I'd rather have rats around than snakes!"

"Not if you had a barn with grain stored in it," Dwayne said. He turned to McCarthy. "We better make ourselves scarce down in the gullies. The Banocci guys will be here anytime now."

"Okay," McCarthy said. "You lead the way."

———

THIRTY-SOME MINUTES LATER THE SOUND OF A truck engine could be heard approaching, then it grew louder as a Studebaker appeared in the grove. Enrico walked toward it with a big grin as the engine was cut. Much to everyone's surprise a short, stocky Mexican opened the driver's side door and lightly hopped down. Then Dominic Rossi and Rick Multari appeared from the other side of the vehicle.

The trio of Banocci men had a raucous reunion, then Rossi pointed to the Mexican. "Hey, guys, let me introduce our driver. Beto Valverde."

Johnny Cullen's temper snapped. "Hey, goddamn it! Who gave you leave to bring in an outsider?"

"Relax, Johnny," Dominic said. "He's in charge of the place where the goods are landed. That's on the Gulf of Mexico. He's in on the action, all right? Him and his guys handle the unloading chores off the ships."

"That's okay then," Cullen stated. "As long as he's part of the operation."

"Believe me," Rossi said. "He's a *big* part of the operation." He looked around the area. "This is a good place, I'd say. Will we use it all the time?"

"As long as we can," Cullen replied. He shrugged. "I guess this is all we can do. Normally, we'd be switching loads from one truck to the other. Anybody have any questions? No? So if this was a real delivery, the goods in your truck would be loaded into our truck. Then we'd head north up to Kansas."

Rossi was getting impatient. "Well, this practice run is wrapped up then. Let's go back home, ever'body. This'd be a good time to take a piss before we're back on the road."

"Watch out for the snakes!" Tim Fagin warned. "They're poisonous."

"We've already been around lots of 'em down by the Gulf," Multari said. "And that includes fat lizards. We know how to be careful."

With that, the men gingerly stepped into the bushes to urinate. Ten minutes later, Beto Valverde was driving out of the clearing with Dominic Rossi and Ricky Multari. At that point, Dwayne and McCarthy reappeared.

"How'd things go?" McCarthy asked.

"Perfect," Cullen answered. "Now all we have to do is wait to hear from Tony Lundari when the first shipment is coming in." He turned to Glencannon, Frank and Tim. "All right! Back in the truck!"

"Shit," Tim muttered under his breath heading for the canvas covered rear of the Dodge.

———

DURING THAT SAME WEEK TONY RECEIVED A number of new house guests. They were Peachy Russo, Legs Spina, Tony Bonvicini, Guido Viola and Freddy Leonardi. These stalwarts were all ex-Forzini gangsters. Their arrival brought up the number of guns to go against the Banoccis and Derbies to eight. Those not included in the battle force were Tony Lundari and Ralph Costiero. Ralph, as the consigliere was required to be with Angelo in Boston while Tony remained in Texas to take charge of that end of the operation. Carlo Banocci and his consigliere Vicenzo Cerro remained in New York City.

———

BACK AT THE RETREAT, DWAYNE WHEELER AND Terry McCarthy were congratulating each other over the fact their mutual undercover assignments would soon come to an end.

"It'll be nice to return to the real world," Dwayne happily remarked.

"It's only a matter of days, my friend," McCarthy assured him.

CHAPTER 43

Red Glover and Dale Wickham drove Ralph Costiero to the Corpus Christi depot for his return trip to Broadview Meadows to join his boss Angelo. The ranking members of the Lundari mob would begin contacting organized crime acquaintances in California to make connections with the West Coast narcotics scene.

With the consigliere back at gang headquarters, Tony Lundari turned his attention to the takeover of the Derby Gang's smuggling. His first step was to call a meeting out on the patio of his ranch house to address his house guests. These would be Chief Capo Fabio Lazzoni and Luigi Pegna, head enforcer of the Lundari gang.

Additionally, the five ex-Forzinis Russo, Spina, Bonvicini, Viola, and Leonardi were also included. Since their own crime organization had collapsed, they were all anxious to be taken in by the Lundari Family.

All were dressed in short sleeve shirts and slacks in east coast informality, with not a one showing any interest in purchasing cowboy-style garb that was espoused by their host. The guest of honor at this session was Beto Valverde. He, of course, was attired as he usually was in the Tex-Mex fashion that was a mixture of American and Mexican cowboy styles.

"Listen up," Tony said, opening the get-together. "I have an announcement to make that will raise your spirits." He paused for effect as he noted all eager eyes were on him. "We'll be starting the takeover on Thursday." He looked at Valverde. "Right?"

"That's right," the Mexican said. "Them two guys Rossi and Multari at the landing have told me that tomorrow the first shipment will come in to be unloaded. My crew is gonna go out to the ship, pick up the load and bring it back to the wharf. I will drive the stuff over in a pickup to the warehouse where the truck is."

"Christ!" Fabio Lazzoni exclaimed. "It must not be very big if you can put it in the back of a pickup."

Tony interjected, "It ain't got a lot of volume or weight, but it's expensive and that means big profits for us."

Tony Bonvicini was confused. "If it's so light, why don't we get more of the stuff?"

"Look! I ain't going through dumb questions again!" Tony snapped.

Freddy Leonardi had an idea. "We could get more trucks. That way we'd make more money."

"That's another stupid idea," Tony stated. He signaled Valverde to continue.

The Mexican resumed speaking. "Them two guys wanna drive over to San Antonio on Wednesday and wait 'til Thursday to head up north."

Tony grinned. "But I got one great big fucking surprise for them. Everyone here is gonna be on a rented fishing boat out on the Gulf when the ship arrives. As soon as it's unloaded and the cargo taken to the warehouse, we'll sail down the lagoon and tie up at the dock. The next step is to whack them two rat bastard Sicilians." He pointed to Luigi Pegna the head enforcer for the Lundaris. "He'll take care of that. With that done, you can all get into their truck and head up north to meet the Micks. There'll be two of them and eight of you. I don't think you'll have any trouble dealing with 'em."

Peachy Russo was worried. "None of us have been at that meeting spot you're talking about."

Beto Valverde spoke up. "I've been at the exact place. I'll be driving you up there. They won't expect nothing for a short time when they see me. I been there before."

"That's when you mugs come out shooting," Tony stated in an emphatic tone.

"Right," Beto said. "I'm gonna have one of my guys following us, so he can take me back to the Gulf. Then you guys take off and do what you gotta do."

Now Fabio Lazzoni spoke up. "Peachy, Legs Spina, and me know the way to where they're staying off U.S. 40 in Kansas. We even got aerial photos and county maps of the place."

"We're gonna have silencers for you guys," Tony elaborated. "Them gats will be .45 Smith and Wesson revolvers. It won't be possible to completely silence the shots, but that don't make any difference. You'll be out in the country and nobody's gonna be close enough to hear anything." He nodded to Fabio. "Finish up."

"The first guy we hit will be in the gatehouse," Fabio said. "After that ever'body's gotta be ready to get out of the truck fast to take care of any reception committee that might be waiting for the load. When those guys go down, we can move into the building and start whacking all the others."

"How many are there?" Pegna asked.

"We figure a dozen or so," Fabio answered. "Remember they'll think ever'thing is on the up and up, so there shouldn't be no trouble for us."

Pegna had another question. "After we're there and in charge, what happens?"

"You just sit and wait while Angelo and Ralph wrap up the arrangements with the people that are supposed to get the dope. Them two are already tending to this. They'll work out an agreement that'll be beneficial to all of us. This'll probably take a week or ten days."

Peachy Russo was feeling sentimental. "Damn! I wish Fat Pauly was here to see all this."

Legs Spina crossed himself. "May he rest in peace."

———

THE NEXT DAY A RUSTY OLD FREIGHTER WITH A Greek skipper and Liberian registration dropped anchor off the Arenosa Lagoon on the Gulf of Mexico. Captain Prokopis Papoulias of the good ship *S.S. Rekin* and his first mate were on the flying bridge waiting for the arrival of a motorized launch.

Both officers shared a good mood. Their agent, a Moroccan businessman with extensive criminal connections, had arranged a cargo deal that would be profitable for years. Twice a week the freighter would meet a fishing boat a few miles off the south Cuban coast to pick up cargo. From Cuba they would steam northwest to the Gulf of Mexico where a motorized launch waited. Each trip was paid for in advance.

The loads would be heavy-duty cardboard boxes that totaled 50 kilograms each. A total of 25 of the containers were in each shipment. That meant no cargo nets need be applied for the loading and unloading.

Now the Captain and First Mate scanned the shoreline with their binoculars, then spotted an outboard launch approaching the ship. It drew up by the accommodations ladder, and a half dozen Mexicans got off the barge to form a human chain from there up to the deck. In only a few moments they began passing the cargo down to the barge. The task was done in fifteen minutes, then the small craft headed for the lagoon.

Another set of binoculars watched the unloading. These belonged to Tony Lundari, who had positioned himself on the bow of a rented fishing boat. Fabio Lazzoni stood beside him. "What's going on?"

"They've loaded the barge and are heading back," Tony replied. He turned around and hollered at Dale Wickham at the wheel. "Let's head to the lagoon. Remember to dock on the far side of the wharfs. We don't want them two Sicilians to recognize any of us."

"I'll go join the others," Fabio said, moving toward the cockpit.

———

BY THE TIME THE FISHING BOAT WAS TIED UP TO the wharf, the cargo had been loaded onto a pickup truck that was ready to be driven to the warehouse by Beto Valverde. That was where Dominic Rossi and Ricky Multari waited impatiently for the load they planned to drive up to the Oklahoma line.

Beto Valverde wasted no time in heading for the warehouse. Luigi Pegna squatted down in the back of the vehicle. He held his pistol while peering from the rear cab window through the front windshield. In less than five minutes he could see Rossi and Multari standing by their Studebaker truck.

The instant Valverde braked to a stop, the killer stood up and began shooting over the top of the cab. The two Banocci men staggered back from the impact of the bullets, then collapsed heavily to the sand. The pistolero jumped down to the ground, reloaded, and fired once more into his victims.

Valverde opened the door and stepped out onto the running board of the truck. He looked down at the blood-soaked bodies. "I don't think you got to shoot them no more. I'll go now and bring your *amigos* over here. Then we head for Oklahoma."

He drove back to the wharf area.

CHAPTER 44

The Studebaker truck crossed the Red River into Oklahoma with Beto Valverde driving. Fabio Lazzoni and Luigi Pegna shared the seat with him. Both wore sunglasses and had their fedoras pulled low. The other six members of the team were in the back among the boxes of narcotics slated for delivery to Kansas. All were poised and ready for the bloody encounters they would face before the evening's sunset.

Valverde turned off the highway onto the country lane, going down to Whiskey Junction. They arrived at the location where the Derby Gang's Dodge truck was parked under the trees. Duke Glencannon and Frank Quinn were leaning against the vehicle waiting. Both gave friendly waves to the arrivals. They assumed it was Dominic Rossi and Ricky Multari sitting in the cab of the truck. The sight of the Mexican did not alarm them.

Valverde stepped down from the Studebaker, loudly announcing. "I got to take a piss."

Glencannon and Frank watched as the Mexican walked toward the bushes. Fabio and Pegna casually got out of the cab, then quickly opened fire on the two Derbies. The unsuspecting victims stumbled and fell, dying before realizing they had been attacked.

The half dozen men in the back of the truck jumped to the ground as Valverde joined them. Under normal circumstances the gangsters would have either left the murdered men where they fell or dragged them out of sight into the bushes. But if the Oklahoma bootleggers discovered two dead strangers in their special spot, it would attract unnecessary attention to the location. Realizing this, Tony had given an order to take the bodies to the Gulf Coast to be put with the corpses of Dominic Rossi and Ricky Multari. The four dead men would be weighted down with adobe bricks and dumped in the Gulf of Mexico by Beto's crew.

Fabio, being in charge, set the group to transferring the cargo from one truck to the other. With that taken care of, Glencannon and Frank's bodies were swung up into the back of the Studebaker and a large tarpaulin placed over them. Beto got into the cab to drive the truck and corpses back to Arenosa Lagoon.

The five ex-Forzinis got into the back of the Dodge truck with the narcotics. Fabio Lazzoni took the responsibility for driving up to Kansas with Pegna in the front with him. The others in the back checked their Smith and Wesson revolvers, tightening the silencers. There was plenty of time—about six hours—but an apprehensive nervousness of the looming showdown ahead of them was as contagious as polio.

––––––––––––––

THE LODGE WAS IN READINESS FOR THE DELIVERY of that very important first load of narcotics. Dwayne

Wheeler and Terry McCarthy were charged with making the phone call back to Carlo Banocci in New York City as soon as it arrived. Johnny Cullen would accompany them to the telephone exchange to inform the padrino of the latest happenings.

Meanwhile Charlie O'Donnell worked at preparing a roasted chicken dinner for ten. He was timing the cooking chore so that the food could be served after the arrival of the shipment. Chief Capo Enrico Galo, the representative from the Banocci Gang, played poker with Jimmy Sheehan and Tim Fagin while Johnny Cullen enjoyed a few beers as he kibitzed the game. Dwayne and McCarthy were in their room, quietly discussing when they might be called in by the F.B.I. to prepare depositions that would lead to numerous arrests.

The three gate guards had been called in from their motor court rooms to stay at the lodge for cohesive reasons. Tom Fitzgerald was on duty at the gatehouse while his off-duty fellow guards dozed in a couple of rooms that had once been occupied by the prostitutes.

All was calm and relaxed, tinged slightly with happy anticipation.

———

IT WAS DUSK WHEN FABIO LAZZONI TURNED OFF U.S. 40 onto the country lane leading to the gatehouse. Luigi Pegna opened the cab's rear window that accessed the cargo area. He hollered at the ex-Forzinis. "Hey! You guys get ready!"

There was a sound of shuffling as the five men took their weapons in hand and moved toward the rear. Fabio had his pistol on the seat between him and Pegna. When he turned onto the lane toward the entrance of the

Retreat, he rolled down his window then grasped his revolver. He came to a stop at the gatehouse.

Tom Fitzgerald stepped out. "Hi ya, Duke—" His eyes opened wide. "Who the hell—"

The .38 slug split his forehead open spattering brain matter on the truck door. Fabio put his pistol back beside Pegna and eased down on the accelerator. The lane was a bit uneven and he needed both hands to handle the truck. He drove slowly, going around to the rear of the lodge.

The poker players and Johnny Cullen heard the vehicle and immediately headed for the back door. They walked out onto the stoop and started down the steps, then hesitated when several men suddenly appeared from the truck.

A round of pops from silenced pistols sounded in the growing darkness. Johnny Cullen, Enrico Galo and Tim Fagin were hit. Fagin, in front, was knocked back against Cullen and both slumped on the steps. Galo fell over the banister. At about that time Charlie O'Donnell appeared in the door and caught four bullets in his torso. He fell back into the kitchen.

Jimmy Sheehan miraculously escaped any bullet strikes. He ran back into the lodge and rushed upstairs, bursting through the door of Dwayne and McCarthy's room. "We're getting whacked! Follow me!"

The two undercover men, although shocked and rendered speechless, sensed the fear and anxiety in Sheehan's voice. He led them to a storage closet in the middle of the hallway. He opened the door and immediately scaled a ladder built in the wall. It led to an attic trapdoor. The Irish gangster reached in, pulling out a Thompson submachine gun. He handed it down to Dwayne, got another for McCarthy, then tossed them each a khaki vest with four pockets of 30-round magazines.

After getting the same fighting gear for himself, he dropped down to the floor. "I stored these Tommy guns up there for a rainy day," He announced. "And it's here. Follow me and—"

The sound of pops could be heard out in the hall. Dwayne looked out the closet door to see two men firing silenced pistols into the rooms where the two gate guards were sleeping. Dwayne brought up the Thompson and squeezed out two quick bursts that spun Pegna and Bonvicini completely around before they crumpled under the fusillade.

Downstairs in the kitchen Fabio Lazzoni, amid the five Forzinis, heard the loud shots. "What the fuck?"

Jimmy Sheehan appeared in the door. Having no military training with the submachine gun, he pulled the trigger and held it down causing the barrel to whirl wildly as it spit bullets. Spina, Viola, and Leonardi went down but Fabio and Peachy managed to shoot back. Sheehan crumpled to the floor.

Suddenly it was quiet.

The ferociousness of the two gangsters evaporated. They looked at each other. "D'you think there's any more of 'em?" Peachy asked.

Fabio shrugged with a disturbed expression on his face.

Dwayne slowly eased down the stairs, holding the submachine gun ready. McCarthy followed behind to give him back up. They heard some muffled talking and stopped for a quick moment, then continued. Dwayne reached the bottom of the stairs and saw Jimmy Sheehan's body in the doorway to the kitchen.

Dwayne decided to take a chance. He took a step forward, turned and squeezed the trigger four short pulls. The spread of bullets caught both Fabio and

Peachy who were knocked backward to sprawl on the floor.

McCarthy joined him. "We'd better check to see if there's any more of those sons of bitches around here."

It was then that they sighted old Charlie's body in the doorway leading outside. They stepped carefully up to the opening and saw Galo draped over the banister of the stoop and Cullen and Tim Fagin sprawled on the steps. Several heavy rivulets of blood dripped to the ground below.

Dwayne and McCarthy made a slow and careful search around and in the building, noting there was nobody else in the area.

"Let's check the truck," McCarthy said.

They walked from the stoop to the vehicle and looked inside. Dwayne saw the boxes. "There's a shipment here."

"That's good," McCarthy said. He took a deep breath. "I don't know what brought on that gunfight."

"Y'know something, Terry?" Dwayne remarked. "If I learned anything from this undercover work, it's that the assholes in organized crime are their own worst enemies."

"I could have told you that a long time ago," McCarthy remarked. He cleared his throat and spat, then gave out a sigh of relief. "It looks like this caper is over."

"Yeah," Dwayne murmured, with that fact now dawning on him.

"You stay here," McCarthy said. "I'll drive to the telephone exchange and contact Steve Williams. Don't touch those boxes while I'm gone."

"Okay," Dwayne said.

"I mean it!" McCarthy snapped. "Don't take any of the narcotics."

Dwayne was furious. "D'you think I was gonna steal any of it?"

McCarthy didn't reply to the question, instead saying, "It's evidence." He gave Dwayne a careful look. "How're you feeling?"

"Pretty much pissed off right now," Dwayne replied. "I don't like your chickenshit attitude."

Chapter 45

Another article appeared in the morning *Wichita Eagle* and evening *Wichita Beacon* shortly after Dwayne's return to Wichita. Local radio stations also carried the news.

Local Private Detective Regains License after Charges Are Dropped

Yesterday, officials of the Kansas Bureau of Investigation announced that private detective Dwayne Wheeler of Wichita has been cleared of all charges against him. His license has been restored and he is authorized to conduct his business under Kansas law.

In a statement to the press, Wheeler declared, "The false accusations against me were made by a person or persons who have remained unnamed. I am now ready to return to working capers as a legally licensed shamus."

The Sedgwick County District Attorney's office has declined to issue any comments regarding this case.

Detective Wheeler has solved several well-known murders in the city.

The first thing Dwayne did when he arrived at his apartment was to telephone Mrs. Davies. Miss Carruthers answered the call and immediately transferred him to the boss lady's private office.

"Ah, Mister Wheeler," she said. "So good to hear from you. And I am most pleased to see the newspapers report that you have been exonerated. I had complete faith in your innocence. Please go to our phone center where Miss Brooks will have an envelope for you. It contains the remainder of your fee."

"Thank you, Missus Davies. I'm sorry to have to tell you that the rest of the prostitutes in the caper were taken away by Babe Robertson. I believe you said you were acquainted with her."

"Yes, unfortunately," the lady commented. "However, I do have news that will gladden your very kind heart. Evelyn has completely recovered from her addiction to heroin and has joined our staff to counsel other unfortunate women."

"Evelyn? Who is Evelyn, Missus Davies?"

"Oh, that's right, you don't know her by that name. Evelyn is Wilma, the lady you rescued. Like most prostitutes she had assumed a false identity."

"I'm really glad to hear the good news," Dwayne said. "I have some other matters to clear up, but be sure and call me if there is anything else I can do for you."

"Of course, Mister Wheeler. Goodbye."

Dwayne hung up and immediately picked up the receiver again. He dialed the Beachcomber tavern.

———

IT WAS THE END OF THE WEEKEND AS DWAYNE Wheeler and Nancy Turner lay side by side in bed after making love. They had enjoyed an informal dinner at their favorite Continental Grill.

His homecoming from the undercover caper had been quite happy. When he left, Nancy was adamant about not having sex with him again unless he was willing to marry her and settle down. When he first called on her at the duplex it was Sunday morning, and he feared she would stick to her guns on that declaration. So he decided to check out her attitude in a cautious manner.

Nancy gave him a kiss and hug, obviously glad to see him. Holly squealed with delight and he even got an embrace from Nancy's mother Maggie. His announcement he was going to take them to Riverside Park for the day was also greeted with enthusiasm.

The three females chattered happily as Dwayne drove over to the park. They began by visiting the zoo and later had a nice picnic of hot dogs and French fries he purchased from a vendor's cart. After some fun for Holly on the merry-go-round, swings and sliding board, they got into the Buick and he drove over to the Riverside Boathouse on Murdock Street. Dwayne rented a boat and rowed his three lady guests down the Little Arkansas River back and forth for a couple of miles.

When they got back to the house, Nancy unexpectedly announced that she and Dwayne were going to the movies. He was ecstatic over this unexpected statement. This was the excuse they used when they wanted to go to his apartment for sex.

Following that day, they continued the practice as often as possible. However, on this last sexual contact, Nancy gazed at Dwayne with a mellow look in her eye and sweet smile on her face.

"Dwayne, we have to talk."

Oh, shit!

———

The outcome of the undercover caper caused quite a stir in organized crime after Dwayne Wheeler turned in his deposition of the assignment and Terry McCarthy filed his official report as an F.B.I. agent.

Over two dozen capos and soldiers had died in various incidents during the caper. Sicilians Carlo Banocci and Vicenzo Cerro of New York City along with Italians Angelo Lundari, Tony Lundari and Ralph Costiero of Boston were all under indictment. The Irish Derby Gang of Boston had been completely annihilated.

Unfortunately, the rest of the organized crime groups on both coasts were still hale and hearty.

———

The village at Arenosa Lagoon was raided by U.S. Customs. Beto Valverde blended in with his people and was not arrested. Finding no one to prosecute among them, the government agents took advantage of the fact they were all illegal aliens. Consequently, all were deported to Mexico.

The U.S. Coast Guard seized the *S.S. Rakin* on the high seas. The captain and crew were arrested and charged with smuggling and the cargo on the ship seized.

———

In Dwayne's deposition he revealed the location of the two graves in the woods by the creek. He identified the bodies buried there as Mary Sue Pickens and Dennis Murphy. The Kansas Bureau of Investigation had the corpses exhumed then notified the next of kin.

Jesse and Lorene Pickens held a private funeral and burial for their daughter while Murphy's widow Judy did not claim the body. However, she did hire a lawyer to sue the Massachusetts authorities for a share of the Derby Gang's numerous bank accounts that had been seized. This was a futile litigation, however, and she lost every dime she had to her shady lawyer. Mrs. Murphy ended up taking her four kids to live with her parents in Cambridge where her father was a janitor at Harvard University. The addition of five mouths to feed was a hardship for the family until Judy found a job at the school's student cafeteria.

DWAYNE WAS BACK IN THE CHIPS. HE HAD received $750 from Mrs. Davies (a $500 advance and $250 final payment) and $750 for his undercover service from the United States Attorney General. That was a grand total of $1500. He was set for six months, even if he didn't earn another penny.

After everything was settled, he went back to his office in the Snodgrass Building and called Millie at Reliable Answering Service, informing her of his return to business.

EPILOGUE

At the end of Dwayne and Nancy's last date she wept and yelled angrily, telling him he was just another worthless son of a bitch who had used her for casual and inconsiderate sex. She dressed hurriedly and rushed out, slamming the door.

Immediately following the incident Dwayne was pulled into debriefings by the F.B.I. He also had to get his detective business back into operation and this involved more contacts with his usual collection of the respectable and not so respectable individuals he dealt with.

Later, when that furor died down, he turned his mind to Nancy. He felt a sincere regret about his side of their affair. He liked the woman, but definitely didn't want to marry her. He consoled himself with the realization that he would have made a lousy husband and the marriage would have been an unmitigated disaster. But he was miserable about losing his friendship with Holly. She was a charming little girl who stimulated his fatherly—or big brotherly—instincts.

—————

DWAYNE TRIED TO ACCEPT THE FACT THAT HE really didn't want a permanent serious relationship with *any* woman. He needed a girlfriend who was as casual about sex as he. Dwayne reached the conclusion that his only chance for that type of situation would be to have an affair with a married woman. However, in Wichita, that was a dangerous undertaking. Local cuckolded husbands had a bad habit of shooting their wives' paramours. And juries always found them innocent by reason of temporary insanity.

—————

ONE NIGHT, AFTER LONG HOURS OF TOSSING AND turning, a realization that he had unconsciously kept hidden from himself exploded into his conscious mind like a clap of prairie thunder. The occurrence was so strong and sudden, that he sat straight up in bed. After a short period of deep breaths to calm down as much as possible, the pure truth of the revelation swept over him. Dwayne muttered aloud to himself in a strong sense of sadness and loss.

"You know something, Self? You're still in love with Donna Sue."

A Look At Book 4:

Wichita Artistique

1940s Wichita, Kansas

World War II is over, but shamus Dwayne Wheeler is about to be caught up in a war of his own. Charged with the safekeeping and transferring of works of art that are sold and traded among a cabal of wealthy collectors, he is content with living an action-free life.

But when Pete Van Dyke—Dwayne's former commanding officer in the military police—asks him to join in on his latest project, he can't refuse. All too soon, risky circumstances come to light when mysterious powers-that-be want to learn more about the cabal's contact in Wichita.

Thrust into a precarious mishmash of U.S. military intelligence, a secret Zionist organization, neo-Nazis, Interpol and the FBI, Dwayne must, once again, fight to keep his head above water in a race against time.

Wichita Artistique is book four in a historical private eye series that follows Dwayne Wheeler—a tough and hardboiled detective.

AVAILABLE NOVEMBER 2022

ABOUT THE AUTHOR

Patrick Andrews was born an Army Brat on January 14, 1936—his sister's arrival just two years later. His father was a paratrooper in the 82nd Airborne Division during World War II. His mother was a good army officer's wife, who, like several of her lady cousins, wrote short-stories and poems.

After the war, Patrick's father transferred into the Army Reserves, and they moved to Wichita, Kansas—where Patrick caught the scribbling bug. When Patrick got a job as a copy boy at the *Wichita Eagle* newspaper, he was ecstatic.

A few years later, Patrick got a yen to be a paratrooper. He enlisted in the Army and took basic training in Camp Chaffee, Arkansas, soon after being transferred to the 82nd Airborne Division in Fort Bragg. His career with the 82nd was rewarding—being promoted to sergeant and tasked with training cadets in West Point before retiring.

When Patrick read James Jones' *From Here to Eternity*, he appreciated the pride and struggling of soldiers. Soon after, he moved to San Diego, California and began writing and mailing manuscripts while working at a union typesetting company. He married and had one child, named William Patrick.

One pivotal night, Patrick was with a couple of his writing buddies, drinking scotch whiskey and playing at writing the *Sixgun Samurai* series. The next day, they drove up to Pinnacle Books in Los Angeles, where they walked out with a book deal. Patrick and his friends went on to write the series' twelve novels—which were also printed in the U.K. by Star Books, the paperback division of W.H. Allen & Co.

From then on, Patrick started writing and selling western, men's adventure, and military fiction. Years passed, and he had 24 published e-books with Piccadilly Publishing in the U.K.

Today, all six of Patrick's Wichita Detective books are getting another chance to see the light of day—with Rough Edges Press—and find refuge on a cozy shelf in Ocean Hills, California where Patrick and his beloved wife, Julie, live.

www.ingramcontent.com/pod-product-compliance
Lightning Source LLC
Chambersburg PA
CBHW011421010726
47494CB00011B/2448